# MELODY OF THE SNOW

## BLAKE ALLWOOD

BLAKE ALLWOOD PUBLISHING

Blake Allwood
Visit my website at BlakeAllwood.com

Printed in the United States of America
Box Elder, SD

First Printing: Nov 2022

Blake Allwood Publishing

Ebook ISBN: 978-1-956727-36-4
Paperback ISBN: 978-1-956727-35-7
Library of Congress Control Number: 2022921624

# CONTENT WARNINGS

Racism

Explicit Sex Scenes

# ACKNOWLEDGMENTS

Special thanks to the following amazing people who helped me get this book finished and into your hands.

Jo Bird: Editor

Renee Mizar: Editor

Ann Attwood: Proofreader

And of course, a big thank you to my husband who puts up with my endless stories and handles the formatting and final publishing of all my books.

# 1

## CAM

"**I**'M SORRY, MA'AM, IT'LL just be a moment."

The older woman stood silently while I finished typing the documentation for my patient in room seven. When I looked back up at her, I saw a sweet face smiling expectantly.

I smiled back, and asked, "How can I help?"

"Oh, dearie, this is for you," she said, and handed me a card with my name printed on the front.

I was about to open it when alarms suddenly blared down the hallway. "Damn, that's my patient."

I shrugged apologetically at the woman as I dropped the card on my desk and ran toward the sound of my patient coding again.

Forty-five minutes later, Mr. Howard was still alive and finally breathing on his own.

Luckily, my shift would be over in thirty minutes, and my replacement was already here. Thank God, Lizzie was known for coming in early.

I quickly gave her the rundown about Mr. Howard, and she cringed when I told her he had coded three times since arriving.

"Okay," she said with a resigned sigh. "Well, at least they have me on a one-to-one."

I nodded and patted her shoulder. "Hopefully, they can get a couple more docs to come in early."

She shrugged. We both knew that was unlikely.

When Lizzie left, I sat down at my desk to finish my documentation. With the three codes during my shift, I hadn't had time to do all my charting.

An hour later, I closed the program and caught sight of the card the older woman had handed me earlier. A moment of regret washed over me. I didn't remember the woman, but that didn't mean she hadn't been a patient. I quickly opened the card and smiled. Tucked inside was a picture of her sitting next to an older gentleman and surrounded by family members. I immediately recognized the man as a former patient.

*You made his last days bearable. We can't begin to thank you,* she had written.

Tears burned the backs of my eyes as I remembered how sad the man had been in his final days. I really wished I'd said something to the woman I assumed was his wife.

I knew I needed some downtime. Like so many in my profession, I was barreling toward burnout.

Of course, that just made me feel guilty. There was such need in the medical field, on all fronts. But the attentive, optimistic nurse I'd once been and who my patients still deserved had disappeared. Maybe I'd been naïvely idealistic when I began my career. Now, I felt completely hollowed out.

I'd just stuffed the card back into its envelope when my phone rang. "Hello?" I asked as I shoved the envelope into the front pocket of my scrubs.

"Hey, you still at work?"

I recognized my friend Tommy's voice. Never one for convention, he'd rarely utter a "hello" before diving into a conversation. "Yeah, but I've just finished and was about to leave."

"Good, let's go out tonight. You need to let your hair down, and I need to get laid."

"Ugh, dude, I told you I don't need to know about your sex life."

"You love it, and you know it," Tommy said. His response to this conversation had been the same since we were old enough to have sex lives.

"Are you still coming with me to Peachleaf for the funeral?" I asked, deliberately changing the subject since all I wanted was a shower and my bed. I also needed a friend with me for moral support when I returned to my hometown to bury my grandma.

"Yeah, of course, but I can't be gone long. I've got my hands full at work."

"No problem—" I said, "—but I'm glad you're coming."

"You know I love..." he began as his voice trailed off and he cleared his throat. "I loved your grandma. Besides, I want some of your mom's cookies. She's the best baker in Colorado." I couldn't help but smile at his attempt to lighten the conversation.

"That she is. Okay, let me finish up here, and I'll let you know about tonight."

"That's a nope. We're going out. Go home, wash the hospital stink off, and I'll be by to get you about nine."

I rolled my neck, willing the day's stress to go away, and knew I didn't have much choice. If I didn't go out, Tommy would just end up at my house bitching about being too young to spend a Friday night staring at my four walls.

"You're a pain in my ass, but okay. I'll text when I get home."

After listening to Tommy tease me about me *wanting* a pain in my ass, I hung up and headed out the door.

I was damned lucky to have Tommy in my life. How my crazy friend could graduate with honors in his bachelor's program, then law school, would forever confound me. I mean, he hardly ever studied, but his mind was like a steel trap, anything that went in stuck there.

Lucky for him, at least. And lucky for me, because I desperately needed my bestie with me as I faced the loss of my grandma and the small town I'd moved away from long ago. As much as Peachleaf held some of my most cherished memories, I'd never been all that eager to return to the tiny town.

# 2

## HUNTER

"**F**UCK!" I YELLED AS my alarm startled me awake by blaring its usual nineteen eighties Guns N' Roses hard-rock anthem. My dad had used it when he'd been a kid, because, as he said, "Nothing like GNR to get the blood pumping." Now, I let it wake me up, because it made me feel close to him.

That didn't mean I enjoyed it waking me after a piss-poor night's rest, though. I'd tossed and turned all freaking night and fallen asleep less than an hour ago. I tried slamming my hand onto the ancient alarm clock to shut it up before giving in and finally ripping the cord out of the wall.

I reluctantly hauled myself out of bed, knowing it was too late to get any more sleep. Even if the alarm clock hadn't gone off, my body clock probably would have, and I'd be up soon anyway. There was no more delaying facing my freaking life once again.

I shuffled down to the kitchen to pour myself a cup of the lukewarm coffee my brother always left in the pot before leaving for his three a.m. hospital shift. I sighed and wondered how Deke survived Medical School just to face that schedule day in and day out.

A box of cornflakes sat open on the counter, and I steamed. "Can't a freaking house guest close the damn cereal box? I don't even charge his ass rent."

After grabbing the milk out of the refrigerator, I poured myself a bowl of cereal before slumping into the chair at the kitchen table.

Halfway through breakfast, my phone rang. I couldn't help the heavy sigh that came with it seeing it was my baby sister calling. *Again*!

I ignored it. Sierra was on the school board in our little town. Of course, she'd have heard the news.

I finished my cereal, put my bowl in the sink, and was about to go back upstairs for a shower when the phone rang again.

"Well, shit," I said and swiped to answer. "Sierra, I don't want to hear it."

"What? That you've done the right thing, and we can fight this?" she asked.

"It doesn't matter, they fired me, and now I'm done with it all. It's not like I wanted to be a cop the rest of my life or anything."

"Brother," she crooned. "You caught the SOB red-handed. That makes you a hero, not the problem."

"Have you told Sheriff Forester that?" I asked, giving it my best snark.

"As a matter of fact, I have!" she said without hesitation.

"I know, sis, but he got off scot-free. We both knew if he was acquitted, I'd be the one to lose."

Sierra sighed. We sat in silence on the phone, before I said, "Okay, I'm gonna let you go. I'm gonna take a shower and drink copious amounts of coffee at Lew's Diner. Then I'm gonna try to figure out what to do with the rest of my life."

"Perfect," Sierra said in a chipper voice. "I'll meet you at Lew's, say, in an hour?"

"Sierra, I need..."

"You need *not* to be alone and we both know it, you block-head. See you in an hour!" she said, and hung up. If she'd been on our grandpa's old rotary phone, I'm sure she'd have slammed it down dramatically.

Leave it to my sister to bring a smile to my face, even through all this shit.

Forty-five minutes later, I was sitting in the restaurant waiting for her to show. The woman was nothing if not punctual and usually early. She got fussy when she had to wait. I already had enough going on without her fussing just because I didn't get to Lew's on time.

I'd finished my first cup of coffee, and the server had just refilled it when Sierra burst through the door, a phone to her ear. The entire restaurant turned to see who was making such a ruckus. Sierra had never learned to be unobtrusive. She was one hundred percent seen at all times.

Sierra was technically my stepsister, but she basically couldn't remember a time when I wasn't her big brother. My mom had married her dad when Sierra was still little, and she'd been as much a sister as anyone could be. She was also a fierce defender of our family, and me in particular. I couldn't ask for a better champion in my corner, even if it bordered on being pushy sometimes.

"Paul, I've told you a hundred times, it's either going to be McGraw-Hill or none of them. No, I don't care that it costs twice as much. Warrenstown deserves the best textbooks, end of story." She hung up the phone and looked at me crossly.

I put my hands up. "Don't be mad at me. I don't care which textbooks you pick."

She sighed and sat down. "I swear this town is going down the toilet," she said in a whisper. Sierra was first and foremost a politician.

"It is what it's always been. Nothing much has changed there in the past hundred years or more."

She shrugged. "Maybe, but anyway." Sierra gave me a once over, then waved at the guy serving us and pointed at the upside-down coffee cup in front of her.

"So, how do you plan on playing this? Shall we go to the press? Do you want to sue?"

"No, definitely not. I'll find another job."

"I thought you said you'd have a hard time getting taken on by another force since you were fired for insubordination."

I winced. I'd said that to the entire family the last time we all gathered for a Sunday dinner. At the time, we were all sure after I'd arrested Alderman Grey for stealing parts from the John Deere dealership, he'd be found guilty. The Sheriff told me to drop the case, and when I refused, he threatened to fire me.

The deputy county prosecutor was as new to the job as I was, and he quickly took the case on, meaning I didn't get fired... at least, not right away. Apparently the small town ol' boys' club still ruled the roost in these parts, because once the higher ups–his boss and mine–got involved in the case, the charges against the alderman were dropped, and I got fired anyway.

"Sierra, I still have the money Grandpa gave me for graduation and can tap the trust he set up for us. I'm fine."

"You're not fine, and you shouldn't just roll over. There's a lot of people who were glad you went after the old fool."

I looked at her for several minutes, thinking about how this wasn't the first time our hometown had tried to shit on the family. My grandparents had been the first interracial couple to marry in this county, and there were still townsfolk around who'd hated them and the rest of us for it.

"Sierra, just take a moment to think. You know the people in the community hated Grandma and Grandpa. Hell, there's still a huge group of haters lurking around every corner. I'd be patrolling, and some redneck would even call me the N word. Let's face it, my work in this county and probably all of Kansas is done. Besides, I don't think I want to be a deputy any longer."

She looked at me, shocked. "You've always wanted to work in law enforcement."

"Only 'cause my dad did. Now, I think I was just trying to fill his shoes."

Her expression turned sad, and she placed her hand over mine. For several seconds, I just stared at how small hers was compared to mine. "Hunter, I didn't know your dad, but I'm guessing he was really proud of you. If he were here, he'd know the best advice to give, but I'm sure he'd want you to do something you love with all your heart."

My dad had loved being a deputy sheriff. He would probably have become sheriff too, despite the town disapproving of his parents. He used to talk about work all the time, driving Mom crazy. I never loved it the way my father had, though. Sometimes I even hated the job with a passion.

Sierra leaned back, sipping the coffee the server had poured her while watching me closely. "If I could wave a magic wand, what would you do with your life?" she asked.

I shrugged, then said the first thing that came to mind. "Skiing."

Her face brightened at my honest answer. I'd been on the ski patrol for ages and skied every chance I got. The fact that my aunt and uncle ran several ski resorts across the Rockies had given me plenty of opportunities to learn.

"Then go make a living skiing," she said.

The server came over to take our order, and she spoke first. "I'm not staying, but my brother will have your triple-stack pancakes and a side of poached eggs with Hollandaise sauce."

"Um," I complained, cocking an eyebrow in her direction. "When did you start ordering for me?"

She laughed out loud. "Since you've ordered the same thing for the past ten years."

She got up, kissed the top of my head, and said, "I love you, Hunter. Don't let the haters win. Do what makes you happy. Even if you have to fight tooth and nail to get it."

As usual, Sierra's absence left a huge hole in the room. Left alone with my thoughts and coffee, I pondered her advice. Should I try to make a living skiing? Maybe. It wouldn't hurt to contact my aunt and uncle to see if they had an opening.

I picked my phone up without thinking too much about it and texted Aunt Monica, my dad's sister.

Me: *Auntie, I was just let go from my job. Sierra said I should think about skiing for a living. LOL. Got any jobs that'll pay me to ski around for fun?*

Two minutes later, I got a ding.

Aunt Monica: *No, we don't pay people to ski, but we do to be in charge of the patrol. How are you with volunteers?*

Laughing, I knew I was about to be preached at about work ethic. Even though my entire family knew I was a workaholic, my auntie loved to fuss.

Me: *I've been on the ski patrol for years, so I know a bit. I could also talk to my head patroller and get some pointers. Tell me more.*

The server came over and dumped the mega plate of pancakes and eggs in front of me. I dug in and felt an odd sense of relief, and not just for my growling stomach. Sierra was a noisy, nosy mess, but she'd given me direction. Maybe the disaster my career had become was just the kick in the ass I needed toward the life I'd actually wanted all along.

"Yeah, that sounds good, Auntie," I said, after hearing she would book me a hotel room to spend the night in Denver. She'd just explained all the work she needed me to do at a resort they'd been assigned to salvage by a bankruptcy court.

All I knew at this point was that the resort was old, but had been renovated in the nineteen eighties. There'd been work done on the slopes, and the equipment had supposedly been upgraded, but the company was notorious for skimping and cutting corners to the point of jeopardizing safety.

"I'm going to need you to go around with the inspectors we hired to check the lifts before we do much else," Aunt Monica instructed.

"Shouldn't be a problem," I said.

"Good. I also need you to take over the ski patrol and ensure all the volunteers are caught up on their training. Really, I want to know if we need to shut down this winter. I sure as hell don't want to drive insurance costs up because we took on this mess."

"Why *are* you taking it on?" I asked.

"Well, since I'm going with you, I can give you more details when I arrive in Denver. But for now, let's just say it's a good business opportunity."

I shook my head as I hung up. My aunt believed in hard work, and that went double for family. She paid well, if not too well, as my uncle often complained. She didn't even blink, though, saying, "You need to pay your people what they're worth, Harris, or they'll quit, and then you're stuck scraping the barrel." So, she paid more than any other employer around, and as a result, Cabot Management had been growing steadily for twenty-five years.

Even though my dad had passed years ago, Mom and Aunt Monica had remained steadfast friends and were more like sisters. When Mom remarried, Aunt Monica adopted our new family as her own, including considering Sierra her niece. "The more family, the better," I overheard her saying to Mom one evening when she'd come to visit.

Where neither my dad nor I had an ounce of business sense, Aunt Monica was all business. Her having married into a ridiculously wealthy Colorado family, who owned and managed several ski resorts in the Rocky Mountains, just made sense. That, and the fact she was over the top in love with my Uncle Harris.

After our phone call, I wasted no time packing and flying into Denver, then checked into my hotel, and stared at the walls. What the fuck was I supposed to do for the night?

It didn't take me long to find an answer. I was in a real city with real gay men. I didn't have to worry about being a deputy in a small college town. Here, I was anonymous, and I wasn't going to waste that hookup opportunity. I thought about downloading Grindr. I'd done that once before when I'd been out of town, but I didn't really have it in me to deal with some tweaked-out guy, like the last time I'd used the app.

So, instead, I did a quick online search for the nearest gay bar, pocketed my phone, and headed out in search of my evening's entertainment.

# 3

# CAM

I SAT STARING AT the television where *Drag Dance*, the popular new show designed to compete with *RuPaul's Drag Race*, ran on a never-ending loop. My mind was elsewhere, flitting between work and my grandmother's upcoming funeral. Tommy reached over and patted my arm. "Cam, I know this is hard."

I nodded. "Yeah, it is. I miss her, and I didn't get up there enough to see her."

"You live in Denver. She lived in bumfuck nowhere. I'm sure she understood."

"Yeah," I agreed, not having the energy to laugh at Tommy's apt description of where we'd both grown up.

We finished dinner and wandered over to the club's dance floor. This was one of the last gay clubs left in Denver, mainly because it catered to gay *and* straight communities. Tommy immediately disappeared into the throng, as he usually did when he was on the hunt, but I hung back, watching the crowd like I loved to do.

Even as a teenager, I preferred watching other people interact more than I enjoyed being involved. I only participated in things like sports, because I was forced to by my dad. Later, when Dad died and Mom and I moved to Peachleaf to live with Grandma, I played basketball, because that and skiing were literally the only things to do in town, especially in the winter.

I'd nearly been lost in thought when an absolutely gorgeous man walked into the bar, snapping me to full attention. At maybe six four or five, he was much taller than me, and had the body of a man who worked out regularly. He had a dark complexion with cropped black hair, and my eyes snagged on the huge biceps bursting out of his tight short-sleeved shirt. He was everything I found attractive in a guy.

From what I thought was a sufficiently obscured place at the bar, my eyes explored the man's body, from the contours of his waist that narrowed beautifully down to the tight jeans that clung to what looked to be very muscular thighs. As my gaze roamed back up the delicious man in front of me, it landed on two penetrating brown eyes staring back at me.

Intimidating and intense, that's what this man was. Yet, something about his unwavering stare held more. I was the first to blink, and it snapped me out of my gorgeous man-induced trance enough to look away before rolling my eyes at myself.

I always thought I saw something innocent, something vulnerable, in people's expressions, and each time, I ended up getting burned. After years of heartache, I was fully aware I liked bad boys. Men who attracted trouble attracted me, plain and simple. But one shitty relationship after another, none lasting more than a couple of months, had taught me that if big-butch men had vulnerable sides, they were buried too deep for me to ever uncover.

Before I could order my second beer, I heard my name being called from the stage.

"Cam, baby!" I immediately recognized the drag queen Madonya's voice.

I got up to try to escape, but when I heard Tommy's voice calling in unison, I knew I'd been had.

"Cam, sweetheart, come on up here and sing us a song, you cute little nightingale."

I turned and flipped both Tommy and Madonya off, which made them antagonize me more.

They began to chant "Cammy, Cammy, Cammy," and as the whole place turned toward me, I shrugged and headed for the stage.

It wasn't like I didn't love to sing. It's just that I was tired and grumpy, and… actually, now I thought about it, that was probably a good reason to let my hair down with a song. Performing for an enthusiastically drunk crowd always got the endorphins flowing.

The two stepped aside as Madonya handed me the microphone. I gave a nod to Larry, Madonya's husband, to cue the music.

My mother had loved Robin S. from her and Dad's wild days, so I'd been singing "Show Me Love" since I was knee-high. The fact that I was a high tenor and could hit the high notes and hold them came with years of practice.

"*Ah, yeah, yeah, yeah…*" I began, letting the music flow and the beat pull the day's stress from me.

Even though I rarely did drag these days, mostly because I couldn't spare the hours it took to put my makeup on, I still enjoyed performing. I never lip-synced. I belted out the songs with gusto, which my audiences always appreciated.

I opened my eyes long enough to see the crowd as amped up as I was to the music. Without asking, and to my secret delight, Larry didn't stop at one song but let my entire set play out. When I'd finally had enough, I took a bow and thanked the cheering crowd.

I smiled as they whooped and whistled, and several people I recognized yelled for me to do one more.

"Okay, okay. But this one isn't a dance song," I warned. I pointed at Larry, who shook his head at me because he didn't like when I sang slower songs at the club. But I refused to budge, and with one look from me, he knew exactly what song I was after. Pouting, he turned on the music.

*"Can anybody find me somebody to love...?"*

As I launched into the Queen song, I temporarily caught sight of the muscleman from earlier. The way he stared at me sent shivers through my body, but I was soon lost to the music, belting out the song as God and Freddie Mercury intended.

Despite Larry's objections, the crowd screamed when the song was over. I smiled and waved as I left the stage and immediately found myself face to chest with a wall of muscle.

"Hi," the man said in a deep rumble that sent another round of shivers through me.

"Hey," I managed in reply as my eyes tracked upward to his strong jaw and piercing eyes.

Everything about this guy screamed sex. Screw karaoke when there were more important things that needed screwing–namely, me. It'd also been a long time, and I'd had such a shit day, so why the hell not?

"Wanna get out of here?" the guy asked, his eyes not leaving mine.

"Sure, I just need to tell my friend I'm going with you. What hotel?" I asked.

He smiled, and before he could answer, I snapped a picture of him, texted it to Tommy, and then showed the man my text explaining that if he wanted to kill me, there was evidence of who did it.

That made him chuckle. The rich sound unleashed a kaleidoscope of butterflies in my stomach.

"The Marriott," the muscleman said, and I nodded before going to find Tommy.

As the usual fantasy of wedding bells rang in my ears, I shook it off and told myself to just Go *have an amazing hookup with a gorgeous man, and don't expect anything more,* and went looking for my best friend. *This isn't the kind of man to fall for.*

# 4

## HUNTER

I WALKED INTO THE bar and immediately laid eyes on one of the most handsome men I'd ever seen. He was tall, though several inches shorter than me, and had that slim swimmer's build that made me thirst to touch him. The fact that I caught him checking me out made me smile. Maybe tonight was showing promise after all.

I was about to walk over to him when the drag queen onstage began taunting him. After others joined in on it, he climbed onto the stage and started singing.

At first, I thought he had to be lip-syncing, because no way did someone randomly sing that well.

Of course, the more I watched from my vantage point, a head taller than most people at the bar, I realized it was actually his voice.

I sat and listened, mesmerized, as he ran through a full set of songs. He was about to leave the stage when the crowd demanded more, and during the pause in performing, I had enough sense to pull my phone out and record his final song.

As he began to sing Queen's "Somebody to Love," I felt my heart beat a little quicker. I wanted to be his somebody to love. *No, fuck that, no.* I needed to find somebody for the night, somebody to get my rocks off with, that was it. Once I started working for my aunt, my next opportunity to get away would be... well, probably too long to even think about.

I made my way toward the stage the moment he began the final bars of the song, recording him on my phone as I went. I wanted to be the first person he ran into as he came offstage, because I wanted him with all I had in me, especially after hearing his sultry singing voice.

The energy between us sparked, and it only took him a moment to agree to a hookup. When he snapped my picture and texted it to his friend, it made me like him that much more.

As a deputy, how often had I advised college kids to do that very thing? "Let someone know who you're leaving with," I'd imparted dozens of times. Even in our small town, several lives could've been spared if the kids had abided by that simple rule.

By the time he returned, I was beginning to salivate at the thought of having this sexy man's body wrapped around mine.

I wasn't one for physical affection outside the bedroom, but when he took my hand as we drove my rental to the hotel, I didn't pull away. This guy felt different, like more than just a quick fuck, although that's all it could possibly be.

Soon I would be headed for the mountains, miles away from Denver, in the height of winter. At best, I'd only get back here in the spring. More likely, though, my aunt would have me working so many hours I'd be lucky to see Denver next summer.

This was a one-night stand, but damn, I was going to enjoy every minute.

# 5

# CAM

I FOUND TOMMY ON the other side of the club talking up a couple of guys, and when I told him I was going home with someone, his face lifted into a feral grin. "It's about time, Cam! Try not to explode on him!" he yelled as I made a beeline back across the dance floor.

I half expected the muscleman to be gone by the time I returned to him. Instead, he sat on a stool at the bar, waiting for me.

"Ready to go?" I asked, leaning in close enough to be heard over the pulsing music.

I must've caught him by surprise, because he startled, and his body brushed lightly against mine. A visible shudder ran through him at the contact, causing a similar reaction in me. It seemed we were definitely attracted to one another, which kind of surprised me.

I considered myself fairly good-looking, at least enough to usually get second glances at the bar, but gorgeous men with chiseled muscles didn't typically go for smaller-built nurses like me who worked so many hours indoors that my pasty skin practically glowed in the dark.

For the first time in a long time, I was looking forward to being with a guy. As we walked out of the club and climbed into the muscleman's rental, all I could think about was the various positions we could try all night long.

The moment we stepped inside the hotel room, he turned and crowded me back against the closed door as his lips sought mine. The kiss was gentle at first, almost teasing, before he took command and deepened it, leaving no doubt about who was in charge tonight.

As his hands began unbuttoning my shirt, his mouth trailed down to my neck, sucking on the sensitive skin as he slid my shirt off and tossed it aside.

My heartbeat was beating extremely fast, and I was putty under those big, delightfully calloused hands.

I let out a small yelp, then laughed when he all but lifted me up and carried me to the bed. I was already only half-dressed, but he wasted no time unzipping my tight pants, greedily searching for my cock, which immediately sprang free since I'd gone commando. His smile grew as his eyes raked over my naked body. Apparently, I met his approval.

Without hesitating, he crawled over me and positioned his head between by legs. His eyes never left mine as he licked across my slit before sucking my cock into his mouth.

"Oh, God!" I breathed as pleasure coursed through my body.

He worked my pants the rest of the way off, never missing a beat, then licked around my head before taking me deeper into his hot mouth. He continued his wonderfully filthy ministrations for what felt like hours as I writhed and moaned on the bed.

When my cock slipped from his mouth, I knew it was my chance to return the favor. I sat up and pushed him off the bed to standing, and began undoing his pants as he stripped his tight shirt off.

"God, yes," I said when I saw his taut torso in all its naked glory. That six-pack needed to be worshiped and I was sitting at the perfect height to lick it. *Fuck, yes!*

He chuckled as my tongue roamed the well-defined ridges of his abdomen, a dark sound that sent a jolt straight to my cock. Then he stepped out of his jeans, leaving his boxers on, and tried to ease me back onto my back.

"Oh, no. My turn," I said, reaching over and tugging his boxers all the way off.

When I patted the bed next to me, the muscled god smiled in amusement, but complied. I then straddled him and began moving my hips, grinding our bare cocks against each other, as I kissed him.

"You're so fucking sexy," I whispered.

He wrapped his arms around me, then flipped me around, repositioning our bodies so his cock lined up with my ass. He slowly began to thrust against me, sliding his cock between my cheeks, and I moaned with pleasure.

"I-I don't usually fuck guys I don't know," I whispered.

"We don't have to," he said, but didn't stop moving, continuing to tease my hole.

"Fuck, if you don't stop, I won't be able to..." I said, deciding that if I didn't take control now, I'd throw caution to the wind and impale myself on his cock.

So instead, I turned back around and pushed him further onto the bed before moving down his huge, sexy body until my mouth was in licking distance of his very large cock.

"Oh, this is nice," I said, teasing the guy whose name I still didn't know. When I looked up, his smile was gone, replaced with a look of pure hunger. Teasing time was over as I licked from his balls up to the head, enjoying the smell of him as I went. Pure man, pure sex. I quickly licked the precum from his slit, and God, he tasted so good.

I slipped him into my mouth and gagged when his cock hit the back of my throat. I couldn't remember when I last gagged during a blow job, but this guy was so damn *big*.

I recovered quickly, wanting him more than ever. I sucked his cock all the way to the back of my throat again and swallowed.

"Yes," he moaned. "Fuck, yes!"

He quickly flipped us around, so I was again on my back, then wrapped his hand around the back of my head and began thrusting into my mouth. I loved it when a guy fucked my mouth like that. I moaned in appreciation while savoring the taste of him.

His six-pack flexed as he glided his cock in and out of my mouth. I glanced up to see that he was leaning on his elbow with his head thrown back, displaying his broad chest. God, could this guy be any hotter?

When it seemed like he was approaching climax, I pulled back. I wanted more than to taste him on my tongue, I wanted him inside me. I ungracefully scrambled off the bed and found my pants in a heap on the floor as the guy tracked my movements, not speaking, just palming his cock as he waited.

I pulled the strip of condoms out of the pocket, then sighed. "I don't think these will fit."

The guy chuckled again, that deep, sexy rumble causing me to shiver. "I've got the right size," he said, and scooted across the bed to find his discarded pants.

Luckily, he also had packets of lube, thank fucking God, because I couldn't take that much man without a lot of it.

He ripped open the wrapper and slid the condom on, and I stared transfixed as he then stroked lube onto his sheathed cock. "Care to rejoin me?" he asked with a smirk, motioning toward the bed. He applied more lube to his fingers as I climbed back on the bed, and he lubed me up while taking my cock into his mouth again. This time, I could tell it was about giving me pleasure as he prepped me. I hoped to God I wouldn't embarrass myself if I couldn't take all of him.

"Fuuuuuck," I moaned, all concern slipping from my thoughts as he moved one, then two, then three fingers in and out of me. It usually took longer to prep me, but I was so horny. I wanted that huge cock in me. *Needed* it.

"You ready?" he asked as he pulled off. I smiled and stroked myself while he positioned himself, lining his cock up to my hole, and draping my legs over his shoulders for better access. His head breached me as he thrust gently back and forth, easing my muscles into accepting him.

"God, it's... so much," I said, again unsure I could take all of him if that was just the head I was feeling.

He smiled at me, his face belaying any concern. "Just relax. I won't go too fast."

I nodded and let him take control. He moved his head in and out of me several times until all the pain subsided, then when I nodded, he pushed back inside me. This time, the stretch didn't hurt, and warmth spread through me as my body accepted him.

"Aah," he said as he pulled back. "Goddamn, you're tight."

I laughed. "To you, everyone is tight."

"But they don't feel this good," he said, and the compliment made me blush. Not that he could tell since I was glowing red from all the excitement anyway.

He continued thrusting slowly, gradually getting deeper and deeper, the stretch becoming more and more pleasurable the deeper he got.

Finally, his body pressed flush against mine, and I knew he was all the way inside me.

"Fuck," I moaned as I languished in the full feeling of being fucked by such a huge cock.

"Ready?" he asked.

"God, yes."

I barely had time to look at him before he began to move. Slow at first, then faster, and faster.

"God!" I yelled, not giving a damn if anyone else in the hotel heard me. This was by far the best sex I'd ever had, and it deserved the vocal praise.

"Yes, fuck, yes!"

We were both working up a sweat. I'd never felt this... so much.

He began to slow his pace. "Want to get on all fours?"

"Mmm," was all I could say. I was feeling so wonderfully used.

The moment he pulled out, I quickly scrambled onto my knees, desperate to have him back inside me.

As he slipped deep into me, the sensation even greater than before, all the stress of the day and past week melted away. All that existed was this night with this sexy, delicious man, and all the wonderfully wicked ways he was having with my body.

He began to ride me hard, reaching down to pull my body up, and kissing me. God, that was so fucking hot.

He thrust into me as he tongue-fucked my mouth, and eventually, I fell back onto all fours again, so I could brace myself against the onslaught.

I came with no warning, then flopped onto my stomach, completely spent. I could tell he was close, too, as he pulled out and began jacking off.

He must have pulled off the condom because moments later, I felt warm ribbons of cum land across my back. He collapsed onto me, our bodies fitting snuggly together, even in the awkward, but intimate, position.

After a few gloriously delightful moments where he held me to him, he got up to get a towel, returning to wipe up my back before doing the same to the bed.

"Gonna have a wet spot," he said, chuckling.

"At least we pulled the covers back."

He climbed back into bed, and we lay together, the muscleman's body partially draped over mine. The pressure of having such a huge man lying on top of me felt so good, especially after we'd screwed our brains out.

"God, I needed that," I said mostly to myself.

He laughed. "Yeah, me too."

I turned my face toward him, smiling. "So, guessing this is a one-time thing?" I asked, and he nodded.

"Yeah, I leave tomorrow morning for a new job, but..." He paused as if searching for the words, and used one of his huge hands to stroke my hair. "This was good. Better than good."

I chuckled. "I've done the one-time thing before, so don't think you have to coddle me." I slipped out from under him, already missing his warmth as I did so. Even with the upscale hotel's heating system, the wind blowing on the exposed windows let in enough cool air to make the room chilly.

"Hey," he said as I began dressing. "What's your name?"

I winked at him before pulling my socks on. "It's best not to know, right?"

He shook his head. "I-I guess."

I leaned over, kissing his amazing mouth, and smiled. "I know."

I grabbed my coat, pulling it on as I made my way to the door. I took one last look at the sexy Adonis still lying naked on the bed and sighed. *Damn, I'd have loved to have more with this one.* The unguarded thought nearly had me stopping in my tracks. Being on the verge of injecting mushy emotions into a one-and-done hookup was exactly why I needed to book it out of there.

I quickly dashed from the room, through the hallways, and out the hotel's front door. I guessed from the choice of hotel that the guy must've been loaded. He was probably some business tycoon I should've recognized, but whoever he was, he was now just a memory, a delicious, sexy, sweat-inducing memory. Not to mention the very real twinge in my backside he'd gifted me.

It was just after four a.m., and I was exhausted. When I got home, I quickly showered, crawled into bed, and fell asleep dreaming of the tall, dark, and handsome man who knew all the right ways to use my body.

# 6

# Hunter

THE MORNING AFTER THE most memorable hookup of my life, I sat across from my aunt as she rambled on about the resort Cabot Management was hoping to acquire.

"Between you and me, we're considering purchasing the dilapidated resort. Its hot springs are a major selling point, and with the right management, it could be a destination, despite its unfortunate location."

"What's wrong with the location?" I asked, suddenly feeling concerned.

"It's nowhere near a prosperous town, which means we'll have to attract visitors to it as a destination in its own right. It has a fairly good following, from what I can tell from the paperwork, but that could be smoke and mirrors. Optimum

Management Services, they go by OMS, is notorious for questionable tactics. I'm afraid we won't know the real situation until we get there and start ironing it out."

"So, my job is to what, check out the place for you?"

Aunt Monica shrugged. "Yes, and like I said, ensure our ski patrol is up to the task. The old guy that used to run it is retiring. Rumor has it he clashed with one of the OMS assholes, and they chased him off when he wouldn't give in to their demands. Regardless, we can't run a ski resort without a strong ski patrol."

"That's mostly volunteers, though. You should be able to find out what's going on without me."

She shrugged again. "My guess is they've had such a bad experience with OMS, they won't tell me anything even if they want to. That company is notorious for a lot of things. But they may be willing to talk to you, if you feel up to this?"

It was my turn to shrug. "Well, you've already flown me out here, plus I haven't got anything better to do, so why not?"

"Oh," she said, almost as if she'd forgotten. I squinted at her, knowing my aunt forgot nothing, and this was the other shoe about to drop. "There's a part-owner we'd have to buy out, or join forces with. I'd like you to find out what you can about them as well."

I laughed. "And now, we get down to it. Auntie, I'm not going to spy on someone for you."

"I didn't say *spy*, and I won't be taking lip from my own nephew, especially if he's about to work for me. I just want to know what kind of person he is. His grandmother just passed away, and he'll be inheriting her holdings. Besides that, I don't know anything about him. Don't even have a name yet, so I can't do my own sp... *research* on him."

I laughed again. "I won't spy..." I repeated, looking my aunt in the eye to make sure she understood me, "...but I'll see what I can find out. If there's something fishy about him, I'll let you know, but you'll have to do your own *research*."

I could tell she wanted to argue, and for a moment I waited for her to do just that, but instead, she shook her head. Reaching over and taking my hand, she smiled. "You are so much like my brother. Owen would've been so proud of you. He *was* proud of you."

She sighed deeply, patted my hand, then held hers out to shake as if we were completing a business deal. "I've got a helicopter waiting to take us to the resort. I'll be there for a few days, then I'll leave you on your own."

I nodded, shaking her hand as we both stood up, and grabbed my luggage from beside me. I'd already packed and checked out of my hotel, deciding I didn't want to stay there any longer. I'd only start thinking about sexy singers in Denver bars and then refuse to leave.

It wasn't like I needed to live in a city. Hell, sometimes even Warrenstown had felt too big for me, but I was still a twenty-eight-year-old man with needs that would be hard to meet being in the middle of nowhere, especially on an old derelict resort in a deserted town deep in the Rocky Mountains.

Oh well, when life sent you up shit creek, you grabbed for the nearest paddle. And that lone paddle was Aunt Monica's job offer. So, I followed her onto a helicopter to fly to my new life, or at least, my new life for now.

# 7

# CAM

I SLAMMED ON MY brakes as a herd of big-horn sheep dashed across the road in front of me. "You okay?" Tommy asked as he woke up suddenly.

"Yeah, good thing the road's been cleared," I said.

Tommy looked down to his right as the mountain gave way to a sheer drop, and gulped. "Um, maybe I should stay awake to help you navigate."

I chuckled. "Whatever."

Tommy had already grilled me about my glorious night with the muscleman. When I glanced over and caught him staring at his phone, I assumed he was looking at the man's photo I'd texted him for safety. "He looks and sounds so sexy. Did you get his number for a repeat?" Tommy asked.

"No, it was just a one-time thing."

He shook his head disapprovingly while looking at his phone again. "I think I'd have tried anyway. He looks like a nice, sturdy tree to climb."

"You're a mess," I said as we descended the mountain.

"Hey, I'm not," he argued. "I just know a hot man when I see one."

We teased one another as I navigated the switchbacks on the two-lane road, which had never been expanded even though the state had plans to do so decades ago.

By the time we reached the bottom of the mountain, Tommy had once again fallen asleep, which was fine. I didn't mind the drive, and we still had an hour before we got to the resort. We'd be here a few days, since I needed to help Mom with Grandma's funeral arrangements and all the preparations around the resort.

Grandma owned forty percent of the ski resort, which I'd recently learned she left entirely to me in her will. She owned that much because she was a freaking bobcat who fought with every ounce of strength she had to keep the place from being ripped out from under her. I owed it to her to keep the place going as best I could.

Besides being popular with the locals, though, the Peachleaf Resort was never a big moneymaker. By the time my grandmother inherited it, the place was quickly falling back into disrepair.

Even though her family had come from money, my grandmother had decided not to throw any more of her own into the property. So, in the early eighties, she found three other families who had all worked for the resort for generations to invest in the property. The three each took twenty percent. My grandmother kept forty, and she reserved the right to approve any sale of the resort.

That saved her when a decade ago, the descendants of the three sold to one of the sneakiest, most underhanded companies we'd ever had the misfortune to come across—Optimum Management Services, otherwise known as OMS.

They sued my grandmother when she refused to approve the sale. After spending way too much money on attorneys and with no end in sight, she finally relented, but negotiated to retain the management of the place and the first right of refusal to purchase their stock.

Grandma kept them on a short leash, until she decided to retire five years ago, and my mom assumed management duties. Apparently, though, there was some perceived loophole that if Grandma retired, OMS would be able to take control and maybe even force a sale of her stock.

So, the litigation began again. Luckily, this time, Grandma had a better attorney, who turned the lawsuit back on them. She ended up winning in court, along with being awarded a rather substantial settlement.

That was just months before she died. Now, who the hell knew what was happening?

Tommy stirred in his seat as I turned down the gravel road toward the resort. I could already make out Moose Mountain looming over the Peachleaf reservoir. When my grandma was a kid, the Army Corps of Engineers had damned the river and created the reservoir, which based on old pictures I'd seen had actually enhanced the beauty of this majestic place. In another five minutes, we'd circle around Mount Chester, and everything would open up into the valley where I'd spent most of my life.

This was my favorite part of the drive. Colorado was beautiful, but Peachleaf Valley? It was a hidden jewel straight out of some fantasy novel.

*A hidden jewel*. That was actually the biggest obstacle in turning the resort around. It was so hidden, potential guests didn't even know it existed.

# 8

# HUNTER

"Wow, what a beautiful place," I said through the helicopter headphones as Peachleaf Valley came into view.

"Yeah, this area has been given featured in travel magazines, because the valley is so picturesque," Aunt Monica responded.

"Well, it gives a good first impression at least," I said, getting a hesitant nod from her.

Once the helicopter landed, I was ready to be back on the ground. It hadn't exactly been harrowing, but the one big gust of wind that had blown up the mountain and thrown the chopper around like a rag doll was enough for me to swear off helicopters for life. I'd much rather take my time and travel by road anyway, thank you very much.

Despite that, I'd been given an incredible welcome to the valley, one I wouldn't forget anytime soon.

We landed at an airport, which was little more than a single airstrip and a trailer that served as a terminal, and were picked up by a driver in a limousine. When it pulled up, I cocked an eyebrow at my aunt, who shrugged before climbing in. It didn't go unnoticed by either of us that both the car and driver were ancient.

"You can just take us to the resort," Aunt Monica told the driver, who nodded and put the beast of a car in gear.

We were only on the road for a short time before coming to a little town. And by little, I meant maybe five or six businesses total, dotted either side of the road. A few fifties-style fast-food restaurants that'd been turned into mom-and-pop shops filled in the rest of town. One place, Polly's Pies, caught my attention, and I planned to check it out later.

Upon passing through the tiny town, the driver turned down a long road that wound its way uphill. There were patches of green as well as worn-out statuary that I assumed used to be in the middle of flower gardens, long ago replaced by lawns.

"So much for first impressions," I said, frowning at the less-than-impressive landscaping.

"That's on the list to improve. Usually, there's snow blanketing everything, but when it melts, like now, the grounds need to look considerably better."

"Is there enough snow on the mountain to ski?" I asked, concerned my new job might already be coming to an abrupt end.

She nodded and pointed up the mountain. "That's where the ski part of the resort is, and it's at least a thousand feet higher than here. The hotel sits right on the water, which is great for summer activities. In winter, they transport people from the hotel to the ski lifts and back by tram."

"Okay, but is there a lodge dedicated to skiing only?"

She shook her head. "Nope, just the main hotel."

"That's problematic. I've skied all my life, and dirty socks and feet are pretty much the theme. Is that what the hotel smells like?"

My aunt laughed. "No, they have a separate area where guests check in and deal with all the equipment. The hotel is dated, but it doesn't smell like feet."

"That's good, I guess," I said, though my face still held the grimace from thinking about staying in a hotel that stank like a ski lodge.

After several minutes, we pulled into a circle drive, still gravel, but the building that sat away from it was spectacular. "Wow, she's a looker."

Aunt Monica peered out the window and nodded. "As long as you don't look too close."

I shrugged, knowing my aunt was looking at every dilapidating detail rather than viewing the project as a whole. I guessed when you were the one paying to fix everything that wasn't up to snuff, it would take a bit of the wonder out of a project.

I followed my aunt out of the limo, waving at the old man who drove us here, thinking I should've probably tipped him. I stopped short at the sight in front of me, letting my mouth drop open in wonderment at the opulent and beautiful building.

Even my stoic aunt smiled at my awestruck expression. She whispered as she leaned closer, "It's spectacular, but wait until you see the water."

I followed her into the building, walking through the communal area, past a battered wooden desk, and into a glassed-in section that looked like it might've been a porch once upon a time. The room looked out on a breathtaking view of sparkling water not much different than when we'd flown over it in the helicopter.

"It's one of the most beautiful places we manage," she said. "The challenge is figuring out how to give it life."

I shook my head. "I'm afraid that'll take someone with a lot more smarts than me. But I can say it looks like it's worth the effort."

"I agree. Now let me show you the rest."

The rooms were awash in pastel pink, with frilly window dressings, pink carpet that'd seen better days, and wallpaper that made me feel just a little nauseous if I looked at it too long. "It looks like the nineteen eighties drank Pepto-Bismol and then threw up in here," I said, laughing.

Aunt Monica nodded, frowning. "I was a teenager in the eighties, and I can't even... well, let's just say there's a lot of updating to do!"

"I'll say," I commented, and followed my aunt down a hallway to where a large pool and two bubbling hot tubs sat empty.

"Here's the best part, the pool and hot tubs are fed by hot springs."

"Except it smells like fart in here."

Aunt Monica slapped my arm playfully, but laughed. "The springs have a lot of sulfur. Believe it or not, that's considered a good thing."

"I guess if you like farts, it's great."

"Come on, fart man, I'll show you the spa."

I wasn't sure why I needed to see everything, but my aunt seemed to be on a roll, so I just went with it. The spa didn't look like it'd been used in a decade. It was dusty and not very appealing, certainly not the calming, relaxed atmosphere a spa should be. No way I'd want a massage down here.

The rest of the place was similar. Lots of potential, lots of ugly. "So, when do I get to meet the ski patrol?" I asked.

Aunt Monica shook her head like she was disappointed I didn't want to start tearing out eighties wallpaper.

"All in good time, but for now, we've got rooms in the executive suites. We'll be staying there for the time being."

I nodded, dreading staying in the pink puke palace I assumed the executive suite would be. Fortunately for me, though, my suite had blue carpet, and the wallpaper, although still garish, was less in your face than the other rooms we'd seen.

That night, I lay in bed thinking about this place and the situation I'd be jumping into feet-first come morning. The bones of the building felt good, if not solid, but the interior and décor needed a major overhaul. I also worried if the lift equipment would be equally out of date, and would the ski patrol even be properly trained? The more my mind wandered, the more daunting my job seemed. What kind of mess had I gotten myself into?

# 9

# CAM

TEARS STREAMED DOWN MY face as I sat between Mom and Tommy, letting my grandmother go once and for all. She had been the cornerstone of my life. Since my dad died, she'd been a second parent.

After the service, I shook hands with a lot of people. Some I knew, but most I didn't. Mom, however, seemed to know them all, and smiled through her sadness as people hugged her and offered their condolences.

The relationship between Mom and her mother-in-law was complicated. At first, in the early years of Mom and Dad's relationship, the two had gone to war with each other, at least, that's the story Dad used to tell. Then, when I was born, something clicked between them. By the time I was old enough to remember, Mom and Grandma had become best friends.

Their close relationship served us all well after Dad passed. He'd hated everything to do with Peachleaf, and wouldn't waste an opportunity to make cutting remarks about his small hometown. Mom never really said anything about it, not until after he was gone.

"Your dad detested Peachleaf, but I... well, I think it's a good place to live and grow up," she'd said.

Mom had been thrust into foster care at a young age and had ended up with a family in Peachleaf. Her foster parents had hated my grandmother, and vice versa, which explained why Grandma didn't care for Mom initially.

Now, with Grandma gone, Mom was alone here. *Maybe*, I thought as I looked over at her, *it was time to talk her into moving to Denver.*

I spent the rest of the day poking around Grandma's small house. She'd grown up in the big house by the reservoir and remained there until twenty or so years ago. When the repairs got the better of her, she boarded up the mansion and moved into the caretaker's cottage.

Honestly, I didn't remember much about the big house, only that it was a dusty mess. At least the roof had been repaired recently, and there were no broken windows I was aware of, so I didn't think it would fall down anytime soon, but it was still a mess that I'd need to deal with soon enough.

The day after the funeral, we had an appointment with Grandma's executor, an ancient attorney she'd hired after Grandpa's death to manage her affairs.

"You already know you've inherited most of your grandmother's estate," Mr. Pauley told me immediately after we sat down, then turned to my mother. "Peggy, you've inherited your home, which was kept separate from the resort estate, so that's free and clear. Unfortunately, it's not as easy for you, Cameron."

"What do I need to know about the partnership?" I asked, and the old man sighed deeply.

"I'm afraid all that is a quagmire. Your grandmother, as you know, had years of difficulties with OMS, the other resort owner. When they lost the countersuit and were ordered to pay your grandmother damages, they immediately filed for bankruptcy. Of course, that means their assets are currently being managed by the courts."

"What does that mean? Weren't they silent partners, except for all the lawsuits, of course?"

He nodded. "Yes, but with your grandmother's death and the fact that OMS is as hateful as any company I've ever dealt with, they've petitioned the court to assign a temporary management company to handle the resort."

He shook his head, and I could see the frustration on his face. "I'm sure this is just another way to undermine your rights to control the day-to-day management..."

"Wait," my mom interjected. "Geneva had full power over the resort's management. That's part of the settlement she made before OMS got involved."

The attorney nodded. "Indeed, and I'm sure now that Cam has taken possession, we should probably convince the court that he can run it. Do you intend to run the resort, Cam?"

I shook my head. "No, but my mother could."

He looked over at her. "Is that true, Peggy? Are you willing to run the resort on your own?"

Mom blushed and looked down at her hands. "I can, at least for a while. But no, I'm sorry, Cam, I don't want to run the resort without Geneva."

"So, what does this mean?" I asked, ignoring the fact that the lawsuit had been filed against Grandma, because Mom was supposedly taking over.

"Well, as you probably already know, you can't give OMS any power to undermine you," the attorney said. "You'll need to exert your objection to the new management to preserve the contractual rights to manage the resort. I can speak to the judge, and we can agree to the new management services, but you'd still need to stand your ground with them. That's the first thing since, even if you sell, the right to manage will be a powerful negotiation tool."

I nodded, feeling some relief. "Do I get to choose the company that does the management?" I asked.

"Technically, of course, but in reality, it would be an uphill battle and one you might not want to fight long-term. I have received notice about the new management company, and they are reputable. Why don't you spend the afternoon researching them, and you can tell me tomorrow how you wish me to proceed."

"What about Grandma's house?" I asked.

"You own that outright. I'm sorry I haven't told you what's in the rest of the will. The big house and properties were never part of the partnership, so those are yours outright. Your grandmother also left you a substantial amount of money, but I dare say, much of that will likely need to be spent on deferred maintenance on the big house. I'm sorry, but that won't leave you much unless the bankruptcy courts decide to give you some money from the settlement."

I sighed. "I'm guessing this means I'm going to have to sell the resort, huh?"

The old man's face showed sympathy. "If it's any consolation, I believe your grandmother always thought you would. I also believe the new management company will improve the overall value of the property, as OMS has a lot of black eyes right now. If you play your cards right, maybe they'll buy out OMS, and when you're ready to sell, your value will be even greater. So, you'll want to retain managing authority as best you can right now, but don't go pissing them off so much that they walk away."

I nodded, feeling a sick dread in the pit of my stomach. I was swamped with memories of listening to my grandmother talk about the past generations who fixed up the old estate. The years I spent skiing the slopes, swimming in the reservoir, and soaking in the hot springs. My happiest memories, my childhood, and my sense of connection to Grandma were all tied to this place.

I would be the last generation of my family to run the Peach-leaf Resort. The prospect broke my heart, and not just because I knew how much Mom and Grandma enjoyed running the place together. By selling, I'd be relinquishing a century-old tradition. That realization weighed heavily on me, but no matter how guilty or nostalgic I felt, I wasn't made to run a resort.

# 10

# Hunter

I DIDN'T SEE MY aunt the morning after our arrival. I'd received a predawn text saying she would be in meetings the entire day. With whom, I had no idea, but I knew better than to question Aunt Monica's business dealings.

Without much to do, I grabbed my phone, flopped back onto the bed, and replayed the video I'd taken of the sexy mystery man belting out the Queen song I couldn't get out of my head.

Wow, he really could sing, and he must've been a natural performer, because he owned that stage. Watching on repeat gave way to memories of our night together, and despite my best efforts to convince myself a one-time hookup was all I'd needed, I craved more. Now that I'd had my hands on him, felt his body beneath mine, and all but worshiped him with my tongue, I was desperate for another taste. Unfortunately, that wasn't going to happen.

If a delicious memory and cell-phone video were all I would ever have of him, I'd better preserve them as best I could. I didn't want to lose the video like I'd lost all my phone content last summer when it had gotten corrupted somehow, so I decided to upload it to YouTube.

I probably shouldn't, not without his consent, but he was performing in public at the time for all to hear, so I didn't see the harm in it. And hell, it wasn't like I had a big following, just some of my college buddies and family members. Being a deputy, having a known social media presence had been a significant no-no. So, I doubted anyone but me would ever see the video anyway.

I'd titled the video "Gay Nightingale," simply because I still had no idea who he was. But he was the face of my fantasies and probably would be for a long time.

After watching the video a couple more times, I decided to spend some time on the slopes to get my bearings before meeting people in my official capacity. True to form, Aunt Monica had thought of everything and pre-arranged for ski equipment and snow gear to be readily accessible for us during our stay.

All suited up, I climbed aboard the lift and was surprised at the smoothness of the ride. Usually, even when lifts were well-maintained, they still slipped from time to time. I would make a point of riding all the lifts I could, just to get some idea of whether this one was a fluke or not.

The first time I skied down the hill, I watched for drainage. We didn't worry so much about avalanches or mudslides at the resort I usually did ski patrol for, but I knew it could be a problem here. I was pleased to see precautions in place, at least as far as I could tell. I had no idea what avalanche precautions were being managed further up the mountain.

I felt my spirit healing the more time I spent on the mountain. The crisp morning air beat against my face despite the mask, but the sting helped ease the lingering anger I felt from being unjustly fired from my deputy job.

The slopes were well-maintained, and because I was early, I could enjoy the new powder the snow guns had created, and were still creating, while I skied.

I couldn't wait to race down after a snowstorm put fresh, real powder down. I could only imagine it would be like skiing down a cloud. The truth was, these slopes were already so much more than the midwestern ones I was used to.

I didn't come off the slopes until much later than I intended. In fact, it was close to noon, and I only packed it in because I was starving and beginning to feel the effects of not having my morning coffee. I hated caffeine headaches. So, I skied into the open-air terminal, shed my boots, and caught the tram back to the resort. I thought catching it would be more of an imposition, but it arrived only moments after I'd settled, and I was still on such a skiing high that I wouldn't have minded waiting a bit anyway.

Despite that, if my aunt and uncle bought the place, the first thing they'd need to do would be to add a proper lodge closer to the slopes.

I returned to the lodge attached to the old hotel, stowed my equipment, and headed to my room for a quick shower before lunch. I walked through reception, and spotted hot coffee on a table inside the lobby.

I grabbed a paper cup and filled it, drinking it black as I traipsed to the elevator and up to my room.

I unlocked the door and immediately heard a familiar voice. My aunt was sitting on the sofa in my room, staring at her laptop and chatting to someone on her phone.

I waved at her and lingered, knowing she was in my room, because she wanted to talk to me.

"Honey, I'll call you back," she said into the phone. I smiled, guessing the honey she'd referred to must've been Uncle Harris.

"I see you went skiing, that's good. What did you think?"

I couldn't help but grin, remembering the exhilaration I'd felt on the slopes, and tossed my snow gear on the entryway floor, where there were plenty of tiles and no carpet that could get wet. "It was good, much better than I expected from your description."

"Well, I might've just figured out why. OMS didn't actually run the place, the old lady that just passed away did."

"Oh, that's good, right?" I asked, and she frowned at me.

"Well, no, actually. Unbeknownst to the courts, she had the management rights, not OMS, which means we may be out of a job."

"Oh," I said, falling into the worn sofa. "What now?"

She shrugged. "Harris is trying to get in touch with the woman's heirs. Until then, who knows?"

"Well, shit, just as I was getting used to the idea." My aunt cocked her eyebrow, and it took a moment to grasp why she was looking at me that way. Then I realized I'd said shit.

I shrugged as I stood. "Sorry, Auntie, but I've been with the sheriff's department long enough now that it's going to take some time before I learn not to cuss around people."

She shook her head. "I should pop your head for it, but I guess I shouldn't expect any less. Just try not to be a foul-mouthed brat when we're around our partners."

I smiled but couldn't make any promises. "It's probably best you don't introduce me to your partners or anyone else you want to impress. Think grunt worker, Auntie, not white collar."

She shook her head, sighing with resignation. "Okay, so you like the slopes. What about equipment?"

"Good, all the lifts felt and sounded good. They barely skipped and didn't seem to have any mechanical problems. Of course, we won't know more until the motors are inspected."

She seemed happy with that, and I could tell she was already itching to pick up her phone. "I'm gonna grab a shower, then I need to eat. Wanna go into town with me for some lunch?"

"That is a good idea. I would say let's eat here, but let's not push that issue yet."

"I saw a place on the drive here that serves pies. I was thinking a warm apple pie sounded mighty good."

She laughed. "Maybe after you eat something of substance. Go shower. I need to call Harris back anyway."

The hot water gently soothed my already aching muscles, but I still showered as quickly as possible knowing my aunt was waiting and because I'd start getting irritable soon from lack of food. Luckily, by the time I was dressed, Aunt Monica was bundled up and ready to head out the door.

We took her rental, which had been dropped off sometime after we got to the hotel, and ended up eating at a little pizza place across the street from Polly's Pies. I was pleasantly surprised at how good the calzone was. It was also ready fast enough that I knew they must've prepared it ahead of time. Usually, small-town pizza places took forever to get you your food.

Done with lunch, we walked over to the pie place, and God help me, the apple pie was amazing. Ridiculously expensive but mouthwateringly delicious. I knew I'd be spending more than a few dollars at Polly's Pies, even if it was costly.

We were just about to head back to the hotel when Aunt Monica got a call. "Harris, did you find anything out?"

I couldn't hear what he said, but from the look on her face, it was good news. "Okay, so if they like us, they'll agree to the contract, excellent."

Then her face scrunched up, and she looked at her watch and sighed. "Yeah, we'll leave right now. Can you call and tell them it'll be at least fifteen minutes before we can be there?"

When she hung up, she grabbed her purse, rushed to the register, and quickly paid for our pies. I followed her out the door as we speed-walked across the street to her rental. "We have a meeting with the new owner at his attorney's office outside town. I'm sorry, I know you don't like all this stuff, but I don't have time to drop you off. I could leave you here and pick you up later, or we can call the old man from the airport to drive you back."

I laughed as I thought of the ancient limo and equally ancient driver. "No, I can sit in the waiting room if you want, but there's no reason for me to stay in town."

"Okay," she said as we both climbed into the car. "You be on your best behavior. No cussing, and I'll tell them you're just hanging out or something."

I chuckled. "I'm sure they won't care."

I couldn't have been more wrong. Unfortunately, the moment I walked into the attorney's office with Aunt Monica, which was just one small room with no receptionist or waiting area, I immediately recognized the owner. My Queen-singing, delicious-tasting, big-city bar hookup had stepped out of my dirty fantasies and into this cramped office in the middle of nowhere. Things were about to get awkward as hell, and I swallowed hard.

When he looked my way, his eyes bulged, which told me he recognized me as well.

My aunt rushed over to him, took his hand to shake, and introduced herself. "Hi, I'm Monica Cabot. This is my nephew, Hunter. We were just having lunch when we heard about the meeting."

"Um, hi," I stammered. "I can just wait outside."

The man blushed and shook his head. "That's not necessary. It's too cold to wait outside or walk back to town. I'm Cameron Kell, and this is my mother, Peggy."

As we all shook hands, the man–*Cameron*, I now knew–kept sneaking glances at me, his face inquisitive. I was struggling to make eye contact, though, considering all the things I'd imagined doing to his body while I got myself off the night before. They were not thoughts I should've been having about someone we were about to be in business with, let alone work for, since I technically worked for the resort. I then made the mistake of looking over at his mother and felt myself blush even deeper.

"Okay, let's get down to business," the attorney said.

I ended up sitting on a chair in the corner of the office, pretending to read a book I'd downloaded to my phone. I could tell Cameron was just as uncomfortable as I was, which was some consolation, and as the attorney explained the legal predicament they were in, I listened to make sure my involvement with this part-owner didn't fuck things up too much.

*God, my aunt was going to kill me.*

"So, do you have questions, Cameron?" the attorney finally asked.

Cameron looked at my aunt. "I've only heard good things about your company, and I assure you I've done a thorough search, and even spoke to a couple of your clients at neighboring resorts. However, I have one stipulation. My mother has helped run our resort for almost fifteen years, and she will remain the general manager. If she has concerns about how you're running things, we'll have to make other arrangements, is that clear?"

My aunt blushed, which was a rare sight, and I almost swallowed my tongue and might have if I hadn't been biting it. No one told Aunt Monica how to run her business, not that we had many options. This guy had the upper hand. At least, that was what I gathered from the attorney's discussion earlier.

"We aren't accustomed to having management outside our own," Aunt Monica countered. "We are very thorough in our work, as I'm sure your investigation demonstrated. In my experience, too many bosses often undermine the very foundation of..."

Cameron lifted his hand to stop my aunt, which blew my mind even more. "It's not negotiable. My grandmother had full rights to manage the property as she saw fit. I've inherited those rights. However, my mother doesn't wish to manage the resort by herself, so since the courts have asked you to take the position in the interest of Optimum Management, I'm happy to agree to that, but only if my mother remains as the property's general manager."

My aunt begrudgingly nodded. "I believe we can work around this, but I'll need full access to you, Mrs....?"

"You can call me Peggy, everyone else does, and I assure you, Mrs. Cabot, as long as your staff are doing their job, we won't have an issue. I can meet with you tomorrow morning with a full report of our current staff, the shortages we still have, and the areas of concern, especially the concerns left with my late mother-in-law's passing."

That seemed to mollify my aunt because her taut features relaxed a bit.

Cameron glanced at me, then asked, "Will your nephew be working at the resort?"

My aunt seemed taken aback by his question, but she quickly nodded. "Yes, I've asked him to step into the ski patrol manager position I was told was being vacated."

"I see. I need to speak to him alone for a few moments. Would you please excuse us?" he asked, standing up and leading the way outside into the cold.

I looked to my aunt but quickly turned away, knowing what this one-on-one meeting was really about.

"So, did you know you'd be working for me when we...?" he asked, sounding almost accusatory.

I shook my head and had to clear my throat. "Um, no, I only found out when we walked in."

Cameron took a deep breath. "Okay, well, this could cause legal problems. I'm assuming your aunt doesn't know?"

"That would be a hell no!" I said, laughing, and a smile broke out across his face.

"Well, she's about to find out, because I'll be asking old man Pauley to draw up an agreement stating that you understand that our past, um, fling won't interfere with your work."

"You mean I agree not to sue you."

He nodded. "I don't honestly know much about all that, except that in the hospital I work for, a couple of nurses dated and had to sign similar paperwork." He hesitated and bit his lip, which I found damn adorable, as inappropriate as that was. "You sure you didn't know about all this?"

I shook my head, put my hand over my heart, and said, "I promise, I had no idea. Believe me, I'm as surprised to see you here as you are me. You can't tell my aunt this, but to be honest, I'm scared shitless of the woman. If I had a clue you were part-owner of all this..."

His relaxed smile warmed me from the inside, and he laughed. "Okay, I believe you. So, I guess that means anything else is off the table."

I shrugged. "Maybe, or maybe not, it all depends on that human resources document I'm gonna sign."

He chuckled and turned red. "Okay, guess we better head back in before they all freak out. How do you want to handle this in front of your aunt?"

I cringed. "Delicately as possible," I said, and could hear the nervousness in my voice.

"Good luck," he said, still smiling as we walked back into the office to a group of confused-looking people.

"We've met before—" Cameron said as he motioned between him and me. "—and will need to have some documents drawn up before we can accept a contract between your company and ours. I'll have Mr. Pauley do that and include them in any other paperwork we need to have signed before we make this official."

My aunt pinned me with a knowing look, and I knew I was going to get it later, before she quickly turned toward Cameron. "I think that'll be fine... Mrs... um, Peggy," she said, turning toward the mother. "We'll see you tomorrow at nine."

Aunt Monica grabbed my elbow and dragged me out of the attorney's office. "What the hell was that about?" she asked when we were out of earshot of the others.

"Well, we sorta, um, went out... while I was in Denver."

She stopped, looked at me with the same *I could squash you like a bug* look she'd given me when I was particularly naughty as a child, then sighed. "Of course, you did," she said, and, without looking at me, led the way at a fast clip to the rental car.

# 11

# CAM

MY MOTHER HOWLED WITH laughter, and even the old attorney's face split into a smile when I told them the nephew and I hooked up a few nights ago.

"I thought his aunt was going to blow a gasket. Oh, to be a fly on the wall when he tells her."

I chuckled. "Mom, be nice."

That just made her laugh louder. "Mr. Pauley, can you ensure this doesn't come back to bite us? I mean, he didn't work for us then and still doesn't, but if we sign a contract with them, then I'm assuming he will be."

"Sort of. But yes, you're wise to get things sorted out from the beginning..." he said, then looked to me. "...Especially if you and he... reunite." That caused Mom to snicker again.

"Mom!" I said, but couldn't help laughing too. "I'm going back to Denver, so that's not likely to happen, especially once this one," I pointed to Mom, is done harassing him. By the way, make sure you make it legal for her to harass him on the job, because that's totally going to happen."

Mom nodded next to me. "Leave it with me. Okay, so just a few things to clear up. First, I'll get all the documents put together that stipulate that Peggy will maintain her position as general manager, which technically puts you in charge of staffing, correct?" he asked, looking at Mom.

She nodded, and he continued. "So, there's no need to stipulate who you want to keep in their positions, which makes this easier. Besides that, we'll get the human resources documents signed, and I'll send it all over to the bankruptcy court, so it's official."

"Thanks, Mr. Pauley. I'm not sure how we'd have worked through all this had it not been for you."

"You're welcome, son. I knew your grandparents and even your great-grandparents for years. It does my heart good to know you're keeping an eye on the place. Hopefully, this Cabot Management Company will work out. We are big on family-run businesses around here. Oh, sorry, I almost forgot..." he said, pulling more papers out of his thick file. "...this is more of a middle finger to OMS, but they filed for bankruptcy to punish your grandmother for beating them at their own litigious game. So, I'd like to petition the court that all OMS stock in the resort be turned over to you. It's a crapshoot, well, it's actually less likely than that, but it would give those SOBs something to fret over for a while and give this old man some entertainment. Is that okay with you?"

"Of course, do what you can. I doubt I'll be seeing any of the settlement anyway."

Mr. Pauley shook his head. "No, not very likely."

"Okay, well, at least we got a decent management company out of it." He nodded and we all shook hands before we left.

"Guess things are going to change fast now, huh?" I asked Mom as we walked toward my car.

She shrugged. "It was bound to change eventually. But at least I think I like this Monica person. You know, she sorta reminds me of your grandma."

"Hardcore?" I asked, causing Mom to chuckle.

"Yeah, exactly. Why don't we slip over to Polly's? You can get the blackberry cobbler you love so much, and I can have a couple of Polly's cookies."

"Oh, that reminds me, Tommy wants your homemade cookies. Says he needs a hookup. Would you mind fixing some before we go back to Denver?"

Mom shrugged. "Better be tonight, and I'm making both of you help. I'm guessing once tough Monica gets her hands on me, I won't be doing much other than working for a while."

"Mom, you're still in mourning, don't you think...?"

"Oh, son, your grandmother was a workaholic. She'd want me to mourn her while getting something constructive done."

I laughed at the truth of that. "Well, don't push yourself," I chastised. "There'll be plenty of time to work your ass off. No need to run around like crazy. Besides, remember that I'm the boss, not Monica."

"Yes, sir," my mom said, and saluted me.

"Okay, well, maybe not *your* boss, but Monica sure isn't, so don't let her forget that, okay?"

Mom smiled at me. "Son, I know what my job is. I'm to make sure this new company is doing *their* job. If they aren't, I'm supposed to let you know. But also..." She paused until I made eye contact. "I'm helping you prepare to sell it all."

I nodded sadly. "Yeah, ultimately, I think that's exactly what you're doing."

She wrapped her arm around me in a side hug as we continued walking toward the pie shop. "Then, leave it to me. Geneva trained me well. I've got this."

# 12

# HUNTER

I FOUND OUT LATE the next day that a meeting was being held for the ski patrol. Luckily, a resort this big had a lot of patrollers, so I was able to slip into the back of the meeting without being noticed.

Before becoming an official employee, I wanted to get to know the lay of the land. I already anticipated some kickback to a midwestern ski patroller taking over patrol operations at a Colorado resort. Not unlike law enforcement, there were always boundary and turf wars, and the ski patrol was basically policing on the slopes. Well, that coupled with ambulatory services, because accidents were inevitable.

The meeting had already started when I found a seat next to an older man in the back. He looked over at me and, after a moment's hesitation, nodded. I glanced around the room, observing a fairly even split of men and women among the patrollers, and a fairly wide range of ages.

"So, some changes are coming our way," the guy up front said. He looked like he was maybe nineteen or twenty, and arrogant.

"Like what?" a woman who appeared closer to my age asked from the audience.

"Well, like, first of all, the new management company will be replacing Dad with their own person."

There were some groans, which caused me to smile. There was nothing atypical about that. Hell, in their situation, I'd have groaned as well.

"What do you know about this guy?" a man I figured to be in his late thirties asked.

"Well, he seems to be registered in Kansas."

"Kansas?" the man replied. "Is he doing cross country? Does it even snow there?"

I made a move to slip out, knowing this was about to get ugly, but the older man next to me placed his hand on my arm, keeping me in place, then he stood and cleared his throat, drawing everyone's attention.

"Before we go much further, I think we have a guest here who might be able to give us some insight on your questions."

I swallowed hard, totally unprepared for what was coming. The man didn't give me away by looking at me, so I guessed I could've just remained silent, but that would probably only make things worse. I sighed, then stood up, straightened my shirt, and addressed the group. "Hi, I'm Hunter Jamison, and I'm the one you're talking about, so if you have questions, I can answer them now."

The man who'd just asked if it snowed in Kansas shifted uncomfortably in his seat, and I struggled not to laugh.

The teenage-looking guy leading the group was the first to speak up. "So, what experience do you have, Mr. Jamison?"

"Thanks, I'm sorry I don't have everyone's names, and this isn't an official first meeting, but my background is in law enforcement. I'm also a ski instructor and have been the head ski patrol volunteer on our small slopes in Kansas."

"Then, how can you take over on real mountains?" the kid asked, causing the man next to me to stand again.

"He'll do it 'cause he's trained to do it, and we'll be helping get him up to speed. Won't we, Evan?"

The kid blushed and nodded. "Now, why don't we finish up our business, and then you can all ask Mr. Jamison your questions, one-on-one."

The older man pulled me out of the meeting, and when we were outside the room, he laughed. "Figured you might want me to stop that in its tracks."

I smiled and nodded. "Yeah, guessing it was about to get hot in there."

"George Medford. Pleasure to meet you."

"Likewise. So, you're the retired general then?"

George chuckled. "Yeah, had a bit of a health scare, and the wife put her foot down."

"How'd you know it was me?" I asked.

"Oh, I looked you up when I heard you were going to be replacing me, or in this case, my son, Evan."

"Oh, wow, I'm sure that didn't go over well."

"Went over just fine. Evan is about to graduate from college and will probably go to work in Forestville, on the other side of the mountain, so he doesn't really have time to run the ski patrol. He only took over from me, so I'd be able to step aside with less advance notice than I'd have liked."

"So, no toe stomping then?"

George shrugged. "Well, I didn't say that, but no more than can be expected with these kinds of changeovers."

I liked George, but then, I usually liked all the guys and gals on the patrol. I think that was kind of why I stuck with it all these years, even though I had to drive almost two hours to do my volunteer shifts in Kansas.

George filled me in over a cup of coffee, telling me that about half the patrollers were volunteers. The rest worked full-time.

"We're like family here, Mr. Jamison."

"Hunter," I corrected him. "Call me Hunter."

The older man nodded. "Well, Hunter, you'll find these patrollers are a tight bunch, too tight in some ways, making it hard for new folks to come in. It's gonna make it even harder for you to get your footing, especially since you're a flatlander...

no offense. But if you stick to your guns and respect the family element, they'll eventually come around."

"I sorta expected all this, but thanks for the heads up. I really need at least a month before I step into my full responsibilities. Do you think your son is up to maintaining his position while I get my feet under me?"

"You mean your skis?" George teased, but shook his head. "No, son, you don't want Evan in charge. He'll undermine you. Don't get me wrong, he won't mean to, it's just in his nature. I recommend you appoint someone who works for the resort full-time as your second-in-command. Mia Lance is a solid choice, smart woman, easygoing most of the time, but every single person here has dealt with her when she needed to be tough." He looked at me a moment, assessing. "Mia doesn't have a lot of tolerance for incompetence, but as long as you know your stuff, she's not likely to undermine you."

I chuckled. "I've been on the patrol since I was old enough to join. But that doesn't mean I don't have more to learn. I still need to go through avalanche training, for example, since there's not much concern about avalanches in Kansas."

George laughed and clapped me on the back. "No, and I'm feeling a lot more comfortable with you knowing you don't think you have all the answers. Mia will be the right one for the job, and of course, I'm still on the patrol. I'll be trying to support you too, as long as *you* continue to be right for the job."

I chuckled. "Well, I guess that's all I can ask for."

"Indeed, it is. Well, we best be getting back in there. They'll be wrapping things up, so they can get back on the slopes." George paused for a moment, before saying, "Just be patient. I know at first, it's going to feel like they're all coming at you, but I promise, given some time, they'll come around."

I followed George back into the meeting and could tell they were getting ready to finish. I could and would be patient as the folks here got used to me, but at the end of the day, they'd have to accept my authority; otherwise, it would put people's lives in danger. That was where I drew the line. Hopefully, with George's help, I'd never have to face that.

As expected, I had a few people come up to introduce themselves and shake my hand. Most, though, gave me a wide berth and skeptical glances. One or two had some tough, but legitimate questions, which I answered to the best of my ability. Luckily though, George, who'd been staying close, ended up sending everyone on their way before things got too heated.

"Well, that's that," George said and handed me a card. "When things are official, why don't you give me a call, and I'll help you set things in motion. Oh, I'll go talk to Mia for you too, if you think that's what you'll be doing."

"I'd like to talk to her about it, yeah, but not in an official way. Why don't you ask if she's willing to show me the ropes instead?"

George touched his nose and smiled. "Probably an even better plan. Call me when you're ready," he said and left me standing alone in the room.

I walked out shortly after and turned a corner just in time to collide with Cameron.

"Oh, shit, sorry," I said, instinctively grabbing him by the waist so he didn't fall to the ground. We both stood frozen for a moment, and my palms itched to touch him more, but I quickly let go.

"No problem," he said, smiling. "I don't mind running into you, as you already know."

*Was he flirting with me? 'Cause if so... hell yeah.*

I blushed at the thought and was about to leave before I embarrassed myself, when Cameron asked, "So, I'm about to go grab some takeout pizza. My mom is making cookies tonight for my best friend, Tommy, and you're welcome to join us. We're leaving tomorrow to head back to Denver."

"Oh, I'm not sure a meet the parents is in order."

Cameron laughed out loud. "No, but a meet your new boss might be. Come on, your aunt is meeting with her tomorrow, and you can get to know her before that. Besides, you've technically already met, plus she makes the best cookies in the world."

I sighed. "Well, it beats staring at my aunt as she texts or talks on the phone all evening."

"Then let's go," he said, winking at me and causing my insides to quiver.

*Why do I like this guy so much?*

# 13

# CAM

THAT NIGHT, WE ALL ate pizza and helped Mom make cookies. Hunter surprised all of us by being a pretty good cookie maker, so much so that before the evening was over, Mom gave him a copy of her prized secret recipe. She hadn't even given that to me, not that I'd ever asked, or remotely been good in the kitchen.

We played board games and poker afterward, and I kept losing horribly, because I couldn't keep my eyes off Hunter. Halfway through a game of Texas Hold'em, where Mom sucker-punched me with a bluff while I was distracted by two very sexy biceps leaning on the table, I gave up and kicked back to watch the three of them play.

For a brief moment, I allowed myself to imagine what it'd be like to have a lover, someone like Hunter, who felt comfortable hanging out with my mom and best friend and playing stupid card games.

I hadn't expected Hunter to be like that. I went to the bathroom and splashed water on my face, just to remind myself there was no way something more could happen between us. He was only here temporarily, until either Mom decided she wanted to take over the business, or I sold it.

And hell, I wouldn't even be here. I still had a job in Denver that I needed to return to. I'd already had three phone calls since I left asking if I could come in to take a shift or two. It had to be crazy busy for them to call me, knowing I was on bereavement leave to attend my grandma's funeral.

Even if Hunter lived in Denver and didn't work for me, I didn't have time for a lover. Not that he wanted to be my lover. I mean, he'd returned enough heated glances tonight for me to think he was interested in a replay of our one-night stand, but I'd always sucked at relationships. Men came and went like my love life was a revolving door, whether I wanted them to or not.

I came out of the bathroom, grabbed them a plate of cookie refills, and then went back to begin packaging the leftover cookies for Tommy to take back to Denver.,

"Mom," I asked, "Do you want to keep any of these?"

She laughed. "No, son, I purposefully keep sweets out of the house. Unfortunately, since I turned fifty, even a whiff of sugary goodness goes straight to my hips and won't budge."

Mom was such a nut, but as a nurse, I figured she wasn't lying. Metabolism did slow down with age, even for people as busy as my mom always seemed to be.

By the time I returned to the table, the game was finishing up. Hunter leaned back to stretch, his shirt riding up to reveal his muscular stomach and sending the most amazing memories of licking those abs through my mind. "Well, I think that's it for me. Cam, thank you for inviting me. Peggy, Tommy, it's been a pleasure," he said. "Now, would anyone be willing to drive me back to the hotel?"

As I tried not to swallow my tongue, my mom answered first. "I can. Cam, you and Tommy need to finish packing since you have to leave early tomorrow."

I nodded, still thinking about how Hunter tasted when I'd traced his stomach with my tongue. I could feel myself blushing as I made eye contact with Hunter, who seemed to have recognized my reaction, because he smirked a little.

"Okay, well, come on, Hunter," Mom said, snickering. Apparently, she'd noticed our reactions to each other too.

I managed to stand and shake his hand, and squeaked an awkward goodbye. I turned to Tommy, who just laughed out loud, the ass. I'm sure if my mom hadn't been there, he'd have said something crude.

As it happened, if I was going to end up face-first in a mattress with Hunter fucking me into oblivion again, I needed all the necessary paperwork signed ahead of time to cover all of our asses.

# 14

# HUNTER

LUCKILY, I HAD BAGGY pants on; otherwise, I was sure I'd have embarrassed myself in front of Cam's mom, my new general manager. I quickly grabbed my coat after Cam eye-fucked me and shook my hand, like we were some kind of perverted business partners.

I had to force all the naughty thoughts out of my head of pulling Cam into his childhood bedroom and having a repeat of Denver, but best not to think about that now, while I was riding alongside his mother as she drove me back to the hotel.

"He likes you," Peggy said as soon as she started the car.

I chuckled. "What gave you that idea?"

Peggy smiled at me and winked, then said, "Cam's heart seems to be the kind people step on without any thought. I guess he gets that from me." She sighed before pulling onto the deserted road. "But even though I'm his mom and clearly biased, you should know he's worth the effort."

I stared out the window into the darkness surrounding us. "Even if we wanted to give it a go, we live in totally different worlds. Not to mention he's part-owner of the resort I currently work at, meaning he's off-limits."

"Different worlds maybe, but Mr. Pauley is putting the paperwork together that allows the other to happen without... issues."

I laughed. "Dating is never without issues, but I understand what you're saying. I'm not looking for love, though. My life is a mess right now. I mean, I'm stable, I've just got a lot going on," I quickly added, in case I gave the wrong impression.

Peggy glanced over at me, smiling. "You don't have to impress me, Hunter. Mr. Pauley already called me and said he was impressed enough for the both of us. If you want to pursue more with my son, you have my blessing, not that you need it."

I nodded, my cheeks burning again for what had to be the hundredth time this week. "Thanks," I said, and could hear the bashfulness in my voice.

When Peggy dropped me off in front of the resort, I wondered what the hell had happened to me these past few days. Usually, I was told I was practically stoic, and never one to wear my heart on my sleeve. Somehow, maybe because so much had changed since I'd lost my job, I was becoming soft. I wasn't entirely sure whether I liked that or not.

I shook the thought off as I took the elevator up to my room. Thankfully, Aunt Monica wasn't there, so I crawled into the big blue soaking tub and let the bubbles wash away the day.

Lying there, replaying in my mind the heated looks Cam had given me all evening, it didn't take long for me to get busy under the suds. Moaning his name as I climaxed alone gave me less relief than I'd hoped it would though. Damn, I wished Cam was here sharing this tub with me right now.

# 15

## CAM

---

WORK, AS EXPECTED, WAS ready and waiting for me the moment I entered the hospital. Once again, I started working forty-eight hours a week. Four twelve-hour shifts. The hospital hired a few agency nurses to relieve some of the stress, but even with that and my short break, it still felt like too much.

I also felt pulled in opposing directions, with one foot in Denver and the other in Peachleaf. I received periodic updates from Cabot Management, which I would scan and then call Mom to discuss. It seemed Cabot was good at what they did, and despite our reservations, they were initiating small changes that had already made our systems more efficient.

Mom even said Grandma would've appreciated some of their more creative ideas for increasing efficiency while maintaining a quality experience for guests.

Just before they closed for spring mud season, I gave her a call. "Mom, you seem to be enjoying them."

"Honey, I'm just saying they are not like OMS. I even think Monica and I could be friends if we spent more time together."

I laughed. "You're such a sucker for hard-ass women."

Mom chuckled too. "I guess your grandma trained me to be that way." She let out a heavy sigh, and I could tell she was thinking about the loss.

"You're missing her, aren't you?" I asked quietly.

"Oh, honey, it's only been a handful of months. Of course, I miss her. You know your grandma ended up being my best friend. How do you go from having someone occupy huge segments of your life one day, then gone the next?"

"Why don't you come to Denver and spend a few weeks with me and Tommy? I'll even take time off and we can play tourist."

"No, I'd love to, but we only have a month before the summer activities start. As you know, mud season is when we clean and store all the winter equipment and pull out all the summer stuff."

"Do you have that much business in the summer?" I asked, kind of surprised I didn't already know the answer.

She chuckled. "Son, our business has changed so much since you were a kid. We have a huge summer business now. Families want to escape the summer heat by coming to the mountains to bike, hike, and spend time in our warm lake."

"It just seems odd that people come to a ski resort in the summer."

"Well, if you were going to consider taking over for your grandmother, I'd tell you to spend the summer here and see for yourself. It's actually become my favorite time of year."

"Wish I could, but…"

"I know, I know, work."

"Yeah, sorry. Speaking of, I volunteered for a night shift tonight, so I should probably go take a nap."

There was silence on the other end, before Mom said, "Cam, I worry about you working too much. At your age…"

"At my age, I need to be working to save, so when I'm your age, I can retire."

"Pst," she scolded. "Son, I'm at least ten years from retirement. How old do you think I am?"

"Just the right age," I said, quoting something Grandma would say when anyone foolishly asked how old she was.

"That's right," Mom said, before saying her goodbyes.

When I returned to the hospital for my night shift, things were buzzing among the staff. "What's going on?" I asked Camila, a fellow nurse.

"We're being bought out by Primmer Corporation Services." She shook her head. "Check your email. They sent all the details, but apparently, this deal has been in the works for over a year."

I sighed, opened up the email, and sure enough, the hospital was to be taken over by PCS at some undisclosed time this summer.

I had come to work here because it was community-owned and not a global conglomerate. Now, I would end up working for one of the largest hospital organizations in the world.

I'd made my mind up before I even began my shift. I wouldn't be working for PCS. Not now, not ever. *Then just what the hell was I going to do for a job?* I thought of Peachleaf and the small critical access hospital about thirty miles away.

But was I willing to leave the city once and for all to move back to the middle of nowhere? It wasn't like I hadn't gotten my fill of small-town life growing up there. Hadn't Tommy and I spent years dreaming of escaping it to live in the big city, exactly like we were doing now?

The biggest attraction for miles around was our resort in Peachleaf, although the town where the hospital was located was a fraction bigger. I wasn't so concerned I couldn't get a job there, and frankly, I knew they were paying about five bucks an hour more than I earned in Denver. Another bonus was that the hospital had been completely rebuilt a few years ago, after which Grandma and I toured it during one of my visits.

Still, I shook off the thought of moving back to Peachleaf permanently. I wouldn't work for PCS, no freaking way, so I'd have to figure something else out. Maybe I just needed to keep my eyes open, practice some patience, and see what opportunities came my way.

# 16

# HUNTER

"**E**VAN, I SWEAR TO God!" I yelled when the ornery brat pelted me with a snowball as I came out of the office. Of course, by then he was already gone. We'd gotten a late winter snowstorm, and although we'd already closed down the slopes, several of the ski patrollers had shown up to take advantage of the fresh powder as one last hurrah before the year was out.

Evan messing with me was just one of many positives since I arrived. As I suspected, most of the patrollers were suspicious as hell, and spent the first month giving me attitude, with Evan giving me lip to boot. Fortunately, George put a stop to that one day when he overheard him.

Things had really changed since then, though, probably because I was a workaholic. I spent every day here on the slopes, in the patrol office, or training, and the patrollers had begun to see me as one of their own. At least, that's what I hoped.

Now that it was mud season, or it would be once this last snow melted, Aunt Monica sent out people to inspect the lifts and other resort equipment. I had no doubt it would all be in excellent shape. Spending the past months with Peggy showed me just how intensely particular she was. Folks who worked here before I arrived said Peggy was nothing compared to how Mrs. Geneva had been.

The fact was, everything I observed showed that. Competent patrols, although that was due to George more than Peggy or Geneva, clean changing areas, and systems that kept skiers safe.

Of course, Aunt Monica had her people making changes too, which had improved the flow, although that wasn't my forte. My concern was the slopes and maintaining them to ensure they weren't dangerous.

One of the first things Aunt Monica did was work with the Forest Service to ensure the avalanche supports were in place, which they were, of course, and there were plans to divert snow melt away from the resort. That was something Peggy said they'd been asking to have done for years but weren't influential enough to get the Forest Service to agree to.

The resort was really doing well, and I found myself enjoying it more and more as the months flew by.

I looked down at my phone when it started ringing, just as I was about to head up and enjoy some last-chance skiing. I saw Sierra's name pop up.

"Hey, sis," I said as I went back into the warmth of the office and sat down.

"Hey, yourself. How goes it?"

"Well, better than well... you?"

"Oh, you know, same old, same old, but Aunt Monica said things were settling down there, so I thought I'd call and catch up."

"Things are going great, Sierra. You should've come out and spent some time on the slopes while you could."

"Nah, you know I'm not into skiing, not like you. But I thought Baron and I might come out this summer, maybe do some kayaking. I hear the lake there is perfect for that."

"Yeah, I'm sure." Suspicion was beginning to take hold since Sierra was never this easygoing when she called. "So, you gonna tell me why you really called?"

I could feel the eye roll before she finally laughed. "I hate that you know me so well. I... well, Hunter, I don't know if you want the details from the county, but I have some news I think you should hear."

"About my former job?" I asked tentatively.

"Yeah, there've been some developments."

I looked out the office window at the fresh powder and the specks of my patrollers playing on the slopes and sighed. "Yeah, go ahead," I said.

"Well, it's come out that Sheriff Forester covered up for Alderman Grey on other illegal endeavors. Forester might've even benefited from a few of them. There's a whole investigation happening now. So far, I know things could end up going south for both the Sheriff and Grey. Have you considered whether you'd like to run for sheriff? I mean, once this mess is all cleared up, I'm sure you're gonna come off as the hero, 'cause you wouldn't back down."

"Oh shit, Sierra, I don't know. I mean, that's all in the past now. I'm trying not to even think about any sort of future working in law enforcement."

"Well, you should think about it. You'd be a great sheriff, and the town could use an honest man on the job."

"We'll see, but don't hold your breath, sis," I said.

She didn't stay on the phone long after making her point. Sierra was like that, especially on a weekday. I stared into the distance as I pondered what she'd told me. Did I want to go back to Warrenstown, where it was all in a day's work hearing backwoods idiots throwing racist crap at me? In all the time I'd been here, I hadn't encountered racism. As sad as it was to say in that regard, Peachleaf really was a special place.

I even made more money doing this, and no one had shot at me or threatened to do so. Not only that, but I spent my days and nights skiing, something I loved. That didn't mean the job didn't have its own challenges, and there was almost always someone to patch up, or worse, but that came with the territory. The last week we were open, I sent a couple of idiot kids to the hospital after they'd left the slope and gone through the damned trees, which wasn't that unusual an occurrence.

For the first time in a long time, I was genuinely happy, and not just from the round-the-clock skiing. Peggy's talk when Cam was last here, and the fact I was enjoying my time here, had gotten me thinking that maybe something more really could happen between him and me. Granted, probably not as long as he owned the place, but Peggy had made it clear on several occasions she didn't want to run the resort on her own. That meant Cam would have to move up here or hire a company, like Aunt Monica's, to run it for him.

Of course, it was only about a two-hour drive to Denver from here, so even if he didn't move up, it wouldn't exactly be a long-distance relationship. I mean, assuming he wanted one with me. Intense attraction was one thing, but relationships were a whole other matter.

I'd been shit at keeping in touch with Cam after he returned to Denver, though it went both ways. I was incredibly busy here at the resort all season and, through Peggy, I knew his hospital job kept him insanely busy too. Plus, she'd said that what free time he did have was spent reading through Aunt Monica's management reports, and helping run this place from afar.

Neither one of us really had time for a relationship, but that didn't stop me for wanting to get to know him better, one way or another. Every time I thought of Cam, I'd end up humming his rendition of Queen's "Somebody to Love," which was the case as I headed outside and strapped on my skis for one last run on the slopes.

# 17

# CAM

IT'D BEEN MONTHS SINCE I let Tommy drag me out to the bar. It wasn't like I didn't need some time outside my head, but having met Hunter the last time I was there, to say nothing of our glorious night together, had turned me off from returning. I didn't want another man coming on to me and clouding the delicious memory of Hunter's hungry eyes glued to me before taking me to his hotel room.

Unfortunately, once Tommy got something in his head, there wasn't much to be done other than give in, either that or endure the infamous Tommy pout, which could literally last a lifetime. The man was an expert at holding onto an issue for decades if need be. Perhaps that was what helped make him such a good attorney.

So, since I absolutely refused to work an extra shift this week, I had Saturday night off. I dressed in my tightest jeans and a fitted T that was still almost new, because all I did lately was freaking work.

I even threw on my bright-red cowboy boots, because fuck it all, now that I'd committed to going out, I was going to enjoy myself.

Tommy picked me up, as usual. He figured that would prevent me from just having a single beer and leaving, which was probably true since I'd done that before.

We'd just settled in and ordered our beers when some drag queen I'd never seen before flounced on stage, screaming, "I'm the nightingale, bitch!"

"You ain't no nightingale! Get off the stage," someone in the crowd yelled.

"Oh Lord, just wait until Madonya hears *Miss Thang* up there screeching on her stage," I said to Tommy.

Just then, Madonya arrived, wig askew and one eyelash off. "Bitch, you get off this damned stage. *Larry!*" she called.

As if on cue, Larry appeared, shaking his head as he took the queen by the arm and escorted her off the stage. "Y'all, I need to finish putting my face on, but until then, you can watch the *real* nightingale doing his thing."

I looked to Tommy for explanation, but he appeared as confused as I was. Clearly, we both needed to get out more. A few moments later, after Larry returned, the televisions around the bar turned on. Tommy's shocked expression matched mine as we watched a YouTube video of my months-old performance of Queen's "Somebody to Love."

"What the hell?" I asked, and Tommy shook his head.

"No idea, but you've got quite the following," Tommy shouted as the entire bar began singing along with the video.

I remembered singing the song, but didn't recall it being recorded, and I immediately felt self-conscious. Usually, Madonya was a stickler for getting signatures and handling all that legal stuff prior to recording any performances, which had only happened once when I was actually working here.

Just as the song ended, Jake, one of the bouncers, came up, and whispered in my ear, "Madonya wants to see you in her dressing room."

I nodded and let him lead me through the crowd, which I was glad for, because a lot of men were already ogling me.

"What the hell?" I asked as soon as I saw Madonya finish applying her signature long eyelashes.

"Bitch," she said, ignoring my question. "It's about time you showed back up. Do you know how many people I've had to stave off? You have the press sniffing around, people asking on the regular for 'the famous Gay Nightingale' to perform. You even had someone from *American Icon* call and ask if you'd thought about competing."

Madonya glanced at me in the mirror as she finished applying her blush, then swiveled in her chair to face me. "I tried to reach you, but your number on file here is no longer working. I even had Jake keeping an eye out for Tommy, but neither of you has shown up for months. And when's the last time you checked your social media messages?."

She smiled sweetly then before standing and walking over to me. "So, you gonna hire Larry and me to manage you or not?" she asked.

My eyes must've been the size of saucers. "Um, Madonya, you know I love you like my second mother, but what in the ever-loving hell are you talking about?"

"Well, *bitch*, you know I don't work for free. You also know I'll be the best manager the Gay Nightingale could wish for, not to mention Larry's knowledge of putting on a show. Where the hell you gonna find talent like this?" she asked as she dramatically waved her hands down her body.

"Madonya," I said, suppressing a chuckle. "I-I don't know what you're talking about. Hire you to manage what?"

"Girl, you really don't know, do you?" she asked, then grabbed each of my arms, grinning. "Baby, you're an internet star."

She called to Jake, who'd been hovering in the doorway. "Jake, bring me your phone. I know you've got that video loaded up."

Jake winked at me as he handed his phone to her. I blushed. I'd had an intense crush on Jake while I worked here, but he usually looked right through me. Apparently, that'd changed.

I watched as the same video of me singing played. "Madonya, I saw this out there, and although I don't know why you recorded it..."

"First, bitch, I don't record and upload performances without permission." I figured she must be really into this, because she only repeatedly called someone bitch when she was excited.

"Second, look!" she said, pointing at numbers on the screen.

"What the actual fuck?" I asked as I saw the video had one million YouTube views. "Madonya, I-I don't get it."

"Well, my clueless twink, you are, as I've already said, internet famous."

"Who put this up?" I asked.

She shook her head, causing her wig to move. I automatically reached up and secured it on her head. "You need more pins," I said and scooted her back into her chair. I quickly went to work securing her wig, something I'd done a hundred times when I worked here.

"Nobody knows who they are exactly, just someone going by the username The Deputy. But it doesn't matter. Your talent is wanted, and you've already got a public following and generated media interest, so you might as well let me and Larry manage this new career of yours."

I laughed. "You know, I have to think about all this. I'm a nurse, not a professional singer."

"Well, you're sure as hell not going back out in that crowd without some backup. Besides, you need to be my opening act tonight, then Jake can sneak you out the back. I swear you aren't safe out there with all them horny men wanting a piece of the Gay Nightingale."

"The what?" I asked.

"Oh, bitch, you really are clueless. Sit here, put on some foundation, so your damned face don't shine like the pale creature you are, then come sing us some tunes. Oh Lord, I'm so excited. This is going to blow people away."

"Okay, I guess," I said, shocked that Madonya was willing to let another person go near her makeup, let alone use it. "What do you want me to sing?"

"Just your regulars, Whitney, Cher, and at least one more Queen song. Hell, do 'Somebody to Love' again. I had Larry set up the cameras already. With our equipment, it'll be better quality than the shaky cell phone mess uploaded by The Deputy."

I laughed as Madonya exclaimed she was late and dashed out of the dressing room to her stage. I'd swear that one had always been a lot, but I adored her. I still didn't think I needed a manager, though, because singing wasn't my thing. Well, that was a lie, it had been my thing. Growing up, music had been my life, even if it was mostly just singing in school concerts and at small events around the county. I even had a musical performance degree from the Kansas City Conservatory, but I'd long ago given up on that dream for a more practical career, which had led to me being the overworked nurse that I currently was.

As I smeared Madonya's foundation on my very pale face, I weighed the pros and cons, and decided she was right. If there was a chance I could have any sort of career in music, I'd be an idiot not to try.

I chuckled as I finished up my makeup and heard Madonya announce me as the Gay Nightingale. "Well, here goes noth-ing," I said to myself in the mirror as I stood up and headed for the stage.

# 18

# HUNTER

"Aunt Monica, Uncle Harris," I said as both of their faces flashed up on my screen. "Thanks for meeting with me. I have some questions."

"Sure, go ahead, Hunter," Aunt Monica said.

"Well, I've enjoyed the work I'm doing here, but I have a chance to go back to Warrenstown and run for sheriff..." I hesitated, wanting to choose my next words wisely, then decided it was best just to go for it. "But I think I'd rather do this type of work full-time." I watched as the two of them seemed to contemplate what I was asking. "I know you don't own the resort, but even if this doesn't work out, do you think you could use me elsewhere?"

Uncle Harris responded first. "Hunter, it's possible, but we only had this position open because of the circumstances. Finding another ski patrol director position is unlikely. In fact, the organizations are all very tight, as you probably already know."

"The only reason this position was open—" Aunt Monica added, "—is because OMS was so horrible. They pretty much made the job impossible. When your predecessor resigned, none of his team wanted the job because of that."

"Do you think you'll be purchasing the resort?" I asked, my hopes quickly dimming.

"That depends on Mr. Kell. We wouldn't dream of purchasing a partial interest, especially when someone else owns the management rights. But the resort is in decent condition, so if he wants to sell, it's a possibility."

I nodded and thanked them before hanging up. "Time to talk to Peggy," I said to the now-blank screen, and went to find her.

I found her in her office, staring at her computer screen. She was probably working through scheduling for the summer season, which opened the week after next.

"Hey, Hunter," she said as I entered.

"Hey, so I have some maybe inappropriate questions, but I need to make some career decisions, and they... well, I just need to ask them."

Peggy turned away from her computer to give me her full attention. "Ask away," she said, motioning for me to take a seat.

"Well, I know things are up in the air here, but I enjoy working with the patrol. I might also have a good job opportunity back home. Do you know if Cam has decided what he's doing with his share of the resort?"

She stiffened a bit and shook her head. "No, he's still considering his options, but, Hunter, you don't need to worry about who owns the resort. Your position is pretty secure, more than any other person here. No one who knows what they're doing would try to replace a patrol director, at least if they don't want a revolt on their hands."

I chuckled at the truth of that, then sighed. "Peggy, if the courts dissolve OMS, which according to Aunt Monica looks probable, can you guarantee the resort won't just close down for good?"

A sad expression crossed her face then, and I knew closing the resort would be painful for her given the many years of time and energy she'd put into keeping it going. "It's not likely, especially with earnings up this year, but still possible." She came around her desk and sat on the corner. "Listen, nothing is guaranteed, but neither I nor Cam will let the resort close if we can help it. I won't speak for him, because there's still a lot to consider, but if push comes to shove, I'm almost certain he'll just hire a management company to take over. Maybe even Cabot, which means you'll be fine."

"And if the courts demand a sale?" I asked, knowing I was pushing the boundaries.

"Well, according to Mr. Pauley, that's very unlikely. If anything, the state will put OMS's shares into an account and designate the earnings to go into debt repayment. More likely, they'll try to liquidate the shares, which means Cam still retains control over the management."

"It all seems so up in the air. I don't know what to do."

"What do you want to do?" Peggy asked.

"I love doing this, but..."

"Listen," she said and came to sit next to me. "When my husband died, I had no idea what I wanted to do with my life. I was working for a state senator and making good money, but I was putting in so many hours I couldn't spend much time with Cam when he needed me most. I had to decide what was most important for him and me, so I gave up my job and moved back here. It was hard at the time, but now I couldn't be happier that I followed my heart. Besides, the old bastard I'd worked for ended up behind bars." She chuckled. "Had I stayed, I'd have been out of a job within a couple of years anyway."

I took a deep breath and held it for a moment before slowly releasing it. "It's hard. I feel like my life has come to a fork in the road and there's no clear path to take."

She nodded, then patted my hand. "It's supposed to be hard. No one said big life choices were easy. Follow your heart, Hunter, and I promise, if I think things are going south, I'll let you know. As long as it doesn't jeopardize my son's confidence, that is."

"Thanks, Peggy," I said, and let her get back to work.

Follow my heart? My heart wasn't in law enforcement any longer. Maybe it never had been. Hell, who was I kidding? I didn't want to be sheriff, and facing an election for the job would only dredge up me having been fired by the previous one. Just the thought of having to rehash that mess with voters and the local media turned my stomach.

I'd always hated when the obvious path wasn't clear. After Dad died, life had been so unclear, and I spent months quaking in my boots as I watched Mom figure out how best to survive. To be honest, that was one of the main reasons I went into law enforcement. I figured it'd be something consistent, something I could rely on to always be there, and it had been, right up until my firing.

Returning to Warrenstown was probably still a safer bet than staying with a resort that could close down either by the decision of a judge or the guy who'd just inherited the place. The only thing was, I didn't want to leave Peachleaf. I was already looking forward to the summer months and spending my days on the water or patrolling the bike runs, and the tightknit community had really grown on me.

I'd made genuine friends here, ones that I'd miss if I moved away, to say nothing of obliterating any chances I still had with Cam. I dug my phone out of my pocket, opened up my contacts, and looked at the frozen frame of Cam's performance that I'd set as his contact photo. "I hope you decide to do the right thing here, 'cause I'm putting a lot on the line," I said, and then looked up to see George watching me.

"Troubles?" he asked, and I smiled.

"Oh, just trying to make life decisions is all."

"Oh, that? Well, nothing better than some hot cocoa to help think through those."

# 19

# CAM

I STARED AT THE list of performances my new manager had scheduled for me. "Corey, I have to work. I can't do all this."

Madonya was Corey when out of drag, which, to be honest, I hadn't experienced very often. Other than right now, the only time I'd seen Madonya as Corey had been when he first got to work before he'd begun transforming into his drag queen persona. That didn't mean he was any less the handful now, though.

"Baby, you realize you'll make twice the money performing as you make scooping up poop, right?" I gave him the eye. "I can't just quit."

"Why not? What've those bitches ever done for you except work you to the bone?"

I chuckled, not that he was wrong. "I have some comp time I can use to cover a few of these dates, but I can't do this forever. I need to get back to my real life."

"Girl, please, I'm going to turn you into a star. You'll never again have to clean up some old man's shit, puke, or whatever you do there."

"Bloody stools," I said, just to hear him squeal.

"Girl, take your time off. This is gonna be so much fun! Besides, I need you to perform more at my club. If I do all this work for you, I need some boosters over there too."

"I thought that was what the fifteen percent was all about?"

"Bitch, please, I need both, and you *know* I'm worth it. Now shut up and do what your fabulous manager tells you."

"Yes, *Mommie Dearest*," I said like I'd done when I was one of Madonya's performers.

He flipped me off, but laughed.

The truth was, I had already gotten the time off. The official announcement that my hospital was selling to PCS had been published in last Sunday's paper. The transition would begin sometime in July. I wanted to be long gone before that started.

Knowing I would lose all my comp time had already prompted me to warn the director that I was going to take time off, so she had enough time to cover my shifts. All told, since I never took time off, I had accrued about three months of comp time, plus another month of sick leave. Taking all of that time now meant I wouldn't be returning to the hospital, my work there was done.

As I was getting ready to leave on what only I knew equated to my last day, my director met me in the break room. "We're going to miss you when, I mean, *if* you give notice. Please, come back so we can all say goodbye."

I nodded, knowing not to respond. If I officially gave notice, all the comp time would just disappear, and I'd be damned if I let that happen. After all the years I'd worked my ass off accruing it, largely at the expense of having a life outside of work, I was going to cash in every single minute.

Tommy had celebrated my decision to leave the hospital for good. Along with not being a fan of the corporate takeover, he'd watched for months, if not years, as I struggled with job stress and burnout. Sometimes I thought that was why he tried so hard to get me to go out to the bar with him on the weekends, knowing I needed the stress relief.

"So," Tommy said as he plopped down on my recliner, "foot-loose and fancy-free, huh?"

"Apparently. But, Tommy, don't you think this YouTube thing is all a bunch of bullshit that'll blow over in a month or so?"

My best friend shrugged, but I knew better than to think he didn't have an opinion. "Possibly, but you'll never know if you don't try. I remember how singing used to be your dream. It was all you ever talked about growing up, that and who the cutest boys were in school."

"Hey, you did too!" I said, throwing a sofa cushion at him. "But yeah, I figured the same thing. That's why I'm going to use the next few months to see what happens."

"Might take longer than that," Tommy replied thoughtfully.

"It might, but if I'm earning what Madonya thinks I can, then it won't be an issue, will it?"

"No, I guess not, and you're sure you want to do this?" Tommy asked. "I mean, performing was your childhood dream, but the music business is its own cutthroat industry. I just don't want to see something that gives you joy twisted around into something you end up hating."

I sat silently staring at the dark television, before responding, "Tommy, I almost want it too much. I'm afraid of daring to hope that, somehow, I might be able to do this, but I'm more afraid of never having tried."

He smiled. "You've got the work ethic to pull it off. Besides, Madonya is fierce. If she thinks she can make you a success, my money's on her doing it."

I nodded, but didn't say anything else. My emotions were too raw with my newfound hope of becoming a professional singer. It meant a lot that Tommy believed in me, and I knew Mom did as well. I had no doubt Grandma would be cheering me on if she were still with us too.

I only began to think singing was a real career possibility after Madonya uploaded her own recordings of my performances, and views immediately began to skyrocket. It wasn't like I didn't know I could sing. I mean, I had the skill, but literally thousands of people had that same skill and would never get an opportunity to really use it. I had no idea why I'd been given this chance.

I owed so much to whoever The Deputy was for uploading their video of me singing, even if they had done it without my knowledge. They'd launched a potential career for me, and although I loved nursing, this was my first dream. Who knew a complete stranger would've helped to hopefully make that dream come true.

# 20

# HUNTER

ONCE I DECIDED TO stop worrying about the resort stay-ing open, it was like all the puzzle pieces fell into place. I finally moved out of the hotel and into a nice little apart-ment over the pizza place in town that had been an Airbnb for tourists. It felt good to have a little separation from work, and I felt bad that Peggy couldn't rent my suite out since it brought in more money than the regular rooms.

The only reason they'd kept me in that one was because it had some semblance of a kitchen. Regardless, I wasn't going to miss living out of a suitcase, and even though the apartment was smaller than the suite, I was happy to have it.

What I loved the most was the little balcony that led to the back of the pizza place, which was landscaped nicely, making it the perfect spot to chill when I wasn't at work. I read more novels than ever before because, as I realized, even though I'd loved my job, working every waking moment was probably unhealthy.

I leaned back in my Adirondack chair, enjoying the smells of the pizza place below, and the gentle sway of the evergreen trees shading me, and thought about everything that had led me here. In many ways, at least in terms of my working life, I truly was living my dream.

Now, if only I had some sexy man to enjoy all this with me. In an instant, my mind flashed to visions of a naked Cam Kell spread out before me. But in these many months after our one-night stand, I'd finally figured out how to shift my mind away from that minefield. Maybe it was time to start looking for someone local, or at least someone willing to be local.

*Not that Peachleaf has many options*, I thought, and I couldn't help but laugh. I'd only encountered a few gay men since working here, and they'd all been coupled up. Grindr was non-existent out here, and even if I could find someone, I'd still probably be pining for Cam.

"Shit," I said, getting up from the chair and going inside. I needed to get my mind off this guy, who clearly had no plans to move back here.

I decided to head over to the resort, take one of the mountain bikes up onto the trails, and try to enjoy my downtime. It was better than sitting here wanting something I could never have.

I climbed into the truck I'd bought used off someone George knew, who kindly gave me a friend-of-a-friend deal on it, and drove toward the mountain.

I was itching to feel the wind in my hair as I biked down the steep slopes. Biking was similar, but magnificently different from skiing. I found I loved both. I'd been a bit concerned that the summer here would bore me, but damn, I was wrong. This place had everything I could ever want... well, except...

I'd just had that thought when I entered the lobby and walked right into the man himself.

"Whoa, Hunter?" he asked when I half-slammed into him. Without thinking, I dropped my bike helmet and gloves, and grabbed his waist in a protective hold to keep him from hitting the ground.

"Oh, hey," I managed to say, even though my brain was scrambled by his being here in the flesh and literally wrapped in my arms. "We need to stop meeting like this."

He chuckled but didn't push me away. "Hey, yourself," he said, eyeing my discarded helmet and gloves as I released him. "Where ya headed?"

"Um, thought I'd do some biking. Wanna come?" I asked like some lame idiot.

He smiled. "I really could use that, but it's been a long time. I might need to take it easy at first. Are you on patrol?"

I shook my head. "No, I'm off, but if you want easy, we could go to the Delta Pass. It takes a bit longer to get there, but there's only a little downhill section, and you'll have time to get your bearings before coming down the main slope."

He smiled. "Delta's perfect. In that case, I'd love to go for a ride."

I fought against dirty visions of Cam doing riding of an entirely different sort as I led the way into the rental area. I didn't take Delta very often, not that I hadn't biked it when on patrol, but for pleasure I tended to go for the more challenging trails that ended in an exhilarating dash down the mountain. Despite being one of the easier trails to bike, it was the area people tended to get into the most trouble either from inexperience or overconfidence.

As we took the lift up the mountain, I slung my arm around Cam, more to balance myself than to flirt, but he blushed adorably and looked at me longingly as he snuggled into my side. God, why didn't I ask him to forget the biking and just come back to my apartment?

The lift dumped us off, and within seconds, Cam was on his bike and rocketing down the trail. "Hey! You said you needed easy!" I yelled behind him, but he was already gone.

I struggled to catch up, surprised the guy was outrunning me. Not that I should be surprised, since I was heavier than Cam. Of course, that meant going downhill, no one could beat me. Backcountry biking, on the other hand, well, I couldn't compete.

I did catch up enough that I could admire his very sexy ass as he rode in front of me. I was back to imaging wonderfully dirty things when Cam began to slow down, then moments later, he was off his bike and sprinting toward the edge of the mountain trail.

Once I saw where he was headed, I grabbed my satellite phone that I kept with me at all times while on the mountain, even when off duty, and called in a possible emergency as I raced after Cam.

He was leaning over the person by the time I got to him. "He's not breathing. Shit, I'm going to start CPR," he said. "Get someone up here right away."

I relayed the situation over the phone as Cam began chest compressions. I would've probably checked to see if there were any other injuries, but considering Cam was a registered nurse, I figured he knew better than me, even if I did have extensive training.

After several agonizing moments, I asked Cam if he wanted me to take over, but he shook his head and continued counting off the compressions.

I stood back, knowing my job was to watch for fatigue so I could slip in when needed.

Cam paused a moment when the kid, who couldn't be more than thirteen, began breathing on his own. Thank God.

"He's got a pulse. Do you have a blanket? We need to keep him from going into shock."

Fortunately, I had my pack on the back of the bike. After running to grab it, I pulled out the silver blanket, opened it, and threw it over the kid. Cam was already searching for other injuries. "Looks like a head wound. Let them know that. Maybe a broken leg, but I'm afraid to move him to find out," Cam said, then looked to the boy. "Hey! Can you hear me?"

The kid moaned, which was a good sign. "We have help coming. Just hold on, okay?"

"Okay," the kid whispered, and I felt the emotion well up in my eyes. Usually, I was in Cam's position, adrenaline pumping, but as I sat back and watched him do the work, I felt all the relief and astonishment of witnessing a life being saved.

I heard the helicopter coming in just as the kid regained consciousness and was thankful that the accident had happened close to a relatively flat spot clear of trees where the chopper could land.

I recognized Sam and her husband Rick immediately. They were both on patrol for us and worked for the county's EMT program.

Rick came over to me as Sam went to assess the patient. "What's the status?" Rick asked.

"Apparent head injury. The patient was unconscious when we arrived. Cam saw him first and gave him chest compressions."

"Patient is conscious," Cam reported as he came to our side. "But there are more than a few other issues we couldn't assess due to potential internal injuries. We didn't want to move him until you arrived."

Rick nodded and quickly went to assist Sam in prepping the boy for transport. They secured him onto a board and within minutes were air-lifting the kid to the hospital.

"He's in serious shape. Do you think they're taking him to the critical access hospital?" Cam asked.

"No, he'll be flown to Denver or maybe Loveland," I replied.

Just then, my satellite phone went off. "Hunter, we think we have the kid's parents, but need some details. Can you confirm what he was wearing?"

I quickly described the kid's yellow shirt, high-top sneakers, and blue bike helmet. "The helicopter just left. I'm not sure where they're headed yet. The kid was pretty badly beat up, but conscious when they lifted off."

After ending the call with dispatch, I quickly assessed the area and took pictures with my cell phone of his destroyed bike and tracks that indicated what happened. "Looks like he lost control of the bike and was thrown," Cam said.

I nodded and pointed back toward the mountain. "Tracks come down through there, so he must've climbed up the mountain off-trail, then come down through here."

After taking some more pictures so I had enough to include in my incident report, I called in a request for someone to come collect the mangled bike.

"Cam, you can go ahead, but I'll need to hang out until they get here. I don't want the bike to be tampered with until we can get it back and document the damage."

"I can stay with you," he said, and sat down on a boulder away from the scene to wait.

"This usually takes a long time," I said.

Cam smiled. "Hunter, I've been a part of all this for years, although not as much recently, but I know rescue isn't fast-moving unless lives are at stake."

I nodded. "Okay, well…" I said, and pulled a couple of Cliff bars out of my pack. "I can offer some sustenance while we wait."

Cam smiled and took the bar. "I probably should've waited for you, but years of training…"

"No, you did fine. Amazing, actually. That kid owes you his life."

"He's lucky we got here when we did. He couldn't have been out for more than a minute, or else…"

"Yeah, or else."

Cam sighed. "Can I tell you something?"

He bit his bottom lip in that way which made my head spin a bit as he pondered.

"Yeah, of course," I said, brushing his shoulder with mine in support of whatever he was about to say.

"I miss the adrenaline rush. I know it's stupid and probably makes me a bad person, but I love being on this side of things."

I smiled. "No, it doesn't make you a bad person. I love this sort of thing too, having to think fast and make critical decisions, but don't you get enough of it at work?"

Cam shook his head. "No, I'm... well, I left my job. Not officially yet, but soon. I'm not going back to the Denver hospital."

"Why?" I asked, wincing when he looked nervous all of a sudden. "I mean, it's okay if you don't want to tell me. Why is your business, I don't mean to pry."

"No, it's okay you asked, but the reason is kind of embarrassing. Let's just say something came up. It's good, though," he quickly added, when I couldn't hide my concern.

"So, no more nursing?"

Cam shrugged, but grinned shyly. "Only time will tell, but I think I'm going to be spending a lot more time here. Do you think maybe you could use some extra help with patrol? I mean, it'll be unofficial volunteering, but I sorta want to stay attached to it somehow, and if I can help someone like that kid..."

I chuckled. "We never say no to volunteers with your experience, and we need someone to replace a couple of the older folks who want to retire, but are you sure? Won't you be getting a job somewhere else?" I was thinking Denver, but didn't say it.

He shrugged again. "Not sure, but I'm more than happy to help while I'm here if you could use me."

"Yeah, we could use you." *And so could I, in all sorts of ways,* I thought, though this wasn't the time to bring that up.

# 21

# Cam

Since I'd left the hospital, Madonya was working my ass off. She had me booked at every available venue in Denver, and was recording and posting new YouTube content constantly.

Finally, after a full month of back-to-back performances, I put my foot down and ran away from home. When I arrived in Peachleaf, I called and told her where I was and that I was not performing for at least a week.

It was crazy, but it seemed like I was working more as a performer than I had as a nurse. I loved it, and it fed a part of my soul that had long been neglected, but I still needed a break.

Madonya was upset, but I think she understood. Besides, I was still getting lots of views, so I needed some downtime to pull out my old guitar and try to remember some of my original songs. I was pretty-damn good at writing my own songs, or had been at least, and even my intensely critical professors back in Kansas City had agreed.

I'd tossed my singing career aspirations aside while getting my nursing degree and then working as a nurse. Sure, I occasionally performed on Madonya's stage, but that wasn't with any hope of turning professional.

Now, I was already making good money with my singing career just as it was getting started, and it looked like my nursing would be cast aside as a result. That bothered me, more than I thought it would.

Running across the injured kid and helping stabilize him reminded me how much I loved that side of my life, and I wasn't quite ready to give it up entirely. That, and I knew with Madonya pushing me constantly, I'd need to escape to the resort every so often like I was doing now, so why not put myself to good use on patrol while I was here?

The thought excited me, and Hunter didn't reject the idea out of hand either. I enjoyed just being in his company as we sat together on the boulder in companionable silence, munching on the Cliff bars he'd brought. It'd been such a long time since we'd seen each other, and I regretted not staying in better contact while back in Denver.

Once the guys arrived to load up the kid's bike, we finished our ride down the trail to the tram. We rode back in relative silence, mostly because my mind was elsewhere.

When the tram dropped us off at the lodge side of the resort, Hunter turned to me, saying, "If you're serious about volunteering, come in, and I'll get you signed up. I know you're an owner and all that, but we have our protocols."

"No problem, sure. Lead the way."

I filled all the paperwork out and even watched a couple of required training videos. Hunter stayed in the office with me as I watched the videos, I liked to think because he enjoyed my company too more than it being another aspect of usual protocols.

Once done, Hunter walked me out to my car. I was staying at Mom's house during my visit, though she wanted to clean out Grandma's place, so I'd have an official home in Peachleaf. Although, I'd inherited Grandma's cottage and the mansion her parents had lived in, but I still hadn't decided what to do with them.

"What are your plans for tomorrow?" Hunter asked.

"Well, nothing fun. I'm going to open my grandma's cottage and help Mom go through her stuff."

"That sounds difficult," Hunter said, his mouth downturned in concern. "Sorry about that."

"Don't be. We've put it off long enough. My grandmother wasn't one to tolerate putting these kinds of things off. Honestly, she'd be pissed we haven't gotten to it."

"Do you need help?" he asked, surprising me.

"I... well, probably not for a while. I think it's gonna just be me and Mom doing the memory lane thing, but yeah, maybe later? Can I text you?"

Hunter nodded, then said, "I'll be working the morning shift tomorrow, but I'm free in the afternoon if you need someone to do some grunt work."

I smiled. "I'm sure we will. Let me talk to Mom, and I'll text."

Hunter lingered for a moment before heading back into the lodge, and I felt like I'd given up a chance for more with him tonight, but the adrenaline from earlier was now gone, and the exhaustion from running like crazy for weeks on end was beginning to weigh on me. I needed the rest.

I drove back to Mom's, collapsed on my old bed, and fell asleep, and didn't wake up until the following morning.

"Pass me that box," Mom said as she scanned another photo into her laptop.

"Mom, so much of this is already done? When did you do all the cleanup?" I asked.

She shrugged. "I didn't. Your grandmother did. When she was diagnosed with cancer, she began getting rid of stuff. We planned to scan in all the old family photos, but didn't get around to it, unfortunately."

I looked through some of the black-and-white photos of my great-grandparents standing proudly in the front entryway of the hotel.

"We should pass all the ones with the resort in them to the hotel, as a way of preserving its history."

"We have several on display there already, some duplicates of these, but since we're scanning them all in, I guess it couldn't hurt."

I smiled sadly at one of the rare photos of my grandparents standing with Mom and Dad. I was in Mom's arms. "I think we should frame this one," I said, showing it to her.

"Those were tough days. On the one hand, we were all so excited to have you, but on the other, your grandparents weren't quite ready to have an orphan as a daughter-in-law."

I shook my head. "Would you have believed back then how close you and Grandma would become?"

Mom stared at the picture. "Honestly, right then, I had a lot of hope, but your father moved us away shortly after this was taken. Your grandparents blamed me for that, even though I didn't want to move."

"Did Dad tell them it was your idea?" I asked, never having heard the story.

Mom nodded. "Said it would be easier if it looked like it came from me and not him. I was so in love with him, though, I'd have followed him anywhere, and there was you to consider too, of course."

I sighed as I put the picture away. It no longer felt the same now that Mom had shared the story.

"Do you regret, you know, Dad and you?"

Mom reached over and took my hand. "I don't regret you. Your father was the love of my life. I was crazy in love with him, but he was a kid, in more ways than one." She chuckled, but there was sadness in it. "He needed more years to mature than he had. Despite all that, don't you ever think he didn't love you. He adored you, and to be honest, one of the reasons he wanted to leave so bad was because he thought this small town would smother you like it had him."

"Oh, Mom, I think he and I were a lot more alike than I remember. I was desperate to get away. Now..."

"Now?" Mom asked, sounding a mixture of surprised and hopeful.

"Well, it feels different. I mean, it's still a boring-ass town unless you want to ski or bike, or do other outdoorsy stuff, but I don't mind boring as much as I did when I was younger."

"Your father was just coming to that same realization when... well, when we lost him."

The drunk driver who crossed the centerline and plowed into Dad's car as he was driving home from work had apparently had one too many drinks that night. That was what her defense had been, *one too many drinks*. She got five years for the DUI, but got out on good behavior after serving six months.

It'd taken Mom and me years to come to terms with Dad's death, and I don't think Grandma ever really did. Regardless, it was still very difficult to talk about, so we usually avoided the subject.

"Okay, time to switch to something else," I said as I got up, walked into the kitchen, and started going through the cabinets.

Mom came in a few moments later and saw me pulling out some of the food, like the canned meat. "Why aren't you taking it all out?" she asked.

I sighed. "'Cause I'm moving in, and besides this creepy stuff," I said, pointing at the canned meat, "it's stupid to throw away food I'm willing to eat."

"Really? You really are moving in?" Mom asked, a smile blooming on her face.

"Yeah, I was debating it, but I think I wanna be home for a while. Maybe even work over at the county hospital, if the whole singing thing doesn't work out long-term."

Mom grabbed me with a squeal and spun me around. "Oh, Cam, I'm so excited. My baby boy's coming home! Okay, this means we need to be going through and picking out what you want to keep."

I smiled back at her and nodded. "I'm going to keep my apartment in Denver. It's small and relatively cheap, and it'll be a nice place to crash when I'm performing at all the places Madonya has me scheduled."

"Smart idea, and while you're here, we can repaint all these bland white walls. Your grandmother had fashion sense, but absolutely no interior-design skills. I swear it was all I could do not to sneak in here myself to paint this place."

"Sounds good, but you know her art was what she valued, not her walls."

"Which is what you've got to think about the most. All the artwork here is valuable, at least to some extent. Some pieces are very valuable, despite not being that old. Do you want to keep them, or..."

I immediately nodded. "Oh yeah, I'm totally keeping it all. But I'd like to loan most of it to regional museums or galleries, places it'll be seen and appreciated. I just don't want to live with every possible space on my walls covered in art. It should be displayed somewhere, though, don't you think?"

"You could talk to the museums in Denver. I'm sure they'd take the collection on loan. Like I said, quite a bit of it is valuable."

"That's a good idea, and I'd appreciate your help choosing the pieces," I said, as I glanced out the big plate-glass window and caught sight of the mansion house that sat a few acres away from the cottage. "Or maybe..."

Mom had already moved back to the photo boxes and was scanning pictures again, paying me no mind. I stared at the large stone structure, ideas brimming, and my heart began to pound. This could work if we could come up with the funds.

I didn't know that much about Grandma's collection, but knew my great-grandparents had collected some of the best pieces from the nineteen twenties and thirties. Even during the Great Depression, they collected art. When their parents died, they inherited significantly more.

Grandma had moved the most valuable stuff to this cottage, which was why it literally covered every wall, but the sculptures and less valuable pieces were still stored in the mansion. The art was my heritage, in some ways more than the resort, and I'd never sell it. As far as I was concerned, it belonged to future generations, provided I had kids, which I fully intended to someday.

I stared at the huge mansion thinking. Even if I found a lover and had a kid or two, this cottage was more than big enough to raise a family. I didn't have any desire to live in the mansion, but that didn't mean I wanted to sell the beautiful structure. I thought of its grand ballroom, envisioning concert performances and community gatherings there, and its various hallways that had practically served as gallery space when Grandma's paintings had lined the walls.

The more I thought about it, the more excited I got. Of course, funding this grand idea could be an issue. If I sold my part of the resort, provided it continued to do as well under Cabot Management, the proceeds should be significant. Enough, I hoped, to renovate the old mansion, and possibly still leave me some money in my pocket. Perhaps, even enough to hire a full-time staff.

I whistled as I cleaned out Grandma's old cabinets of the food and knickknacks I'd never use, all the while planning this next adventure. *The Kell Museum of Art*. God, I loved the sound of that.

# 22

# HUNTER

I TEXTED CAM AFTER finishing my shift.

Me: *You ready for my help?*

Cam: *Sure, if you don't mind packing up canned meat of a questionable origin.*

Me: *As long as I don't have to eat it, count me in.*

He called a few minutes later. "Hey," he said when I answered.

"Hey to you, so where am I going?"

"Where are you right now?" he asked. I told him I was in the lobby of the hotel.

"Okay, go back to the lodge, and tell me when you get there."

I chuckled, but did as he asked. "Okay, I'm here."

"Do you see that big house on the water?"

"Yeah, that's what you're moving?"

He laughed. "No, lucky you, but if you walk the road to that house, you'll run across a two-story cottage, same stone as the hotel and the big house. That's where you'll find me."

"Okay, I'm headed out now."

"Cool, see you in a few."

I walked along the road that hugged the reservoir. I'd seen the big house since it was visible from most vantage points around the resort, but I hadn't taken this road before. During the winter, I didn't even know the road was here because it'd been covered in snow, which, I'd assumed, meant that house in the distance was empty.

The walk was beautiful, with the mountain reflected in the crystal-clear water. I'd spent some significant time in the lake this summer, swimming and water skiing. The hot springs that fed the reservoir kept the temperature remarkably warm, though never hot, because, after all, it was still a Colorado mountain lake.

After walking for just over ten minutes, the cottage Cam must've been talking about came into view. It looked like it should be in one of the old-time villages in England. Of course, it was much newer, but it gave off that homey, lived-in feel.

When I reached the front door, I noticed it standing open. "Hello!" I called, and was immediately greeted by Peggy.

"Hey, Hunter, what brings you over?" she asked.

"Oh, I, um, agreed to help Cam."

"Cam?" she asked, and looked confused. "Okay, well, come on in."

"Cam, Hunter's here," she called toward the stairs.

"Thanks, Mom. Can you send him up?"

Her crooked smile suggested she knew more than she was going to say, and I couldn't help but return a grin like a naughty schoolboy who had just got caught stealing a cookie from the cookie jar.

I dashed up the stairs and found Cam sitting on a bedroom floor, surrounded by boxes. "What's all this?" I asked.

Cam looked up and smiled. "Well, it's mostly art, but some other stuff too."

"Art, like what's already on the walls?" I asked, pointing to the walls that even in this room were covered..

"Yep, but these are the pieces my grandmother didn't have anywhere to hang."

"Wow, your grandmother was into art, apparently."

"Great-grandparents. I doubt my grandmother ever bought any herself. She wouldn't have had anywhere to store it if she had."

"I can see that. Anyway, how can I help?"

"Nothing really in here, but come with me." I followed Cam into another room. It, too, had wall-to-wall art. "I want to take this bed apart and move it into the master bedroom. Then I want to move that bed into here."

I looked at him, confused. Cam just smiled. "I don't want to sleep in the bed my grandmother passed away in."

"Yikes," I said, and quickly nodded. "Okay, makes sense."

I took the bed apart while Cam returned to the other room, where I assumed he was putting the plethora of art in boxes. Then I went to the master and took apart that bed, happy to see the mattress and box-spring had already been discarded. The bed was beautiful, though. It looked old, with gold inlay and a picture of a woman with dark hair from what appeared to be the nineteen twenties. I wondered if maybe she was a relative of Cam's.

"I see you finished. Want me to help?" he asked from the doorway.

"Yeah, sure. Hey, who's this woman?" I asked, causing Cam to cringe. "Well, I've been told it's my great-great-grandmother, but the story sometimes changes to her being my great-grandmother. So, I'm not sure, but I do know I don't want her watching me in my sleep."

I nodded in agreement. "Okay, let's move this into the other room."

We changed the beds out and, to be honest, I much preferred the nice king-size four-poster bed over the dainty great-granny bed. But with all the art on the walls, I'd have been creeped out sleeping in the room anyway.

Cam caught me frowning at all the art and asked, "It's a lot, isn't it?"

"Um, yeah, maybe too much."

"I totally agree, which is why I'm packing it up."

"What're you going to do with it all?" I asked, and Cam flashed a shy smile.

"Well, I have an idea. Let's see if Mom has the key to the big house."

He left and came back a few minutes later, key in hand. "Come on. I'll show you."

The cottage and main house were closer together than I'd thought when I approached the cottage. Probably because the cottage sat closer to the water, almost like it was built as a lake house.

The main house, which had appeared to be right on the lake when looking from the resort, actually sat back a ways and further up the mountain. The views from its front porch were breathtaking. "Wow, this is incredible," I said as I waited for Cam to unlock the door.

Cam turned around, smiling. "Yeah, you won't be able to tell, 'cause the windows are boarded up, but that view is different depending on which window you look out of."

"How long has it been boarded up?" I asked as the door creaked open.

"Oh, I was around nine or ten when my grandpa died, and the upkeep was too much for my grandmother, so she shut it down then, but I remember it from before."

I followed him into the house and stood staring at the amazing chandelier and wide grand staircase that flowed upstairs from the middle of the room. "Let's go to the grand ballroom first," he said, leading me to a room on the right. "This is where they hosted parties, but according to my grandmother, it's rarely been used. Regardless, it runs the full length of the house. You also have the Conservatory over here," he said and led the way into a glass enclosure just off the ballroom. "I don't think this key works, but you can see there are patios on the front and back of the Conservatory, so guests can meander through all the different doors."

"Wow, really, wow," I said as I stood transfixed by the opulence.

"That's not all," he said and led me out of the ballroom and into a series of rooms on the other side. "Remember, this was built before open concept became a thing, so you have several smaller rooms off the main entryway, but here's the parlor, as my grandmother called it. It's the biggest room on this side of the house."

The tattered wallpaper and motheaten carpet didn't diminish what was once a beautiful room. There was even a marble fireplace that still had burn stains from years of use.

The library, which led from the parlor, was a dark hunter green, with meticulously crafted built-in bookshelves and one of those strange-looking rolling ladders you'd see in pictures of old libraries. The bookshelves encircled openings where I assumed paintings had hung, but all the books still seemed to be in place. I pulled one down and smiled at what looked like a first edition *Winnie the Pooh*.

Figuring it was worth a lot, I slipped it back into its dusty spot.

Cam next showed me a dining room and tiny kitchen behind a grand staircase. The dining room was spectacular and probably the best-preserved room in the place. The kitchen, however, was smaller than I had in my house back in Warrenstown. I must've looked perplexed, because Cam chuckled.

"Remember, only servants used the kitchen when this was built."

"Oh, well, that explains it, I guess," I replied, but it still baffled me how such an opulent home could have such a tiny kitchen.

We went upstairs, and the opulence continued. Marble floors that led through the entry and up the stairs spilled into the bedrooms before polished wood took over. The bedrooms were mostly empty, though a few still had beds and miscellaneous furniture pieces in them.

Finally, we went to the third floor, where there were several small rooms I assumed had been servants' quarters.

"Cam, this is an amazing place. What are you going to do with it?"

He sat down on a dusty old straight-back chair and pointed at one next to it for me to take a seat. "Well, I think this could make a good museum. I have so much art that should be seen, not boxed away, and really, who wants to move into a giant mansion in the middle of nowhere? Personally, I don't have any interest in living here, but it seems a shame not to share it in some way."

"An art museum? Here?" I asked, feeling excitement grow inside me.

"Yeah, is it stupid?" he asked, that shy look he sometimes got returning.

I shook my head and sat on the edge of my seat. "No, it's a great idea. You should talk to my cousin, Josiah. He's Aunt Monica and Uncle Harris's son. He's going to go nuts over this, especially if they buy the resort." I stopped my rambling dead in its tracks. "Um, I don't think I was supposed to mention that last part. Can we delete it from this conversation?"

Cam just laughed. "Hunter, it's not like everyone doesn't know that's what Cabot Management is doing here. Hell, they're barely getting paid for the work they're doing. It doesn't take a rocket scientist to see they're just checking things out before they invest."

I nodded and kept my damned mouth shut like I should've before, then I sighed. "Seriously, you should talk to Josiah. He graduated a couple of years ago with a fine arts degree. I think he wants to be a museum curator or something like that, even though he's a pretty amazing artist himself."

"I figured your aunt would've made her kids work in the family business," he said, and laughed.

"Well, trust me, she tried, but Josiah is as stubborn as she is and never had an ounce of interest in the resort business.

Amelia, however, that's a different story. She's all business, smooth like Uncle Harris, but there's no doubt she'll be the one running Cabot Management one day."

Cam looked thoughtful as he stood and led the way back downstairs. "I wouldn't mind talking to your cousin. I don't know shit about museums, and with my crazy singing schedule, I don't know when I'd do any of this."

That took me aback a bit. "Singing schedule?"

"Oh, yeah, sorry, I guess I haven't mentioned it. "I'm singing now, well, trying it out. I've been doing gigs around Denver full-time for the past month. I ran away this week, 'cause my manager is nuts and would only give me a break when forced."

"You're talented enough." I thought of the video I'd recorded of his bar performance that I'd all but memorized at this point.

"Well, yeah, thanks. I like it, but if your cousin knows how to make this big house work as an art museum, I'd love to try it."

We were just coming to the foot of the stairs when Cam snagged his foot on a piece of carpet and stumbled forward, almost taking us both down the last three steps.

"Whoa," I said, catching him by the shoulders and then holding onto him as we finished descending the stairs.

"Shit, I'm a klutz," he said, sounding embarrassed, before looking up at me when I didn't immediately let him go.

"I don't mind," I said, gazing into his beautiful golden-brown eyes.

"I, um, yeah, me neither," he said.

I leaned down and kissed him softly, and was relieved when he sank against me rather than pulled away. Just as tongues were beginning to meet, the front door opened. We broke the kiss and turned guiltily toward the doorway, and found ourselves facing a very amused Peggy.

"Mom, you have horrible timing."

"I disagree, but you can get back to that later. We should try to finish cleaning out the stuff you don't want while I've got time off. Hunter, come on back to the cottage, I need help with some heavy boxes."

Peggy was still smirking as she turned and left us standing there, and Cam just shook his head. "Well, guess if I'm moving back, I need to get used to my mom being all in my business again."

I laughed. "Oh, as someone who recently escaped mine, I can give you pointers on how to hide and run when necessary."

Cam hummed in amusement, then, taking my hand, led me out of the old house before locking the door behind us.

We walked like that the rest of the way to the cottage, hand in hand, my heart swelling like a middle schooler who had just had his first kiss. Today was a fucking amazing day.

# 23

## CAM

---

IT TOOK THE REST of the week to take down all of Grandma's paintings and store them in the upstairs bedrooms. Hunter came by occasionally to help, but with Mom hanging around, I remained cockblocked all week.

To be honest, I was beginning to get more than a little frustrated. I wanted Hunter again and was determined to have him, and he seemed to feel the same, but life and responsibilities kept getting in the way.

I had to head back to Denver for a full schedule of performances this weekend, and if I didn't already know that Madonya would be working me around the clock, I'd have invited Hunter along.

So, Friday afternoon, I decided to take things in hand... well, in the butt at least, and applied a plug just in case an opportunity with Hunter presented itself. If not, I could at least think of him when I got home to take care of myself.

I packed up the last paintings that I didn't want to keep in the cottage for myself. I'd loved a few of them all my life, including one by a female painter from the time of Hildreth Meière. Grandma told me I had a good eye when I'd told her I liked it.

With that done, I could unleash Mom and her paintbrush. "No pastels, no bright nineteen nineties colors," I warned her. "Just something smooth and easygoing."

"Ugh, I'm not painting your walls beige," she said, and I laughed.

"Mom, seriously, no crazy colors. You know my style."

She rolled her eyes, and I'd swear I heard her say "boring," but God help us both, if she thought my style boring, at least it would keep my walls from becoming neon yellow or candy-apple red.

Mom had to return to the resort after our visit to handle some mishap with supplies for the snack bar, which left me alone for dinner. We'd eaten a late lunch, so I wasn't particularly hungry, but I was craving something sweet.

Of course, my mind immediately went to Polly's Pies. My mouth began watering as I thought of Polly's cobbler, or maybe

I'd order the apple pie with some of the homemade ice cream she also made this time of year.

I quickly locked the cottage up and headed to town.

My eyes shot straight to the display case as I entered. Sometimes Polly made other pies I liked better than blackberry cobbler, and if she happened to have any in stock, I didn't want to miss out. I fell into line, because there was always a line at Polly's.

I glanced around the place as I waited, and my attention snagged on a very tall, very sexy man in line whose eyes honed in on me like heat-seeking missiles. I could feel my blush turn crimson as Hunter's stare intensified, and I was about to break the silence when he turned and ordered.

The teenager behind the counter, a kid I had only seen here a few times when I came in for my obligatory blackberry cobbler, took his order but glanced at me and smiled. She disappeared out the back and returned a moment later with a whole pie and a box of homemade ice cream.

Hunter paid, then came over to me. "I heard you like their apple, so I got a whole pie. Wanna come to my place and share it?"

I had to swallow hard, because inappropriate images sprang to mind of smearing Hunter's body from head to toe with apple pie and licking it off. At least, inappropriate when standing in line at a very public eatery, which was why I quickly nodded and followed him out the front door.

"You can just leave your car. I live right over there," he said, shifting the food to his other hand as he reached over and grasped mine.

It was all well and good at least one of my hands was occupied, because God help me, I was going to rip that man's clothes off the moment he let go.

I was able to maintain my composure long enough for him to walk me into his apartment and put the pie down. "Do you want your piece now?" he asked.

I shook my head. "No, Hunter, the only *piece* I want is you. I-I..."

Before I could embarrass myself with mushy blathering, Hunter's arms wrapped around me in a firm but gentle embrace. "Yeah, me too," he whispered, his breath hot against my ear, as I melted into his touch.

# 24

# HUNTER

I NUZZLED CAM'S NECK, taking a moment for my mind to catch up to the fact that the guy was back in my arms after so many months dreaming about him. "I want you so bad," I admitted, then took Cam's earlobe into my mouth, sucking on it while he quaked nicely in my arms.

"My God, Hunter, me too," he said as he let his head fall back, so I could suck and lick my way down his delicious neck.

I wanted to take my time and enjoy all the parts, sensations, and ways to bring him pleasure that I'd missed the last time–and achingly still the only time–we'd been alone together like this.

Moving behind him, I let my hands roam under his shirt and across his body, slowly taking in every subtle ridge and dip from hips to chest. When my fingers brushed over his hard nipples and his breath caught, I tweaked them, causing Cam to moan with desire.

I dipped my head for another taste, kissing his neck and inhaling the intoxicating scent I'd yearned for since I first touched him.

He turned and lifted up on his toes to kiss me. I grabbed his ass and pulled him tight against me, letting our cocks rub together and showing him how much I wanted him.

I gave Cam's firm cheeks a squeeze before reluctantly letting go in order to pull his shirt off. I dove in for another taste of his lips before slowly working my way down, nipping at his jaw, then his neck, and collarbones, before reaching his bare chest. When I moistened one of his nipples with my tongue, then bit down, he gasped.

Cam's hands tugged at my shirt as I attacked one nipple, then the other, smiling up at him with desire. He gave me a smirk, then pulled my shirt the rest of the way off before pressing his palms against my chest, and I reveled in the feel of his fingers tracing every muscle.

"Bedroom," I said, grabbing his hand and leading him down the very short hallway, kicking our shoes off along the way.

We lay down on my bed with me on top of him, grinding my cock into his, and wanting to go fast, but needing the slow, easy glide.

"I want you naked," he finally said between kisses as he thrust against me.

I nodded and lifted up long enough for him to unbuckle my pants. When he reached for his, I batted his hand away. "Let me," I said as I shimmied out of my pants and underwear, and used my feet to kick off my socks.

He grinned and watched me as I undid his pants, slowly stripped them off his legs along with his underwear, and tossed them aside before taking his delectable cock into my mouth. "Mmm," we both moaned at the same time.

"Fuck, you taste so good," I said when I pulled back, making eye contact with him.

Nowhere near having gotten my fill, I began licking around the head, letting my tongue linger in the slit before going deep, choking him back all the way.

He arched against the bed, prompting me to suck him harder, taking him to the edge. I didn't always like to be edged, but tonight, I needed to bring him there, then back, time and again. I wanted him yearning for me before I took his ass again.

Cam cried out my name, which sent electric pulses to my cock. Fuck, his sexy voice all riled up in the throes of passion sounded as sultry as his singing voice.

"I'm gonna..." he started to say, and I pulled back and smiled at him as he dry-humped the air.

"Oh my god," he said, "that's cruel."

I laughed and kissed his inner thigh. "You'll thank me later."

"Mmm, are you going to fuck me? That cock of yours is all I've thought about for months."

I cocked my eyebrow, but wasn't going to argue with him. I had honestly thought about him for months too, but the whole package. His scent, his body, his face, his fucking voice.

I crawled on top of him then, in a sixty-nine position, lining my cock up with his mouth and taking his in mine again.

I fucked Cam's mouth, and his moans assured me he was enjoying himself too. I deliberately went slow, sucking and savoring, and wanting to take him to the edge again. I also wanted to fuck him senseless, and needed him pliable for that.

When his moans grew louder, I reached over to grab lube I'd stashed in my nightstand. He groaned in disappointment when I pulled off him, then smiled when he saw the lube in my hand. I then took some condoms out of the drawer, and he put his hand on mine.

"Um," he began, and I noticed he was blushing now. "I'm on PrEP. I've also been tested, and there's nothing to worry about."

I smiled. "Same here, but I want you to feel comfortable."

Cam leaned up and kissed me sweetly. "Hunter, I do feel comfortable with you, and I want to feel you come inside me. I know that's probably stupid." He began to move away, but I held him in place.

"Listen, it's not stupid. I want all that too, I want everything about you, so if you trust me..."

I let my words trail off in question, and Cam smiled in reply. "Then let's do all of that without those," he said, pointing at the condoms.

I shuddered at the thought of what it would feel like being inside him unsheathed. I was a huge advocate of condoms, but I was also disease-free and on PrEP. I trusted him when he said he was too.

Cam lay back down, and I squirted some lube in my hand and began coating myself, then him. That's when I realized he was wearing a butt plug.

"You prepped for me?" I asked.

"All day," he said with a smirk. Fuck, the little minx had been thinking about this all day and hadn't given any sign?

He moaned so deliciously as I toyed with the plug and replaced it with my fingers. By the time I had my third finger in, he was whimpering and whispering my name.

Cam was so pliable, so perfect for me. I watched as his lean body squirmed under my preparations. I lubed his cock with my right hand and began to stroke him, enjoying his moans as they got louder and more desperate.

I positioned my cock against his hole and waited, the sight causing my breath to catch. I'd wanted this for so long, to feel Cam beneath me again, writhing and eager for my cock, that I almost couldn't believe it wasn't dream.

Before I made a move to push inside him, Cam wrapped his legs around my waist and did the work for me. I laughed when I noticed the perturbed look on his face. "Taking too long," he said.

"No more waiting." I chuckled and slowly slid deeper into his body, watching him take me in inch by inch.

He didn't react to my length or girth this time, the fact that he'd prepared for me beforehand sent a rush through me, and I thrust all the way in.

Cam arched again, but this time he yelled, "Hunter, fuck!" I pulled back, afraid I'd hurt him, but when I looked into his eyes, all I saw was ecstasy.

I continued to take it slow, letting my cock get used to the tightness of him. He squirmed with pleasure as I moved my cock around, letting it stretch his hole wider than my girth.

"Fuck, yeah, fuck, God, this is so... God, Hunter," he exclaimed, and with a naughty grin, I shoved my cock in hard and deep, just to hear him react.

"Aargh," he moaned before stopping me to get on all fours. "Take me hard, Hunter, I need it!"

I obliged, driving into him with all I had in me, and he arched back again. Cam's moans turned to short cries as I took him, each thrust claiming him as my own. "Hunter, fuck, Hunter," he chanted between cries. *God damn*, was all I could think. I was going to take advantage of this sexy ass while I had the chance.

He went eagerly as I shoved his beautiful face down into the pillow, dominating him more. He purred under my aggression. Fuck, if that didn't make the need to plow into him even stronger.

As much as his muffled moans into the pillow were turning me on, I wanted to see his face covered in my cum. I pulled out and rolled him onto his back, and put my cock up to his mouth before I began jacking off again. He continued to moan as he stroked himself, and within seconds, I came all over his face and into his open mouth.

He had to swallow and breathe before taking the rest. Fuck, I was coming a lot. More than usual.

I looked down and saw he was about to come too, so I quickly moved into position just as the long white ribbons of Cam's release pelted my face. Cam's cum was still dripping from my chin when I turned to smile at him.

He didn't hesitate. He leaned up and, taking my mouth with his, combined our flavors in a sensual kiss.

"Fuck," I said when he leaned back. "That's... fuck."

Cam chuckled. "Not used to snowballs, huh?"

"I fucking love snowballs," I said and lay on top of him, laying claim to his mouth and getting another taste of our cum.

Finally, overcome with the afterglow, I collapsed next to him and nuzzled in. "Damn, you're so fucking much. I-I'm..."

"Happy?" Cam asked, and I nodded, then burrowed my face back into his neck.

# 25

# CAM

I snuggled up against the man I'd been fantasizing about since last we screwed several months ago. If I could just lie like this for another week or two, I'd be perfectly happy.

He got up, found a washcloth, and cleaned us up as much as possible before slipping into bed next to me.

Hunter turned toward me, lifted my face, and kissed me. "That was amazing."

"Mmm, each time is," I said.

He nodded. "I'd like to do that more. A lot more, if you're willing?"

"Too damned willing," I said, and dipped my head down to kiss his gorgeous chest. He smelled so fucking good, something between clean, raw masculinity, and coffee. I just wanted to lick him all over again.

"You want some pie now?" he asked, and I laughed because no matter how delicious Polly's apple pie was, eating was the last thing on my mind. Well, unless his mouthwatering body was on the menu again.

"Um, sure, but not for a minute. I want to do this a little more," I said, flicking his left nipple with my tongue.

Hunter wrapped his big arms around me and chuckled in a low deep way that sent blood coursing to my cock. *Really*? I thought. *All he has to do is chuckle and I'm hard?*

Hunter was clearly my type. The kind of man I wanted, looked for, and seldom found for more than a night or two. Men like him—gorgeous and muscular, with legs for days, kind eyes, and a dirty mind—rarely went for slimmer guys like me. At least, that'd been my experience, and probably why I had largely given up on dating.

"You're thinking really hard, and it's screwing with my afterglow," he said after several moments. Of course, I had been biting my lower lip, which was probably what gave me away.

"Yeah, I do that sometimes," I said, but leaned up and smiled. "Come on, let's have that apple pie, then I think we might be able to have some fun with that ice cream."

"Hmm, Cam à la mode?" he asked, causing me to laugh.

"Hunter à la mode sounds tasty too."

Hunter rolled over on top of me, pinning me down and kissing me. "Maybe both à la mode." He began to grind his cock against mine, and I knew it would take us some time to get to that apple pie.

# 26

# HUNTER

AFTER WE'D TRADED SLOW, luxurious kisses, Cam curled up next to me, neither of us quite ready to leave the bed. I kept thinking, *He's an itch that when scratched just itches that much more.*

Honestly, I didn't quite know what to do with that realization. Men had come and gone from my bed and my life, and if we were compatible in the bedroom, great. If not, neither one of us stuck around long. Cam, though? Why the fuck did I want him like this?

I couldn't get enough of him, and not just between the sheets, although sex with him had been the best of my life. He was everything I liked physically, and his body fit with mine like a glove, never mind his eagerness to let me be aggressive in bed.

Fucking him was like fucking happiness itself. Parts of me I didn't know existed took over when I was making love to this man.

We were still learning about each other, and I wouldn't be surprised if he considered me little more than a fantastic repeat hookup at this point, but Cam was the whole package. I hadn't seen that when we first hooked up, but on the days we'd hung out together since then, even with Peggy around, he was funny and witty, always teasing and poking at me until he got me to laugh. He was also a kindhearted man, saving lives and wanting to do right by his family, and then there was his sultry as hell singing voice I longed to hear again.

I knew deep down I'd never felt this way about someone before, but I also didn't want to scare the man off with any big declarations so soon. Hell, were we even technically dating at this point? *Okay, enough*, I thought. *Time to feed this man more than just my cock.*

"Come on. I'll fix us some pie," I said, leading him to the kitchen. Neither of us bothered with clothes.

As I took the pie out of the container and began slicing it, Cam slipped in behind me, his naked body hugging my bigger one from behind. God, I thought I almost purred. *That's another first*, I thought.

"I like how this feels," Cam said, rubbing his body up and down my back like a damn cat before laughing and releasing his hold. "I'm probably freaking you out, aren't I? I'm sorry, I just can't seem to keep from touching you."

I put the cutting knife down and turned toward him. "You don't have to apologize. It feels fucking amazing every time you touch me."

"Really?" Cam asked, and ducked his chin. For the first time today, he looked shy.

I lifted his face so he would look me in the eye and nodded. "I fucking *love* it," I said, emphasizing the word that mattered most in that sentence.

Cam's face lit up with a smile. "Then let's do more."

We spent the night curled up on my oversized sofa, eating pie and ice cream, and just enjoying each other's company. I'd paid to have the damned thing shipped from eastern Kansas, which had been worth every penny given how well Cam and I fit on it together. My brother took over the rest of my house in Warrenstown, including paying the mortgage and utilities. That was all thanks to Sierra, who'd threatened to kick his ass if he didn't pay up. God, I loved her.

"You disappeared," Cam said, drawing me back to the boring show on TV.

"Yeah, sorry, just thinking how much this sofa works for snuggling with you."

He sat up and faced me, eyebrow cocked. "Really? That's what you were thinking?"

I laughed. "Sorry, you thought I was pondering the meta-physical elements of the universe?"

That earned me an eyeroll. "You're such a guy," he said, then lay back down with his head resting on my chest.

"And that's a problem?"

"God, no, just commenting," he said.

We fell asleep like that until sometime during the night, Cam woke up and complained about me being a furnace before pulling me back to the bedroom.

Just as I was dozing off, Cam slipped between my legs and took my cock into his mouth.

He moved his talented tongue around the head, then alternated between licking and sucking before shoving my cock down his throat and swallowing, each time blowing my mind with how intense it felt.

My climax approached faster than I expected, and I pushed him back, but he held firm and continued bobbing up and down my length with increased speed.

"Aah," I roared as I came, emptying into his mouth.

Cam pulled back with a smirk on his face before tonguing off a spot of cum that had escaped him.

He crawled up the bed and lay next to me, and I was rousing myself to return the favor when he placed his hand on my chest to hold me in place. "Shh, you can worry about me later. I just wanted to feel you squirm from my attention."

I kissed him, tasting myself on his lips, which made me want him that much more, but I did as he asked, and turned both of us on our sides, so I could spoon his body instead. It wasn't long before Cam's breathing changed slightly and I knew he'd fallen asleep, cozy and content snuggled in my arms. *I could get used to this,* I thought, just before drifting into blissful sleep.

## 27

# CAM

"R EALLY?" I asked Madonya as I stood in her dressing room at the club. "They want me to star in *Drag Dance?*"

"Of course, honey," she said as she dabbed her impeccable makeup. "You're a sensation, the Gay Nightingale. Besides, I've trained you how to perform with the queens. I assured them you were perfect for the job."

"What do they want me to sing?" I asked. Madonya looked away, and had I not known her for years, I would've missed her tell. "Girl, what shit have you gotten me into?" I asked, eyebrow cocked.

She laughed. "It's not that bad, just a new song. A local artist wrote it. It's a great drag song called "Bitch, My Shoes." Fabulous title, don't you think?"

I squinted at her, but she just ignored me, switching over to putting her long eyelashes on. "Madonya, you know not all songs work for me. I need to hear it before I agree."

"Oh, you're such a princess. *Larry!*" she yelled, and damned if her husband wasn't right there waiting. "Can you play the song I found for Cam to perform?"

Larry looked at me apologetically, then opened his phone and played it. God, it was horrible. When it mercifully ended, I shook my head. "Slasher music for a drag show?"

Madonya shrugged and looked at me through the lashes she'd just applied. "Well, you can work with it, right?"

"I mean, not without a band or something. I can bang out some stuff on the piano, thanks to my training, but I'm no expert. I'll need help turning that into a real song. *Shit,*" I said, ready to stomp out like the princess Madonya had called me.

"Girl, I already got all that set up, so don't get your panties in a wad. Now, you're going on first tonight, and I don't want you fucking up in front of my crowd. God knows I've built your skinny ass up so much they think you're the queen of the night."

I knew she was trying to get my mind off the horror that was that song. "Okay, but listen to me, Madonya, and you too, Larry. I'm not going to go on live television and make a fucking fool of myself. That song is horrible and has to be fixed. I don't give a damn if RuPaul herself wrote it. I'm not singing it without a major overhaul."

Madonya swirled her chair around and stared at me. "How *dare* you. The queen would never write something that horrible. You take that back."

I pinned Madonya with a look. "So, you know it sucks."

"Well, of course, I know it's dreadful, but you and I are both too broke to buy a new song. Besides, you're talented enough to turn that steaming pile into something singable. But don't be dissing my girl RuPaul, you hear me?"

"Whatever, Madonya," I said, frustration getting the better of me. "Let's get this over with. I'm going to sing one song tonight, then I'm headed to my apartment. My head is starting to hurt from all this."

I left before she could respond. I adored Madonya, but sometimes that girl could push me to my limits, and she was right, I was performing in a few minutes. Although I knew the number like the back of my hand, I still didn't want to fuck it up, not when we'd come so far building up a following.

Luckily, I was able to slip behind the bar and had just enough time to down a shot of tequila, which helped calm me, before I took the stage to sing one of my favorites, Robin S's "Show Me Love." The crowd went wild and cheered for an encore from the Gay Nightingale, but as I'd already told Madonya, I just didn't have another performance in me tonight.

I left out the back way, where I'd learned to park my car, so I didn't get stuck in a crowd of people. Madonya's song was bad, but it *was* time for me to stop singing other people's stuff. So, even if I had to completely rewrite the thing, at least it would be original.

When I got back to my apartment, I opened my laptop and pulled up my files from years ago. I'd written several songs, ranging from slow ballads from my Adele period, to dance music written during my infatuation with the nineteen nineties.

I enjoyed reminiscing as I went through the audio files, but none of the songs worked for *Drag Dance*. I thought about writing a new song, but when I'd written these at music school, I had access to all kinds of modern tech, which meant I could hammer the songs out on the keyboard, and the built-in software would turn my banging into music.

Besides, I wasn't in the right mindset to write songs. Although I could write music in pretty much any genre, I'd never been good with lyrics. Some of my fellow students in the Conservatory were poets, and I managed to talk a couple into helping me put words to my music, but it backfired when they stole the song. I could've pressed charges, but since both were now teaching high school, and neither were famous songwriters or singers, I figured it wasn't worth the effort to fight for it.

I flopped down on my bed and my thoughts drifted to Hunter. God, I wish he were here to fuck my mind into oblivion. I hated when anxiety took over like this. That was when I had a wonderfully naughty thought.

I grabbed my phone and gave him a call. I cursed when it went to voicemail. Well, shit, there went the phone sex idea.

To distract myself, I went to the kitchen, fixed myself a sandwich, then fell onto the sofa and flipped through the channels until I found *Drag Dance*.

The show featured a lot of different styles of music, so I wouldn't have to worry about being limited to only one genre. Most of it had a good beat, something that let the divas strut their stuff. The slasher song sure as hell wouldn't work, probably not even if I significantly revamped it.

As soon as I closed my eyes, Hunter came to mind. Memories of him taking charge, using me, and working my body until I was putty in his hands were accompanied by a faint but steady beat.

As I thought of him using his fingers to prep me, that low rumble of his voice vibrating through me, some bass joined the mix.

I continued stroking myself, imagining all my feelings and anxiety rolling out of me as I gave myself over to Hunter completely. I came with a loud moan, and only after I'd quieted down did I hear another sound—the song playing in my head.

Slowly, the music took shape, getting stronger and becoming more real. This was more than just a string of notes and lyrics.

It was a manifestation of the incredible lovemaking between Hunter and me.

I got up, and after washing my hands and doing a proper cleanup, I went to the closet, pulled out my ancient keyboard, and began hammering out the melody. Adding the beat and the bass was harder. I needed a more skilled musician who could help me find the right feel, because that intense deep rumble I couldn't quite capture was the sex that drove this song.

When I played the melody, even though the bass wasn't right yet, I knew I had something special.

It was late, and I knew Madonya and Larry would be heading home from the club soon, so I used my phone to record myself playing the song and quickly texted them.

Me: *Find someone to help me make this work. I'll need a lyricist.*

I knew I wouldn't hear back from her tonight. Knowing Madonya, she was probably mad at me, which was par for the course. I also knew she'd listen to the recording repeatedly until she had a good feel for it. Then, if Madonya's past was any indication, she'd find exactly what—or, in this case, who—I needed.

I fell asleep thinking about the music, or more accurately, what it represented. This song positively oozed sex and sensuality, and there was no doubt in my mind, it would be exactly what my performance on *Drag Dance* needed.

# 28

# Hunter

"WHAT THE HELL?" I asked as I walked into the lobby, thinking I was meeting my aunt and uncle, but running headlong into my mom and sister. "What're you doing here?"

Sierra laughed. "What a warm welcome, brother!"

"Oh, shut up and come here!" I said, and pulled her into my arms. "God, it's so good to see you."

Mom's face never dropped her smile as she leaned over and kissed me. "We missed you too," Mom said, and your aunt insisted we come out and see the place you're working at."

"Beautiful, isn't it?" I asked.

Both of them nodded, eyes wide with wonder as they took in the surroundings. "When you come into the valley, it's like something from a fantasy novel."

"It is. So how long are you here? You staying in the hotel? Catch me up."

Both women laughed and led me up the stairs to the same suites Aunt Monica and I had occupied when we first arrived. "Well, I took off work for a week, so that's probably all we have," Sierra said.

"Same here, but we're hoping you'll be willing to show us around. I know Rocky Mountain National Park is a drive, but oh, I want to see it," Mom said. "I haven't been to Colorado in years."

"We can do whatever you want. This is perfect timing, because my team is fully trained now, and I can afford a few days off."

"First, I want to check out the resort. Your aunt can't stop talking about it, although the room is... *interesting*," Mom said, making me laugh.

"Outdated, but the bones are good and well-maintained." She just nodded. "Come on," I said, leading them back down to the main lobby. Just as I was going to lead them through the lodge to show them my office, Peggy stopped me.

"Hunter, are you going to be able to come by and help me pick out paint colors? My son and I don't have the same taste, and when I screw it up, I'd prefer to put some of the blame on you."

I chuckled. "I'm afraid I got surprised by a couple of sneaky guests, Peggy. Meet my mom, Sue, and sister, Sierra."

"Oh, sorry, I didn't realize," Peggy quickly said. "I'm Peggy Kell. I work with Hunter."

"What, were you needing help with paint colors?" Mom asked, not even trying to mind her own business, and I couldn't hold back a knowing grin.

"Peggy, my mother is a real-estate agent as well as an interior designer. If anyone can help with paint colors, it's her."

Peggy's eyes lit up. "Oh, yes, if you could just stop by my son's cottage? I love color, and I'm not shy about it, but Cam, not so much. I offered to help paint his place, so he'd spend more time here in Peachleaf. Okay, too much information, sorry, I'm rambling."

Mom laughed. "Trust me, I know all about the particular tastes of a son. We'd love to help, wouldn't we, Sierra?"

Sierra just shook her head, resigned, but smiled. "Sure, why not."

Before I could do anything else, Mom linked her arm with Peggy's, and the two women were talking about paint. "Well, guess the tour will have to wait."

Sierra elbowed me. "It's so good to see you, Hunter. I've missed you."

"Yeah, same here, sis. How's things?"

Sierra and I hung out while Peggy and Mom got to know each other. "Dad is retiring. The bank he works for is merging with a much larger one, and he said he's too old to learn how to work for a huge corporation."

"Wow, I mean, really? I never thought he'd ever retire."

Sierra chuckled. "None of us did. Truth is, Hunter, I think he and Mom are looking for something different, since they both took what happened to you badly."

I sighed. "Yeah, last time I called home, he was pretty much in rant mode."

She laughed. "I think he'd have taken out the Sheriff if he wasn't afraid of going to prison."

I nodded. "He basically said as much to me."

We looked into Peggy's office, and she and Mom were still talking and gesturing wildly. Of course, I had no doubt they'd long ago stopped talking about paint colors, especially when I saw Peggy showing Mom a picture of Cam.

Sierra must've gotten a clue too, but even though she smirked, she didn't say anything. That was her way. She was a wait-and-pounce kind of sister. She'd be pulling all the details about Cam out of me before long. Regardless, I didn't mind them knowing I had a crush on a cute boy. Cam was all that and so much more.

"Honey," Mom said after noticing me and Sierra hovering in the doorway. "Do you mind if we go with Peggy to see the house? It sounds absolutely lovely."

I shrugged. "Why don't you all go? I'll make sure everything is still running smoothly here, then I'll walk over."

"Mind if I join you?" Sierra asked.

"No, not at all," I said, and led the way from Peggy's office before she or Mom had time to harass me about Cam, which, from the looks on both their faces, was coming next.

"So, there's a boy, I think," Sierra said as we walked back toward the lobby.

"You do realize I was trying to avoid that conversation."

Sierra laughed. "How's he related to that Peggy woman?"

I sighed, knowing I'd already lost any argument I might have about privacy. "Well, I've just started going out with Peggy's son, Cam."

"And?"

"And nothing. We've had a couple of dates."

Sierra snorted another laugh, loud enough that several people looked our way. "Dates, huh? Whatever you wanna call it." Then she looked me up and down and smiled. "You look happy. Like really happy."

I put my arm around her shoulders, which was easy since I was more than a foot taller than her. "I am. It's this place. It's sorta magical."

"I can see that. Warrenstown was getting you down. I mean, I miss you and would've loved you to run for sheriff, especially now all the shit about your being terminated has hit the fan, but I prefer seeing you happy."

"Come on. I'll introduce you to some of my patrollers."

By the time I'd introduced my sister to everyone in the office, a good forty-five minutes had passed, so I steered us toward the cottage. I knew both Peggy and Mom were extroverts, but there was only so much strangers could talk about, right?

"Oh, Hunter," Sierra said as we walked down the road that hugged the reservoir, "this is one of the most beautiful places I've ever been."

"Just wait," I said and pulled her over to the water. "We're in Colorado, so feel how cold the water is."

She shivered before even touching it, but obliged me anyway. "Wait, that's warm! Why is it warm?" she asked.

"The water that fills the lake is from a hot spring. In fact, the basement of the hotel has a spa where you can soak in the water."

"Really?" she asked. "Aunt Monica didn't mention that."

"Well, it's old and smelly, and only a few people still use it, but in the winter it's nice. At least the outdoor pools are."

Sierra scrunched up her face. "Old and smelly? That doesn't sound like something Aunt Monica or even Uncle Harris would allow in one of their resorts."

I shrugged. "It isn't theirs yet, but if they buy the place, I'm pretty sure they'll renovate the whole thing. The hot springs really should be one of the key selling points to tourists, along with the skiing and lake access."

"Show me later, I'll be sure to wear a nose plug," she teased as I steered her back to the road. A few moments later, we reached the cottage, and Sierra drew in a breath. "Oh, this is adorable. Your boyfriend owns this?"

"Not boyfriend, we just started dating, but yes, the guy I've seen a few times owns this."

"This is charming, like a little piece of heaven."

I smiled as we walked through the open doorway and then laughed at the two moms sitting across from one another, chatting like they'd been friends their entire lives. "Oh, Hunter," Peggy said as soon as we entered. "I can't thank you enough for introducing me to your mom, her ideas are amazing. Cam's going to love the color she's recommended."

I winked at Mom, who was beaming with the compliment. "Sorry, I won't be able to help. I'm going to be showing these two women the sights."

"Oh, nonsense," Mom said. "We're happy to help. Aren't we, Sierra? Besides, I can't wait to see this beauty get a much-needed facelift. I'm going to take before and after pictures and put them on my website. Peggy already said it's okay."

I looked between Mom and Sierra with an open mouth, and Sierra just shrugged. "It was bound to happen," she said, but genuinely smiled. "Fortunately, I love to paint, so I'm game."

"Really?" I asked, truly shocked these two would spend their vacation painting a stranger's house.

"Mom nodded her confirmation, then stood and, taking Peggy's arm, led her outside. "So, tell me more about that gem," she said, pointing up the hill at the mansion house.

Sierra and I followed as Peggy gave Mom the history of the place, telling her about her deceased mother-in-law and the woman's parents. I hadn't yet heard all the history and was fascinated. Cam's family had quite a connection, not only to the resort, but also to this area, for several generations.

What would it be like to live somewhere for that long? It was no wonder Cam had struggled with the decision to sell the resort. There was more to consider than simply business. In many ways, just like the cottage and mansion and his grandmother's art collection, it was his heritage. This place was a part of him.

Sierra, Mom, Peggy, and I began painting the cottage the next day. Peggy treated us to dinner and made me blush with memories of an apple pie she'd bought from Polly's. I couldn't hide a huge grin while eating my slice, because every bite made me think of Cam.

Peggy made me promise not to tell Cam about the paint job, as she wanted to surprise him. So, once we were done, we helped her put the house back together. Well, Peggy and Mom told Sierra and me where to move stuff.

By the time Wednesday rolled around, I insisted Mom and Sierra do some touristy stuff. We drove to Rocky Mountain National Park and oohed and aahed over the wild animals like all the other tourists.

We ate elk burgers in Estes Park and spent the night at the Stanley Hotel, which was much more up-to-date than Peachleaf, even though it was older. Of course, it didn't take much to imagine the upgrades my aunt and uncle could make if Cam sold the resort to them.

It was fun to be out with my mom and sister, which in turn made me miss the rest of my family. "I wish Deke could've come," I said on the drive back to Peachleaf.

"He would've, but his residency is kicking his ass."

"Well, good, someone needs to kick his ass," I said, making us all laugh. Deke was technically our half-brother, not that the distinction mattered in our family. In fact, even after Dad died, Mom was pulled even tighter into Dad's family, and Sierra, then later Deke, were embraced as their own, same as me.

We pulled up to the hotel late at night and I let Sierra and Mom off at the main entrance, then drove home to my apartment. It'd been a few days since I'd talked to Cam, and I was feeling withdrawal.

He told me he was busy writing a song, and I had my family here to entertain, but now that I was back on my own, I felt his absence. Busy or not, I needed my Cam fix, so I called him.

"Hey," he answered groggily.

"Hey, yourself. Were you asleep?"

"Yeah, stayed up over twenty-four hours with that, um, song."

"Wow, inspiration must've really struck. Have you finished it?"

"No, damn it, I can't quite get it right, but it's coming along."

I consoled him as best I could over the phone, but mostly I wanted to hold him in my arms. By the time I let him go, because, frankly, he was beginning to fall asleep on the phone, I wanted him so much it hurt.

I fell asleep stretched out on my sofa with my clothes still on and didn't wake up until dawn. Of course, it reminded me of when Cam and I had fallen asleep on the sofa, and my longing for him came back full force.

I was able to go back to sleep after stripping and climbing into bed, but my dreams were filled with him, touching, holding his hand, holding him. God, I had it really fucking bad.

# 29

# CAM

"No, no, no, no, no, you keep using the bass like an afterthought. That's not how this is supposed to work. Like I told you, it leads the song, *has to* lead the song."

I'd said that at least a hundred times, and Pete, the guy Madonya had hired, was about as frustrated as I was. "Let's call it a night. I'll see if I can figure out a better way to explain it to you tomorrow."

I'd just fallen asleep when Hunter called. "God, it's good to hear your voice," I said as I began drifting to sleep.

"Cam?"

"Yeah?" I asked, barely keeping my eyes open.

"You go to sleep," Hunter said. "I'll talk to you soon, okay?"

I didn't remember if I even told him goodbye, but I woke up the next day with Hunter on my mind. The deep rumble when he chuckled that caused me to go weak at the knees was a running theme in my dreams. As I slipped in and out of sleep, I kept thinking about that sexy rumble and how I wanted to capture it in the song.

Come morning, I grabbed coffee, opened my laptop, and began searching for music that represented what I wanted. I didn't take long for me to grow frustrated. If I searched for low voice, bass, anything like that, it gave me a bunch of country singers. God, that wasn't what I was looking for.

I managed to find Marvin Gaye and Barry White, which weren't exactly what I wanted either, but at least I was getting closer. Regardless, together, I thought I could communicate what I was looking for.

I showered, rushed through the drive-thru to grab some breakfast for myself and Pete, then went straight to Madonya and Larry's bar, where we'd been practicing during the day.

Pete cringed when I walked in, telling me he dreaded "take three" since we'd been at this for three days straight. "I think I have it," I said.

I unlocked my phone and pushed play on Barry White's album. The guy just shook his head. "Listen," I said, reaching the end of my rope. For real, I'd done everything to break this down to him, so this was my last hope. "I'm assuming since

Madonya picked you that you're a gay sista, so sit down and let me explain."

Pete nodded silently and did as I asked as I went over to his keyboard and turned on the beat. "Imagine a man, taller than you, tight V-shaped waist. Muscles bulging from every angle in his tight clothes, and when he comes close, you can smell the masculinity rolling off him." I paused for effect, letting the image I'd drawn sink in. I was speaking in a low voice now. "Just looking at him causes your body to break out in a sweat. Imagine your desire to touch him, feel him. Now, imagine letting his big hands roam up and down your body, slowly, before his rough calluses scrape over your nipples, sending electrical pulses through you."

Pete was beginning to breathe hard, so I knew I had him. "Now, imagine him speaking to you, soft but deep, as he kisses your neck, your ears, and when you shiver, he chuckles. That deep low rumble vibrates through you while you're so close, desperate for your cock to be set free so he can wrap his mouth around you and take you while that rumbling chuckle engulfs you. Now, he has his fingers inside you, probing deep, and you hear that deep chuckle again."

I paused long enough for Pete to look at me. "That's the bass you're playing. That's what leads this song."

He swallowed hard, and I would've laughed if I still wasn't so fucking perturbed. He thought for a moment, added some notes to the bass, and thank the fucking stars, he finally seemed to understand.

I hummed along, putting in the melody where I thought it should go. "Fuck I think we've got it. Hell yeah!" I yelled when he finished.

"I might need a cold shower, but yeah, I get it now."

"Thank God, okay, play it again from the top. Let's see if we can put it together and record it so Madonya's lyricist can put the words to it."

"Dude, I hate to tell you this, but you have to write down what you said, because this beat doesn't really match the sex you're talking about. That's why it confused me. This is pure sex to a dance beat."

I smiled wickedly. "My man moves it like that."

He shook his head. "I need a man like that."

I laughed and refocused him. "Back to the music."

That night, Madonya listened to the song and grinned from ear to ear. "This is fucking awesome. Likalya is going to wet herself when she hears this!"

"*Lick all* what did you just say?" I asked, not sure I heard her right.

"Likalya, just some hoe I used to work with. She does entertainment for *Drag Dance* now."

"Oh, that's how you got me in."

Madonya winked. "Baby, you can't be in this business as long as I've been and not run up on a few divas. Now, get your skinny self on the stage. I want *three* fucking songs tonight, 'cause I'm about to turn your ass into a star!"

I couldn't help but laugh. Madonya was a mess, but I loved her crazy self, even if she was all about the business.

# 30

# HUNTER

MOM AND SIERRA STAYED through the weekend after Aunt Monica called and said she wanted to call a family meeting. Not even Mom could get her to tell us what the meeting was about.

By Sunday, everyone was here in Peachleaf except Deke, but he was Zooming in. We all gathered in the living room in Mom's suite. "Okay, I know you're all curious about why I wanted to meet," Aunt Monica began, with Uncle Harris standing by her side.

I looked over at my cousins Josiah and Amelia, who looked as confused as the rest of us. "So, as you know, we've been researching this resort for the past few months, thanks to Hunter's help, of course, and it looks like the courts are getting ready to close out the bankruptcy. We might have a chance to purchase the resort then."

None of us spoke, still waiting for some explanation about why the entire family was in on this conversation.

When we all stared blankly at her, Aunt Monica sighed. "So, getting financing will take months, maybe longer. This is a long shot since the resort isn't in a major town, and all our assets are currently locked up tight. I have a feeling if we want to purchase, we'll have to present an offer either to the courts or to OMS. Either way, we'll need cash to do it."

"And," Mom said, seeming to finally be catching on. "You want to use the trust money?"

My aunt nodded. The trust was several million, set aside after my grandfather, Dad and Aunt Monica's father, sold his considerable assets to an investor and university back in Kansas. He'd surprised everyone by including Mom, Sierra, and Deke in the trust. It was beginning to make sense now why all of us were asked to attend.

"I guess I don't understand, isn't that all invested? I know you manage it, but I get quarterly earnings reports," Sierra said.

Aunt Monica nodded. "Yes, it's with the same broker we use for our company, but because of the way it's laid out, we can use the money to invest in anything we see fit, as a family, that is."

"So, Mom, you want us to sink everything into this?" Amelia asked.

"Hear me out before you say anything. Hunter can attest to the overall value of the estate. Yes, it's out of the way, but so many resources here are not being capitalized on. One, it's not one of the major ski resorts, which means we can attract some of the more ardent skiers. We can create several more advanced runs that might make that even more possible." She looked at me and, having discussed that with her already, I nodded confirmation.

"Two, the hot springs aren't being utilized, including the spa and other facilities in the basement. The reservoir could become a huge selling point because it's warm enough for entertainment activities, not to mention the view."

"Isn't this really risky?" Deke asked from the computer screen.

"Yes," Uncle Harris said. "It's entirely too risky if you ask me. We can guarantee part of it through our company, but not all of it."

Aunt Monica looked at him crossly, then sighed. "It is a huge risk, certainly, but one I think we should consider."

"Has Cam decided to sell?" I asked.

She shook her head. "No, and that is a huge contingency. We need more than sixty percent ownership if we're to invest in the facilities like we want to. Several million dollars in upgrades are needed, not to mention building a lodge closer to the lifts, or..."

My mind sorta shut down then. Was I willing to sink everything our family had into this resort? The money we'd all inherited from my grandfather had slowly increased over the years. The trust had been set up more than a decade ago, then almost crashed completely a year later when the economy tanked. Since then, it had steadily grown to a substantial sum.

"Aunt Monica, I love the idea, but to be honest, that's Mom's retirement. I intend to use it the same way down the road. I'm not sure we should take on such a risky endeavor."

Several of the others nodded in agreement. Aunt Monica wilted a bit, then sighed. "I don't disagree, but before we take a vote, I want you all to spend some time wandering around the grounds and think about the option. Deke, we'll text you some pictures and videos."

No one responded, and I guessed that was appropriate, sort of. None of us were ready to put everything on the line, not even me, and I really wanted this place to work out for me and my career, not to mention a sexy man I craved like I craved chocolate.

The meeting was over, and we all wandered out to go our separate ways. "What do you think?" Mom asked as she came up behind me while I stood on the balcony looking out over the water.

"I think it's dangerous and maybe foolhardy."

"I agree, but it is a beautiful place."

"It's an amazing place, but I've researched the history since Peggy told us about the big house on the hill. It's struggled before. Hell, it's struggling now. There is no guarantee anyone can pull it off, not even people as skilled in this business as Aunt Monica and Uncle Harris."

Mom sighed. "I always thought it was generous of your grandfather to include me and your siblings in the whole trust thing. I'm financially set from work, even if the trust money goes belly up, so if you think it's worth the investment, I'll join."

"Mom, that's…"

She put her hand up to stop me. "That's fair, and I'm sorry it's putting so much pressure on you, but you're not a child. You can handle it."

She gave me an affectionate shoulder bump as she pushed off the railing and went back inside. A few minutes later, Sierra came out and basically said the same thing, and that if needed, she could twist Deke's arm as well. I couldn't help but laugh. Deke had grown up with my grandfather as if he was his own. So, I didn't expect him to feel the same about the trust as Mom and Sierra did.

That being said, I knew he was going to have a shit ton of debt when he finished medical school. I assumed he'd use the trust money to pay it off. Was I willing to put that at risk, even if our aunt wanted us to?

I just couldn't see it.

The next day, I talked Peggy into letting me have the key to the big house, telling her I wanted to show my cousin the property.

Without a second thought, she handed the key over to me. That, more than anything, showed how much trust had been built between us over the past few months.

Knowing Josiah wasn't one for hiking, I borrowed one of the electric golf carts the maintenance crews used and drove us up to the big mansion on the hill.

The moment I pulled up to the house, Josiah's eyes almost bugged out of his head. "You have access to this?" he asked with wonder.

"Well, sorta. I know the owner, which is why I wanted to show you. Come on."

As we walked through the mansion, me giving Josiah the same grand tour that Cam had given me, my cousin's eyes grew to the size of saucers. "Is that a Montrose Pierce? When he looked at the painting closer and saw the name, he shook his head. "Why the hell is a Montrose Pierce hanging in an abandoned haunted mansion in the middle of the Rocky Mountains?"

I laughed. "I'm not sure it's haunted. And it's not exactly abandoned, just... unoccupied for the time being. That's actually something I wanted to talk to you about."

He didn't even hear me, because he was already examining an ugly statue that resembled a stump with a nail sticking out. "This can't be. I mean, who would leave exquisite work like this sitting around collecting dust? These need to be properly preserved."

I let Josiah freak out as we went from room to room, and he literally did freak out in every single room, except the kitchen, of course. When we reached the third-floor servants' quarters, I sat him down in the same two chairs Cam and I had sat in before.

"The owner wants to turn this place into an art museum. And what you've seen here is what they left behind. There's so much more art, Josiah, and some of it is really nice."

Josiah was staring at me with his mouth agape. "Nicer than these pieces?"

I shrugged. "We both know I'm not the artist in this family. There's a shit ton more art, though, and I know it was moved out of this building because the owner thought it was worth more than what's left."

"Tell me more about this guy," Josiah said, switching from art geek to serious curator at lightning speed. He was all business now, and, once again, I could see his mom in him.

"Smart, talented, hardworking, handsome, what do you want to know?"

"You're dating him?" Josiah asked like we were both in high school again, sneaking onto the local university campus so we could ogle cute college boys.

I laughed. "I am, and he's part-owner of the resort. But..." I said, waving my arms around the room, "...he wants this to be a museum. You know all about that sort of business, so what would it take to make it happen?"

"A fuck ton of money, to start with, and that's not even to renovate the building. Why does he want to put a museum in the middle of nowhere?"

"'Cause it's his heritage? I don't know exactly, but if you could give me some information that would be beneficial to share with him, I'd appreciate it."

Josiah stood up and left the room without telling me where he was going. I followed him to the second floor and into one of the bedrooms. "You're telling me this is one of the pieces he didn't want?" he asked, pointing at a painting of a forest scene featuring a half-naked woman bent over a baby next to a stream.

"He didn't say that, just that his grandmother didn't consider it as valuable as the other stuff."

"If that painting is the least valuable, he could sell it and the other pieces around here and have more than enough money to fund the renovations and establish a museum."

I stared at what I considered an ugly painting and shrugged. "Okay, wow. That's helpful."

"'Tell you what, let me dig into this and get you some actual numbers. It looks like all the pieces here are from the turn of the nineteenth century to the Great Depression. Is that what you understand as well?"

I shrugged again. "I mean, if you're asking about the timeline, that makes sense, but again, you're the artist. I'm a deputy turned ski patroller who thinks a lot of this stuff is ugly as sin."

Josiah finally managed to laugh, though he was still clearly in business mode. "I'll do some research and then let you know. Colorado might have some grant money available too. Maybe a foundation could kick in some support. But for real, just what he has left in this mansion alone could probably finance the project."

"Josiah?" I said, prompting him to look at me. "Don't tell anyone about all this, okay? If it's worth this much, maybe I shouldn't have even shown you. The owner said he'd be interested in talking to you, but he doesn't know you're here."

"If you want my advice, tell him to box up all of this and put it in proper art storage. It's a miracle no one has broken in and stolen or vandalized anything, or worse, the art destroyed by the elements. As it is, there will be tons spent on restoration from the dust that's settled on it all."

"Okay, I'll tell him."

Josiah prattled on and on with names of artists I'd never heard of as we rode back to the hotel. He was beyond excited about the project, which was kind of fun to see, and I wondered in my own selfish way if maybe Josiah would consider taking over the museum if his mom and dad ended up buying the resort.

"Wouldn't that be the shit?" I said, causing him to stop talking abruptly and look at me. "Sorry, my mind was wandering." I pulled up to the back of the hotel, parked the golf cart in its designated spot, and plugged it in.

"Did Mom put you up to this?" Josiah asked before we walked inside.

"Put me up to what?" I asked, confused.

"About showing me all the art pieces and tempting me with curating a museum."

"Um, no, Aunt Monica doesn't know about it, so far, that is."

He studied me. "You do know I did my master's thesis on Art Deco design and my doctoral dissertation on the Art Nouveau movement, right?"

I laughed. "Josiah, you're my favorite cousin, but I have no idea what Art Nouveau means. New art?" I guessed. "I'm sorry, but if all that shit in there was Art Nouveau or whatever, it's a coincidence. I don't play manipulation games, especially when our family's trust money is on the line."

He nodded, and I could tell he was deep in thought. "I want to meet your boyfriend, like sooner rather than later. Is he around today?"

"No, I wish, though. He lives in Denver."

"Then you can set up a meeting with him and me before I fly out. Let me know."

He turned and disappeared into the hotel. Of course, I didn't need much reason to call my... well, Cam. I needed to get the boyfriend idea out of my head, because despite my family calling him that, we were just dating. Not boyfriends, not yet.

The thought made me smile, though, because I sure as hell didn't mind the idea of Cam Kell being my boyfriend.

# 31

# CAM

WHEN THE BLUE, YELLOW and green-haired pixie Madonya had hired to write lyrics for my song first came into the bar, I almost went full princess again. The woman couldn't have been over five feet tall, and was absolutely covered in tats. Madonya introduced her as Megan.

I didn't really believe she'd be able to write the lyrics I intended for this song, but I also knew better than to judge based on looks, so I checked myself and gave her and Madonya the benefit of all my doubts. The moment she heard the music and the sexy beginnings of the song, thanks to Pete, she went right to work, and damned if her lyrics weren't spot on.

We spent several hours together, tweaking and testing out her words to my music, and even getting some feedback from

Madonya and Larry. By the time we left the bar, I felt like with some help, I'd finally captured exactly what I wanted the song to be.

I'd just crashed on my sofa, excited by how well the song was coming along but mentally drained, when my phone rang. I smiled when I saw Hunter's name flash on the screen.

"Hey, your ears must've been burning, 'cause I was just thinking about you."

He chuckled, and my heart pounded with the thought of that deep, soul-stirring sound mixed into a song. "Yeah, I've been thinking about you too. Do you remember I told you my cousin is an art geek?"

"Yeah," I said.

"Well, I shared with him your idea about turning your mansion into a museum, and then gave him a tour–I hope that's okay, your mom let me borrow the key. Anyway, he thought it was weird you wanted to build a museum here in the middle of nowhere, but he also thought it was cool."

I sagged in my seat, because for real, it was kind of a stupid idea. A museum for what? Skiers? "Well, thanks for asking him."

"Wait, there's more. He looked at the art you had left in the mansion and said you could probably sell those pieces and have enough money to renovate the building and fund opening the museum. In fact, he said you needed to pack all that up and put it in fancy art storage or something."

I laughed. "*Fancy art storage*, that's how he put it?"

"Ugh, no. I think he said climate-controlled, but you know, not in a drafty old mansion house in the mountains."

"Yeah, I probably need to have it all assessed, and your cousin's right about storing it all properly. Maybe I'll have time for all that once the resort is settled and everything."

"So, when are you coming up?" he asked.

"Not sure. Maybe next week, why?"

"Josiah, the geeky cousin in question, wants to meet you and discuss this museum thing in more detail."

"Oh," I said, chewing a fingernail, a bad habit I'd never quite broken. "How long is he staying there? I might be able to come up tomorrow. For a few days, at least."

"Yeah, I'll ask. So, what're you wearing?"

I blurted out a laugh at the sudden shift in conversation. Phone sex would've been nice, but Hunter was still at work, in an office I knew had thin walls, and where he could be interrupted at any time. Still, just hearing his deep, sexy voice brought a different kind of satisfaction, and we talked for about an hour before he had to go. He was working a late shift tonight since a group of kids wanted to do some night riding, and the trails were lit up. I guessed that was a new activity his aunt had implemented.

After we hung up, I mulled over what Hunter had said was his cousin's reaction to the museum. I could barely contain my excitement. I wasn't that into the art scene, not like I should be, considering I owned the kind of art collection I did. I'd taken some art appreciation classes in college, but they only ever discussed old art from centuries ago. Never anything like what my family had collected.

The art collection, according to the estate papers, had last been insured in the early nineteen nineties, and we paid insurance based on that assessment, but I knew it was no longer accurate. Hell, you only had to watch *Antiques Roadshow* to know that much.

First and foremost, I needed to know how much the collection was really worth before getting ahead of myself. Mind made up, I grabbed my phone and called Tommy. "Hey, I'm headed up to Peachleaf tomorrow to talk to a guy about the mansion and all the artwork. You willing to come with me?"

"Um," he said. "I mean, Dad has been after me to visit Grandma. I guess she threw a fit when I didn't come by last time I was there."

"Good, see you tomorrow morning at nine."

"Wait, why nine?"

"'Cause you'll be sleeping the whole way anyway."

Tommy laughed and told me he'd be ready. I resolved to go over to his grandma's house to visit too. She'd been good to me when we were kids, and I should've made more of an effort to stay in touch. Tommy and I were bussed to the same school growing up, and it didn't take us long to become fast friends, being the two queer kids in a tiny school in the mountains, but we actually lived miles apart. Mom and I lived in town then, and

Tommy's family owned an old ranch out in the county. Too far to easily hang out when we couldn't yet drive, so his grandma would schlep us back and forth in her big old Suburban.

Both of Tommy's grandparents were still alive, and still living on the old ranch, but the rest of the family had long ago moved to Denver. The older couple had to be in their eighties by now, since they were older than my grandmother. I couldn't help but think their time living so remotely had to be coming to an end soon.

The next day, I picked Tommy up and was surprised to find him ready to go. Usually, on our early weekend morning drives to Peachleaf, he was dead to the world. Apparently going up on a Monday, at a time he was used to being at work, made all the difference.

Tommy stayed awake the entire time we were on the road, and we talked the whole way, so the trip felt faster than normal. It wasn't quite lunchtime when we got to Peachleaf, but my stomach was growling. I pulled over and texted Mom.

Me: *I'm in town. Wanna grab a sandwich there at the resort?*

Mom: *No and blech. You shouldn't either. I've got a meeting, but I'll see you after, say about one?*

Me: *LOL, still bad, huh? Okay, around one it is.*

One of the families that invested in the resort back in the eighties had also owned a small café in town, so it made sense when they took over preparing meals for the guests. According to Mom and Grandma, the food had been decent, at first. But after the matriarch and main cook died, it went downhill fast. By the time they sold out to OMS, Grandma didn't have the energy to try to replace anything, staff included, so the same old cooks who'd been there for decades continued to cook the same old lousy food.

"Well, Mom says the food is still bad at the resort, so guess we're having pizza."

"No problem, I love the pizza here," Tommy said, smiling.

I quickly texted Hunter to let him know I was in town and across the street from his apartment having lunch. I hoped he was home so I could at least run upstairs and steal a kiss.

Hunter: *Shit, you're already here? I'll let Josiah know, but I'm on the trails. Can I meet you around one?*

"Damn, what's up with one o'clock here today?" I asked, and Tommy gave me a strange look.

I didn't bother to explain. Instead, I drove over to the pizza place and parked, then texted him back I was meeting Mom at one.

Tommy and I ate our pizza, the same kind we'd ordered here since we were teenagers, then went over to Polly's for dessert. I had a slice of apple pie, my new favorite thanks to Hunter, and grabbed a dozen cookies to share with him and Mom and Hunter before we headed to the resort.

We planned to drive to Tommy's grandparents' ranch the following day, so I hoped to spend some time with Hunter today. If I had my way, it would be alone time. Maybe after I met with the art geek cousin of his.

# 32

# Hunter

***

Poor Cam wasn't prepared for what happened when he arrived at the resort. I always felt sorry for anyone who had to deal with my overbearing family, especially all at once. I should've given him fair warning.

I walked into the hotel lobby around five after one, expecting to find Cam talking to his mom. Instead, I saw my entire family–sister, mom, aunt, uncle, and both cousins–sitting in a circle that included Cam, looking dazed, like he'd just been hit by a two-by-four.

"So, you think you'll be renovating the mansion into a museum?" I heard Aunt Monica ask as I walked up and cringed.

Cam glanced up and gave me a quick squinted look that told me I was gonna get it later, but he smiled at my aunt and said, "Yes, I'm considering it. I don't see myself living in the mansion house, but I do think it'd be a nice place to display my grandmother's art collection."

"That's such an unusual idea for this area," my cousin Amelia said.

Cam nodded. "Yes, it's a bit strange, but I don't have any interest in living in the huge drafty thing and much prefer the cottage where my grandmother lived. I'm not interested in selling it, though, and a museum feels appropriate."

I could tell Amelia was about to become argumentative, so I jumped into the conversation. "I think that's enough of the third-degree, or Amelia, shall we begin discussing some of your interesting life decisions?"

My cousin gave me a smirk, knowing full well I was talking about her dating a guy who ended up being affiliated with Mukhabarat, and more specifically, Egyptian intelligence. That would still be a story for another day, but not today. Luckily, it was enough to shut her down.

Cam stood and moved toward me in a *save me from your crazy ass family* way, and I couldn't help but chuckle. Meanwhile, Peggy sat across from him, smiling ear to ear, totally enjoying the third degree.

"We are about to tour the mansion house, Hunter," she said cheerfully. "Would you like to join us?'

The fake smile Cam had plastered on his face was answer enough for me, and I feared it might become permanent if I didn't rescue him from my family soon. Fortunately, everyone jumped at Peggy's mention of a tour and began heading for the door.

I stayed with Cam as my family piled out of the lobby behind Peggy. When it was just Cam and me, I whispered, "Shall we make a run for it?"

He laughed, a genuine smile blooming across his handsome face. "I would say yes, but I think my mom wouldn't let me hear the end of it. But I think it's totally unfair you told your family about the museum. Before you got here, I felt like they were all about to start asking about financials and make me produce spreadsheets about the viability of my idea."

"I only told Josiah, but you wouldn't be wrong about everyone wanting details. Remember, though, you don't owe them anything. This is your property, and you're free to do with it as you choose."

He nodded and laced our fingers together, and we slowly followed the chaos that was my family down the small road toward the mansion. We walked past Cam's cottage, and I was thankful everyone paid it no mind. My family snooping through what was about to become his real home would've been too much.

The mansion house, however, was something different. I could tell the moment we began walking through the space together that my aunt's analytical mind was considering the possibility of Cam's idea.

I watched as Josiah quietly revisited each dusty art piece and knew he'd have loved to sit down with Cam one-on-one. Of course, had he kept his mouth shut, that was exactly what would've been happening right now.

No one asked questions, which surprised me. Instead, each person wandered around doing their own assessments. I could tell Mom wanted to design it. I could tell Aunt Monica and Amelia wanted to monetize it. The only person not showing interest was Uncle Harris, but that wasn't surprising since he was all about business, and this was not a business venture.

Finally, we all ended up on the patio outside the Conservatory. "So, you would really dedicate this as a museum?" Aunt Monica asked.

Cam nodded, but didn't elaborate.

"Would you be willing to put the house in conservatorship, so if public money is spent on the building, you can't just pull the home back and sell it?"

Cam considered for a moment. "The home is part of my family's estate, and it'll house my family's art collection. So, no, I won't surrender ownership entirely. Still, I would be willing to lease the property to an organization or nonprofit designed to ensure a museum is established and maintained within the property."

Aunt Monica nodded. "The art is impressive, but not so much that it could be considered a museum."

Cam laughed. "This is just a part of the art we own, not even a quarter of the total amount."

That seemed to mollify my very nosy aunt, who then walked back inside while everyone else followed, except Josiah.

When everyone else had left, Josiah asked, "Would you feel comfortable showing me some of the art you plan to display?"

Cam looked at me before answering. "I don't mind showing you since you're related to Hunter and Monica, and I trust both of them, but I'll ask that you not disclose what we own."

"Of course," Josiah said. The fact that he'd already blabbed to our family made me question his ability to keep his thoughts to himself, but I'd have a little chat with him about that if need be. So, as the family walked back toward the resort, Cam, Peggy, Josiah and I detoured to his cottage.

I hadn't realized that Cam hadn't yet seen the paint job, so when Peggy opened the door to the cottage, he walked in and gasped, forgetting Josiah was with us.

"Mom?" he said, turning toward her in astonishment. "This is gorgeous! I can't believe you picked these colors. They're perfect."

Peggy smiled triumphantly. "Thank you, honey, but I had some help. Hunter's mom picked them out, and she, Hunter, and his sister helped me paint."

Cam walked through the house, his smile growing larger and larger as he went through each room. "Mom, Hunter! This is amazing!"

"Ready to move in?" she asked, sounding hopeful.

Cam nodded. "Yeah, I really am!"

She handed the key to Cam then, and they hugged in front of us.

I glanced over at my cousin, who was staring open-mouthed at several very tasteful paintings that hung on the walls. I nudged him, and he swallowed.

"These... I can't believe you have these. And they are original?" he said, almost whispering.

Cam looked over at him and smiled. "They are. This one..." he said, pointing at a landscape, "...has been with my family since the late eighteen hundreds. But most of the rest is newer, after the turn of the century."

Josiah finally got his wits about him, and said, "This really should be better protected. Do you know the value of that piece alone?"

Cam shrugged. "Well, we have an insurance estimate."

"And the insurance company knows it's just hanging on your living room wall like this?" he asked, sounding practically scandalized.

Cam and Peggy just snickered. I could see a quiet resolve not to take him upstairs to the rooms that were literally stacked to the ceiling with paintings that used to hang on these very walls. My poor cousin would probably have a heart attack.

"M-may I make a suggestion?" he asked, and Cam nodded. "For the time being, I think you should allow your collection to be displayed at one of the more prestigious art museums. They can help you ensure it's not damaged and tell you how best to conserve the pieces. From what I've seen in the mansion house, as well as what's here in your cottage, these pieces are vulnerable." He looked at the landscape painting again, this time with a pained expression. "Too vulnerable," he said, his voice once again a whisper.

"Thank you, Mr. Cabot. I'm happy to speak to anyone you'd recommend for that."

Josiah just nodded, and, dumbfounded, walked out the door, barely responding to what Cam had said.

"Well, I should probably go with him. I agree with him, Cam. You should consider having the art stored somewhere safe, at least until you know what to do with it."

He raised up on his toes and kissed me. "Find out what he recommends, and I'll look into it, okay?"

I hummed as I kissed Cam back, then rushed to catch up with my bewildered cousin, knowing if I left him wandering down the road like this, he'd likely end up in the reservoir.

# 33

# CAM

"What do you think?" I asked Mom after Hunter and Josiah left.

"I think we don't really know what you've got here. I'll talk to Josiah and Monica and see if they can help me identify someone we can trust with the art," Mom replied.

"Okay, but from the look on Josiah's face, I'm feeling a bit nervous about what we've got. I mean, I'd hate for someone to break in and steal a bunch of valuable art."

Mom shrugged. "It's been hanging on these walls for a long time, but we'll see what we can do. I think with a little nudging, we can get Josiah to help you with it. Why didn't you show him the upstairs?"

"Truth? I thought it might kill him. I mean, we have it all stored in cardboard boxes. That might not be something he can handle."

"Probably wise, I have a list of all the art insured by your grandmother in the nineties. If you don't mind, I can hand that over to him and see what he says."

"Oh, yeah, Mom, that's a much better idea. That way, he doesn't have to know it's all in my guest bedrooms upstairs."

We walked back after locking up the house, both of us clearly more concerned now than we'd been before.

I got a phone call from Tommy as we neared the hotel. "It's about time you woke up," I answered in greeting.

"Shut up, I need my naps, and I never get to take them. This is my vacation time, in case you forgot."

I laughed. "I didn't forget. You ready for me to pick you up?"

"Yeah, maybe we can drive to Forestville for supper. I can't do pizza for two meals in a row anymore."

"Tommy, hold that thought." I stopped and looked at Mom. "Hey, why don't we treat Hunter's family to dinner in the cottage tonight? It can be my way of thanking Hunter and his mom and sister for helping with the paint job."

"Sure. What do you want to fix?"

"Only thing I know to cook, enchilada pie."

She laughed. "You need to learn to cook more than that, but yes, I think that's a nice idea."

We resumed walking as I got back to my best friend. "Hey, Tommy, I think I'm gonna cook supper tonight. Wanna go to the grocery store with me?"

"Um, I guess, or you can just come here."

"Nope, we're going to cook in my new house. Mom got Grandma's cottage painted, so we're moving in."

"We?" he asked.

"Okay, *I'm* moving in, but you'll either have to sleep at Mom's or on the sofa 'cause all the bedrooms here are packed full of stuff."

Tommy laughed, "Since I have the option, I'll stay with your mom. I've been riding the trails since we arrived, and I don't want back pain on top of already sore muscles if I'm going to face my grandparents tomorrow."

"That'll be fine, I'm sure," I said, thinking about inviting a certain someone to help me christen my new home the old-fashioned way.

# 34

# HUNTER

MY FAMILY QUICKLY AGREED to dinner at Cam's new home. I thought everyone had their own motives, of course, but except for Amelia, they were all on their best behavior. I guessed even in her harsh, uncouth way, Amelia was too. I just wish the woman would stop giving Cam the third degree over every damn thing in his life.

We were just sitting down to eat when Cam walked downstairs with a very alarmed-looking Josiah. "Couldn't resist showing him upstairs, huh?" I asked when Cam walked by.

"Well, he did ask," Cam said with a shrug. Peggy had given Josiah a list of the artwork when we first arrived, and my cousin had shaken his head like he didn't believe the pieces could be originals.

"I've seen a lot of prints made of this one," he'd said. "It's possible you have a print."

That was when Cam had taken him upstairs to see the painting. Poor guy was freaking out now, not that we hadn't suspected he would. Of course, most amusingly, Josiah's face went from alarmed to utter shock when he saw Cam's friend Tommy.

"Hey, you made it," Cam said as his friend walked in. "I'd like to introduce you to my best friend, Tommy Jones. Tommy, this is Josiah."

Cam went around the room then and introduced everyone. To my delight, Tommy's face reflected Josiah's when Cam finally introduced them.

Everyone returned to their own thing, and I bumped up against Cam, and chuckled, "Is Tommy single?"

Cam pinned me with a look of *don't even think about flirting with my friend*, before simply asking, "Why?"

"'Cause, if the heated looks those two are sharing are any indication..." I said, nodding toward Josiah and Tommy, "...those sparks are about to turn into a three-alarm fire."

Cam glanced toward his friend, and I saw the smile bloom across his face as he saw it too. "Cool. Tommy needs someone to sweep him off his feet."

"Player, huh?" I asked.

"Worse than, he's of the *screw 'em and lose 'em* sort."

"Have you ever been one of his conquests?" I asked, feeling jealous all of a sudden.

Cam laughed out loud, which caused everyone to look our way. "Um, that's a *hell no*," he said, shaking his head like it was the funniest thing ever, then squeezing my bicep, he whispered, "I'm only attracted to big bears."

"Roar," I whispered back in his ear, nipping at the lobe and causing him to shudder and chuckle simultaneously.

That night, my family sat around the cottage chatting with Cam, Peggy, and Tommy like they'd all known each other for ages. Cam rarely left my side, which felt right in so many ways, like we were a real couple rather than just two guys who'd hooked up and found each other again.

I cringed several times during the evening as Aunt Monica brought up the resort and whether Cam was ready to sell or not. Being a gracious host, he just smiled and answered her very diplomatically, which I knew from experience drove her insane. My aunt wasn't one to be put off. She was like a dog with a bone when it came to business, well, or anything really.

Regardless, Cam was hard in his own way. He handled my family like a trooper. When I saw his mom talking to mine, I realized he'd come by his spunky personality naturally. Damned if I didn't like him even more as I saw his strength up against the master manipulators of my family.

Cam shut the front door and sagged against it as the last guest left for the evening. "Finally," he said. "I thought they'd never leave."

"What? You don't like my family?" I asked, walking over, and pinning him against the door.

Cam smiled and tilted his head up before taking my mouth with his. "I like your family fine, but I like the idea of christening my newly acquired home even more."

I almost said something to the effect that this had been his grandmother's cottage when I realized that would just be cock-blocking myself. Instead, I let him lead me upstairs to the bedroom he'd chosen as his own.

I was ready to rip his clothes off and fuck him senseless the moment we entered the room, but I also wanted tonight to be special. This was his new home, after all, and if I were lucky, I'd be invited back here often. So, I took my time with him.

Undressing led to caressing, as I slid my rough hands over every inch of bare skin I could reach, knowing how much he loved being touched. Cam whimpered as my tongue replaced my roaming fingers, which circled his hole and began to slowly work him open to take me as I peppered kisses along his back. Even as I fucked him, slow and deep, I knew this was more than just sex. Something had changed for us, and even if I couldn't yet put words to it, this was more than anything I'd ever felt. As I slid inside him, my heart seemed to have leaped over the edge once and for all.

He leaned back against me, our bodies moving in rhythm as I kissed him from behind. My heart all but stuck in my throat as I wrapped my arms around him.

"You're so…" I couldn't think of the right words, but Cam smiled, and I knew he understood the sentiment at least.

After we were both satisfied, I held him to me, kissing his neck as he hummed his pleasure. Cam Kell had somehow become everything to me. I had no idea when exactly it happened, but the man now owned my heart.

# 35

# CAM

---

Wow, I THOUGHT TO myself, *that was so much more than anything we'd done before.* We'd had amazing sex each time we'd been together, but something had shifted this time. It just felt like so much more...

Hunter turned toward me and smiled. "You okay?"

I smiled back and snuggled into him. "Yeah, better than okay. You?"

"Same." He wrapped his arms around me and pulled me close. We drifted in and out of sleep before Hunter started to get up to leave.

"Um, wait, where are you going?" I asked as he slipped his pants on.

He gave me an odd look. "Home, why?"

"You don't want to spend the night?" I asked, feeling a bit frustrated.

He stared at me for a moment, before he replied, "I mean, sure. If you'd like me to, but you know, I didn't want to assume."

I sat up then. "Assume what? That we're more than fuck buddies?" I could feel myself getting upset. I shook it off. "No, sorry. You've made no commitments to me. I should be..."

"Wait," Hunter said as he returned to the bed and wrapped his arm around me. "I like you, Cam. I like you a lot. Much more than I probably should at this point. I just didn't want to put pressure on you or make you think I was pushing you into anything, especially with my family and all."

I let out the breath I hadn't realized I'd been holding. "Listen, Hunter. I'm not, well, I guess I'm not your typical gay guy. I want to pursue a relationship, not just find the next hookup. I should've probably come clean about that sooner."

Hunter leaned over and kissed me, and when he pulled back, he was smiling. "I feel the same way. I'm ready to be boyfriend material. I just wasn't sure when or how to have this conversation."

I felt my eyes grow wide. "You wanna be my boyfriend?" I asked, and chuckled inwardly at how much that sounded like a teenager.

"I really do. If you do, that is?" he said, his face only inches from mine.

I threw my arms around him, pulling his tight body down onto mine again. "I really, really do!"

Hunter laughed and kissed me deeply, letting it turn into something more again, and this time, the *more* I'd felt earlier had a name. We were making love.

# 36

# HUNTER

I woke up humming. Last night was too fucking amazing. Cam was still asleep, so I gently removed myself from the bed and slipped downstairs to fix coffee and breakfast. I was just turning off the eggs when Cam's sex-rumpled self stumbled into the kitchen, looking sleepy and adorable. Damn, I really did have it bad for him.

"Hey, I fixed breakfast. I hope you like bacon and eggs, which I assume you do since I found them in your refrigerator."

Cam came over and slipped into my arms, burying his face in my chest. "I hate mornings. Have I ever told you that?"

I chuckled and bent down to kiss his head. "No, but I can kinda tell from how you're acting."

We stayed like that for several moments, me inhaling his scent while he clung to me. "Mmm, is that coffee I smell?"

"Yep," I said, and frowned when he pulled out of my arms to grab the cup I'd set out for him. After pouring his cup and doctoring it with milk and sugar, he walked around the kitchen island and sat across from me.

I took that as a sign, plated our food, and then came to sit beside him. He leaned into me then and said, "My *boyfriend* fixed me breakfast."

I chuckled again and leaned back into him. "He did, and he hopes you enjoy it."

"I like this whole boyfriend and breakfast thing."

"Same," I said, and dug into the food. When we were done, I rinsed the dishes as he rushed up to shower, saying he had to meet Tommy this morning since they'd be going to his grand-parents' ranch. I was a little disappointed he had other commit-ments today. Mostly, I could take time off since it was summer, and I'd have loved more than anything just to spend the day snuggling with Cam and discovering all the nuances of our newly declared relationship status.

But that wasn't happening, at least not yet. He dashed off immediately after returning downstairs, giving me a quick peck on the mouth, and pressing a spare key in my hand, asking me to lock up when I left. I didn't read much into him giving me the key, figuring the gesture was more about protecting the art collection littering his house than leaping that far forward in our new relationship.

I sat on his front porch for a while, staring at the reservoir and the boats on the water. This was an amazing place, and as I got to know Cam and his sweet personality better, it became clear this place fit him to a T. He was just as amazing.

# 37

# CAM

"Oh my god, Tommy, you've got to stop already. I've already told you everything I know about Josiah."

Tommy huffed and fell back on the seat as we drove to the ranch. "Well, you don't have to get pissy about it. I mean, I was just asking."

"For like the hundredth time." I laughed. "But it's good that you have someone you're actually interested in for a change."

Tommy looked at me, and I could tell he was about to deny being interested when he caught himself. *Okay, that's different,* I thought. For real, Tommy didn't do relationships. He didn't even do repeat hookups, if our conversations over the years about him not getting tied down were any indication.

Another tell that he liked Hunter's cousin was that he stayed awake the entire trip from town to his grandparents' ranch. Even though the ranch was in the same school district as Peachleaf, it took a full hour to get there. That was how remote it was.

"So, did you tell your grandparents I was coming with you?" I asked.

He smiled. "Yeah, Grandma's pretty excited to see you."

"Same here. I've missed her. It's been too long since I came out."

Tommy nodded. "Yeah, me too. Dad was out last month and said they weren't doing too well. So, I'm glad we're able to come for a visit."

I reached over and patted Tommy's hand. He'd told me about their conversation, and it wasn't good news. Tommy's grandparents were as hardheaded as him, and had made it clear they were going to "die on the ranch, like his granddad's parents and their parents before him."

Unfortunately, neither Tommy nor his dad lived anywhere near them any longer, and moving closer didn't appear to be a real option given where they worked, and because the ranch was so isolated, there was no one close by to keep an eye on his grandparents. I knew that weighed on Tommy, though he didn't often say.

When we arrived, his grandmother met us at the front door, as she usually did when we showed up. She grabbed us each into a big hug, and when I gently squeezed her, I could feel how frail she'd become. Damn, I was beginning to understand why Tommy's father was so concerned.

When we went inside to find his grandfather sitting in his old recliner, I was even more concerned. He greeted us with shaky hands, his Parkinson's clearly having worsened significantly. He didn't even try to speak.

Tommy's grandma busied herself in the kitchen and, a few moments later, brought in a tray of homemade cookies and coffee, pouring us all a cup. The old-fashioned silver tray and china cups only used for company made me smile.

"So, when did I become company enough for the fancy dishes?" I asked, causing the older couple to smile.

"Well, now that you and Tommy ain't so wild you'd likely break 'em, it just made sense to pull out the fancy stuff. 'Sides, we don't ever get to entertain no more."

I leaned over and kissed the old lady's cheek, causing her to bat at me. "I appreciate it," I said with all the affection I'd ever had for them.

Tommy's mom and dad had divorced when he was still young. His dad worked on the fishing vessels in Alaska at the time, so he was gone most of the year, and his mom had new boyfriends all the time, and she didn't seem to have the time or interest in raising a kid. So, Tommy ended up here on the ranch with his grandparents.

I spent many weekends on the ranch, helping do various chores. In return, Tommy got to spend equal amounts of time with me either at Mom's place in town and later at the resort, where we typically got into untold amounts of trouble.

Regardless, I'd become very fond of Mr. and Mrs. Jones. After we finished eating, I could tell the older couple were growing tired. "Tommy, show me around the place," I said, knowing it would give them a moment to rest.

Mrs. Jones smiled as we left, but didn't bother to get up. That spoke volumes as to how frail she'd become. I'd never seen the woman sit still for long in all my time coming out here.

"It really is that bad, isn't it?" Tommy asked when we got outside and out of earshot.

"I mean, they're getting older, and yeah, I think your grandpa's Parkinson's is worse. Much worse since I last saw them."

"They'll never go to a home, even if Dad pushes. I-I think it'll break them," he said. Tommy rarely got emotional—sometimes I thought law school trained it out of him—but his voice broke in talking about his grandparents' futures.

I put my arm around my best friend and pulled him into an embrace. "I'm so sorry, buddy. This can't be easy."

He just shook his head. We walked around the huge ranch, and for the first time, I noticed what had to be years of deferred maintenance. "Wow, Tommy, a lot needs to be fixed out here."

He nodded. "Yeah, and Dad already signed over his part of the inheritance. Said he didn't need it, although the value is well in the millions now. His new wife is rich, and they're making plans to stay in Alaska permanently. It's where they met, and she has family there."

I heard the sadness in his voice. "So, you'll own this?" I asked.

"Already do. They made it legal a few years back to avoid inheritance taxes. I didn't pay much attention back then."

I squeezed him again, knowing all the stress he must be feeling, then let him go and walked toward the old barn where he and I spent copious amounts of time hanging out. "You know, I'm sure you can turn all this into a resort thing. The terrain is ideal for cross-country skiing, not to mention all the fun we used to have on your dad's old snowmobile."

"You forget, I'm an attorney in Denver, not a hotel person."

I laughed. "I think they call it the hospitality business, but yeah, I know the dilemma, but if I decide to keep the resort, maybe we could include this in the packages we offer. Your grandparents' place is huge, and didn't you say they had paying guests here at some point?"

"No, but their parents did, and there is the ranch hands' housing. Granted, it's likely in need of serious repair too, but the building is still standing and the plumbing works."

I didn't say anything for a while, letting all of the new information sink in. Mostly, I just wanted to get Tommy's mind off the inevitable. I knew the moment he got home, he'd have to have a long talk with his dad about moving Mr. and Mrs. Jones into a home. Somewhere that they could be better cared for. But that didn't have to be decided upon right now as we continued looking around.

We returned to the house, and sure enough, we caught both elderly folks snoozing. "We're going to leave you to it," Tommy said as his grandmother made a move to get up. "But, Grandma, I'm going to come back in a few weeks and spend some time here. Are you okay with that?"

Mrs. Jones lit up. "Oh, Tommy, that would be so nice. I'll get your room cleaned up." She didn't complain when we said we were leaving. I suspected she was already worn out from the little time we'd spent with them.

He smiled as he hugged her and then his grandpa before I did the same. We left, but I knew we both felt a bit concerned about doing so. As soon as we were in the car, Tommy asked if I knew any fellow nurses up here who could check in on them.

"No, but I can ask around," I told him. I didn't say anything else. I could tell Tommy was overwhelmed and not ready to face all this yet. I didn't want to make things worse by pushing the issue. Right now, I just needed to be a supportive best friend. Tommy might be flighty, crazy, hyper, and mostly nuts, but he was also responsible and loved his grandparents with all his heart. He'd do what was best for them.

# 38

# HUNTER

"Everything okay?" I asked when I saw Tommy and Cam back at the resort earlier than I'd expected. Cam had said they might spend the night at Tommys' grandparents' house.

Cam smiled sadly, and I knew to drop the subject. Clearly, the visit hadn't gone as well as they'd hoped. Tommy didn't say much other than the usual pleasantries, then wandered out alone to the wide veranda behind the hotel. When he left, I asked Cam again if things were okay.

He shook his head, then shrugged. "It's fine, just having to face the fact that people we love are getting older."

I nodded, assuming he was talking about Tommy's grandparents, although I didn't know any details. Cam and I grabbed a cup of coffee from my office since the coffee at the resort kitchen tasted like warmed-up piss, and took a cup to Tommy as we all sat in rocking chairs on the veranda facing the slopes.

A few moments later, Josiah appeared and sat next to Tommy. I could see the sadness in Tommy's face from here. As oblivious as my cousin seemed to be most of the time, even I was confident even he wouldn't miss the man's dejected demeanor.

"I think that might be the best medicine for both of them," I whispered to Cam as I observed both men quietly chuckling together in their chairs across the veranda.

"Yeah, that's good. Tommy could use a distraction."

"How about you?" I asked.

Cam was silent for a long time as he rocked back and forth in the old rocker. "Truth? It's hard to see the people who were such a big part of our lives passing away, or getting so old they can't care for themselves." I took Cam's free hand in mine in support and waited for him to continue, if he wanted. Cam gave my hand a squeeze, and sighed. "Seeing Tommy's grandparents, so frail and sick... I know it tore him up, but it reminded me of losing Grandma too. I wasn't ready for her to be gone. I mean, she was only in her seventies. I have patients all the time who reach their mid-nineties. It feels like I was cheated out of more time with her."

"Yeah, same with losing my dad. He was taken from us far too soon."

Cam looked at me and brought my hand up to his lips to kiss my knuckles. Such a sweet man. We'd never talked about our fathers, which was kind of ironic seeing as our mothers had become such fast friends. The truth was, as close as I felt to Cam already, we still had a lot to learn about each other.

"I hardly knew mine. At least, I don't remember him that well, not the sort of memories you'd hold near and dear. I spent a lot of my childhood trying to come to terms with that and the car accident." He shook his head sadly. "It seemed like he'd come home just to leave again, always so busy with work, then I turned around, and became a workaholic myself, go figure."

I absorbed the details Cam had just shared while we sat silently for a bit, still holding hands, and looking out over the hillside. Even in summer, the slopes looked spectacular, then I started thinking about Dad and, as painful as it still was to talk about losing him, I felt I owed it to Cam to be as open as he'd been with me.

"I always thought my father was the most awesome dad ever, and still do, which made it hell when he was gone. One minute he was there, and the next... I still wonder why I went into the same profession that ended up killing him. I guess, maybe to just be close to him again in some way?"

When I turned to look at Cam, instead of responding, he leaned over and gave me a gentle kiss, before he settled back in his chair, still holding my hand, and we sat like that for a long time, just watching the activity around us. For years, my family had tried to get me to talk about Dad and his death, including making me go to therapy as a kid. None of it helped as much as holding the hand of someone who understood what it meant to lose a parent so young. Even though our circumstances were different, I knew Cam was all too aware that no matter how many years passed, that deep sense of loss never really went away.

# 39

# CAM

"Hey, Cam, can you meet me at my office? I have news," Mr. Pauley, my family's attorney, said over the phone. It'd been a while since I'd spoken to him, so I was surprised by his call.

"Perfect timing, I guess," I said. "I'm in town at least for another day or so. Can you meet now?"

"Of course," he said. "Come on over."

"Should I bring my mom?" I asked, concerned about what he had to tell me.

"You certainly can if you want. Rest assured, it's good news, and I'm sure she'd like to be in on it. If you want her to be, at least."

"Good news? Okay, that's awesome. We'll see you soon," I said, and quickly hung up because my nerves were beginning to get the better of me.

"I practically ran from the cottage to the hotel and burst into her office without knocking. "Mom!"

"Yeah?" she asked, looking alarmed as she peered up from a mountain of paperwork on her desk.

"Mr. Pauley just called. He has news, good news, about the estate. Can you come with me?"

"Sure, just let me tell my staff I'm leaving," she said before locking up her office and heading for the lobby. A woman who was every bit as old as Mom waved at the check-in desk as she saw us approaching. "Rachel, I'm going to run an errand with Cam. Call if you need anything."

Rachel, who'd worked at the resort for as long as I could remember, gave us a thumbs up. We all knew the woman could handle just about anything, almost as well as Mom could.

We rushed out of the hotel to Mom's car, without even discussing who would be driving. When at the resort, I usually hung out with Mom so much that I defaulted to riding around with her.

"So, what's this about?" Mom asked once we were on the road.

I shrugged. "Mr. Pauley didn't exactly say, just that the news wasn't bad. I'm guessing he has news about OMS's bankruptcy."

"Oh, well, that's pretty quick. I didn't expect to hear anything on that for at least another few months."

When we walked into the old attorney's office, he welcomed us with a bright smile. "I'm glad you could both make it. Come on in."

He waited until we were seated across from him before handing me a document. I had only ever seen a few court documents, and only because of Grandma's lawsuit with OMS. Mom and I read through it as the attorney sat across from us, smiling.

*This court rules that the corporation of Optimum Management Services shall be dissolved, and all assets be liquidated to pay back its creditors.*

I looked up at the attorney, unsure why this was such great news. "So, what does this mean? Will we be paid along with the other creditors, and what about OMS's portion of ownership?"

Mr. Pauley laughed. "Read on. You didn't go far enough."

I looked back at the document.

*In the case of Peachleaf Resort, Optimum Management Services stock will hereby be relinquished to Geneva Williams-Kell in payment for debts owed her by the defendant.*

"Wait, seriously?" I asked, and nearly dropped the document as I jumped up out of my chair. "I-I own it all?"

Mr. Pauley laughed and stood up to shake my hand. "You do. I told you it was a long shot, but apparently, the judge wasn't a fan of OMS's tactic of wiggling out of its legal debt to your grandmother. Of course, I take a little credit, because I made it clear in my petition that was what they were doing."

"I don't get it, though. Why dissolve the entire company?"

"They were a mess. It was stupid of them to file for bankruptcy anyway. Their attorney should've warned them this was a likely outcome. They owed more money than they could pay back, and continued running all these huge resorts into the ground. More than one of their creditors testified that if they were allowed to go on, all the properties would be worthless."

I stared at the papers in my hand for another long moment, then looked to Mom in disbelief. "I fucking own it all?"

Both Mom and Mr. Pauley laughed.

"Son, you fucking own it all," Mom said.

I grabbed Mom into a hug and shook Mr. Pauly's hand again. "Oh my god, I can't wait to tell Hunter. Wait, what does this mean for Hunter's family? For his aunt's business?"

Mom's face fell. "Well, it means either you're going to sell to them, or you'll have to hire them as your management company."

"Yeah, okay, we should talk about this before I tell Hunter, huh?"

Mom nodded. "Might be best," she said, but she was smiling again.

As soon as we left the attorney's office, Mom drove us to Polly's for a celebratory pie to go, and then back to her house, where she popped a bottle of Champagne.

"Here's to finally having control of your family's legacy again," Mom said.

We clinked glasses, and when I saw a tear escape her eye, I sighed and pulled her into a hug. "I know. I wish Grandma could've been here to see this day too. That hateful company put her through hell."

"But you won. Don't you forget that, you won, and she would be so proud," Mom said, sniffing back the tears.

"*We* won, Mom. And Grandma would be proud of us both. This may have been Dad's family's resort, but you're as much a part of it as any of them were."

"Hear, hear," she said, and we clinked glasses again, then dug into the pie. Although this had brought up another layer of sadness about losing Grandma, knowing that horrible corporation would be no more offered some bittersweet comfort. The courts had done right by Grandma, even if it'd taken longer than she'd had in her.

As we were celebrating, I got a call from Madonya. Two calls, actually. I should've known better than to ignore them both, because, a few seconds later, my phone buzzed with an incoming text.

Madonya: *Bitch, you better not be screening my calls. Call me NOW!*

I groaned. "Sorry, Mom, I have to get this."

She smiled like she always did when I got distracted too easily. I figured I'd spare her having to listen to my manager screeching at me through the phone, so I went into the living room to call Madonya back.

"Girl, it's about time you called me back! Where the hell are you?" Madonya asked, not even bothering with a hello.

"I'm in Peachleaf, celebrating something monumental with my family. What's so important?" I asked, feeling a little annoyed.

"Well, you need to get your princess ass back to Denver, like now. *Drag Dance* wants you in New York City tomorrow to perform your song, so we need to catch a flight out tonight. Girl, they're going to use it as their finale. Can you believe it? We've hit the big time, baby!"

I sat on the sofa, mouth agape and too stunned to say anything. I knew they'd told Madonya they were interested, which was the whole reason why I was preparing the song, but when we hadn't heard from them, I assumed maybe they were thinking next year's show.

*Drag Dance* was one of the most popular TV shows right now. The season finales always drew millions of viewers, and they only booked the most well-known talent to perform the final song.

"Wha... how? Why?" I finally managed to ask.

Madonya just laughed, sounding practically giddy. "Girl, have you taken a look at your views on YouTube recently? It's off the charts!"

"Um, not since you shoved it in my face that one time."

"Take a look, just do a search for the 'Gay Nightingale,' then get your ass down here. I'm booking our flight for ten tonight. Move it, sister, or I'm sending Larry to drag your skinny ass off that mountain!"

She hung up without a goodbye, and I just sat stock-still on the sofa, still holding the phone up to my face and staring off into space.

"Honey, are you okay? You look like you just got horrible news," Mom asked, coming to sit beside me.

I shook my head. "Mom, I'm going to sing my new song on *Drag Dance*. For the season finale."

"I love that show!" Mom's eyes grew wide as realization dawned. "You're going to be a superstar."

"I mean, yeah, maybe. My manager certainly thinks so."

Mom jumped up and pulled me into a hug. "Not maybe, honey. This has been the most amazing day."

I couldn't help it. As Mom held me, tears of joy about everything that'd happened today poured out of me. I was so overwhelmed.

"Shh, honey," Mom cooed as I wept. "You deserve all this and so much more. Your grandmother would be so proud. I know I am."

That just made me cry that much more.

After forever, I pulled back and wiped away the remaining tears when it hit me. "Shit, I've got to find Tommy and get back to Denver. God, Madonya wants to fly out at ten tonight. I barely have time to get there if I leave now."

"Oh, don't rush. I'll call Roland at the airport and see if he can fly you down. Ever since he met his new woman, he's flying down there constantly anyway. This way, you can at least give him another reason to go."

"Really? I mean, that would make it easier."

"I'm sure. Go on, get Tommy, and tell him the news. I'll get the flight set up."

I'm glad Mom mentioned the plane, because it took a full hour to locate Tommy. I found him and Josiah sitting by the water, stuck together like glue.

"Tommy, hey, I have news," I called out as I got closer to them.

Both men jumped, and if I hadn't been in such a hurry, I would've laughed at Tommy for being skittish around a man. I'd never seen him behave that way before. He must really like Hunter's cousin.

"Hey, I've got to leave in a few minutes. Mom got me a plane down to Denver. I'm flying to New York tonight to perform on *Drag Dance.*"

Tommy and Josiah's eyes both grew wide at the announcement. "Wow, that's great. Congratulations," Tommy said, and jumped up to hug me. "I can't believe this is really happening for you."

"Yeah, but you need to come on. There's room enough for both of us on the plane."

I was just about to turn to leave when Tommy shook his head. "No, I'm not going back to Denver, at least, not right now."

He looked over at Josiah and sighed. "I talked to Dad, and he said Grandma and Grandpa both refused to leave, and it would take a court order to pry them out of their home. So, I called my firm and told them I was taking leave."

"What?" I asked, my turn to look startled. "But, Tommy, they'll..."

"Yeah, they did, but to be honest, I was going to quit anyway." Tommy had a love-hate relationship with his law firm. He loved the money he made. He hated everything else.

"Okay, well, that's a lot to unpack, and I don't have time to do it with you right now."

Tommy's serious expression turned into a smirk, then he shoved me playfully. "Go and get famous, then come back, and we'll gossip until the cows come home."

I laughed at the old saying he'd adopted from his grandparents.

"Okay, and okay. I'm gonna go then. Mom's taking me to the airport, so here's the key to my car, just don't wreck it." I said, handing it over and hugging Tommy again, I shook Josiah's hand, because it felt rude not to, and ran back to the hotel.

I didn't find Hunter in his office, so I tracked down one of the patrollers and asked her to call him using their two-way radios.

"Yeah?" I heard Hunter answer.

"Can I use that?" I asked, and the woman smiled as she handed her radio to me.

"Hey, Hunter, it's Cam. I have to rush back to Denver, but I wanted to tell you bye before I left."

It was silent on the other end for a moment, before he said, "Okay, I'd come down, but I'm on the back side of the D-lift. It'd take me an hour to get back."

"No worries, just call when you can," I said, and handed the radio back.

I knew all his patrollers were required to carry two-way radios while on duty and might be listening to our conversation, so I didn't say more. Besides, there'd be plenty of time for celebrating with him after I returned from New York.

I then went looking for Mom and got to her office just as she hung up the phone, shaking her head. "Mom, I'm ready," I said.

"Good, that was Roland, and he's ready too. I swear to God, I could hear him smiling over the phone. All you lovebirds are making me nauseous."

"*Mom*," I said, sounding like I used to when I was embarrassed by something she said, then I smirked at her. "You might be old as these mountains, but you can still get you a man if you want one. You know, Mr. Pauley is single."

Mom's mouth fell open, and I had to dash out of the way as she came for me. When she caught me, we were both laughing, and she hugged me. "I'll get you for that comment later, but I'm so happy for you, Cam. Now, let's get you down the mountain.

You know the winds can pick up after dark, and I don't want you in the air when that happens."

Within the hour, I was flying down to Denver, just beginning a scary, but exciting, new adventure.

# 40

# HUNTER

I RUSHED INTO PEGGY'S office, hoping to catch Cam before he left, but the moment she saw me, she shook her head. "Sorry, Hunter," she said before I even spoke. "He left about forty-five minutes ago."

I sighed heavily before flopping down into a chair. "Did he say when he would be back?"

She shook her head. "No, and I doubt he even knows. This whole music career thing seems to have come out of left field."

"Yeah, I saw him perform the night we first met. He's amazing."

Peggy smiled at me. "He is and always has been, but it's a dream he gave up on after graduating from the Conservatory." She shook her head, looking almost pained. "It was so hard to watch him give up on his dreams of a career in music. All that talent just got tucked away inside him, no different than how his grandmother's paintings have been stored away, unknown and unappreciated until now."

As she said it, she glanced out the window of her office, a thoughtful, but contented smile on her face. I could tell how proud she was of him.

"Well, I'm done for today. Wanna grab a pizza?"

Peggy's eyes shot to mine, and she looked startled. "Um, I guess, but don't you still have family here?"

"Mom and Sierra left this morning, the rest of the family are doing their own thing, and I miss Cam... already. So, do me a favor and let's share a pie."

Peggy offered to drive, saying she'd also pick me up in the morning for work, since we both lived in town, and we talked the entire time about Cam's acceptance into the Kansas City Conservatory, how excited he'd been, and about how disillusioned he became. Our conversation about all things Cam continued as we settled into a booth at the pizza place.

"Once he graduated, it's like he lost all hope of ever making it. I tried to get him to try out for those television singing competitions, but instead, he entered nursing school, and that's the last we talked about it."

"I guess I'm confused about why he's taking his shot now. As I said, I saw him perform at the bar in Denver, but wasn't he a regular performer there while still in nursing school? That's what he told me, at least. What's changed?"

"He did perform there, years ago, but what turned things back around was this," she said and took her phone out, taking a few moments to find whatever she was looking for on it, and then handed it to me.

I recognized the YouTube video immediately. I swallowed hard. "Um, *this* is the video that restarted his career?" I asked, not even bothering to hit the play button.

She smiled. "Yes, more or less. He's been performing a lot lately, but when I was driving him to the airport earlier, he told me that video is why *Drag Dance* was so interested in him performing. Just look at the number of views."

I did look, and almost swallowed my tongue. It was in the tens of millions. When had that happened? How did that happen? I mean, I barely had any followers on YouTube. I just uploaded the video, so I could watch it again in case my phone crapped out and I lost all my files. Maybe I shouldn't have titled it "Gay Nightingale." *I bet that...*

"Hunter, are you okay?" she asked, interrupting my racing thoughts, and I froze. Would she even believe me if I admitted I was the one who uploaded the video? And that was the night Cam and I had hooked up. I did not want to go anywhere near that conversation with his mother.

"Um, yeah, it's just amazing is all. That's actually the night I met him." I wasn't ready to admit to her it'd been me recording

Cam's performance. Not that anyone would be able to figure out my real identity based on my username, The Deputy. Sure, I was there at the bar that night, and I had just left my job as a sheriff's deputy, but I took it seriously when the department had warned us against having public social media accounts. I guessed, in this case at least, my code name was wording a little too well at keeping me in disguise.

Regardless, I hoped Cam wouldn't be mad when he found out. I mean, he was going to be famous, right? But then, what did that mean for us? We'd just declared ourselves boyfriends, after all. Boyfriend or not, if I were smart, I'd be the one to tell him before anyone else figured it out.

Peggy cleared her throat, snapping me back to attention. "You're lost in thought."

"Yeah, it's a lot to take in. I mean, he's already sorta famous, just from this video, right?"

Peggy nodded. "But one thing I know about my boy is that he is who he is. Don't worry. This won't change him. If anything, it'll just make him more stubborn. He gets that from his grandmother."

I chuckled. Obviously, I'd never met the infamous Geneva, but from what I'd learned, she was tough as nails. I hadn't seen much of that in her grandson yet, but I would take Peggy's word for it.

"Hunter, can you come meet us in an hour?" Aunt Monica called to me over the two-way radio.

"Um, yeah," I said, and quickly put the thing down. I'd just lectured the patrol about not using our radios for personal business, and here I was doing so myself twice in one week.

I turned my bike around and started pedaling back down the trail, enjoying the wind in my hair as I rode. Summers were definitely a plus I hadn't expected to enjoy much when I signed on for this job. Who knew the slopes were this fun in the off season?

I parked my bike at the patrol hut, rushing in and grabbing a Gatorade from the refrigerator, because damn, the late summer sun could dehydrate you in a minute up here, then I headed up to the hotel suites where my aunt had officially set up shop. As usual, I cringed at the ugly nineteen eighties décor as I entered.

"You wanted to see me?" I asked.

"Yes, thanks, Hunter. I'll call your cousins, and they can come join us, then we'll video call the others."

"Okay," I said. "Let me go clean up a bit then."

She didn't acknowledge me as I left, which wasn't good. My aunt wore her emotions on her sleeve, and I could tell she was feeling nervous or frustrated about something. If she was including the whole family in this conversation, it meant she felt that way about this resort.

By the time I returned, my cousins were sitting across from Aunt Monica. Uncle Harris, Mom, Sierra, and Deke each occupied a box on Aunt Monica's computer screen.

"So, I just received word from the attorney who hired us to manage Peachleaf."

We all knew better than to interrupt Aunt Monica after she'd called a family meeting to order, so we waited in silence to hear what she'd learned. My aunt took a deep breath and let it out slowly. "Optimum is being dissolved. The company's assets will be liquidated to pay back its creditors."

"That's good, right?" Amelia asked. "So, we should be able to get this place for a discounted price."

Aunt Monica shook her head. "No, the courts returned the shares of Peachleaf to its now full-owner, Cameron Kell."

My mouth fell open. Cam hadn't mentioned it to me, neither had Peggy. "How long ago? When did this happen?" I asked.

"A few days ago, although I'm just now getting word." Aunt Monica looked at me for several long moments, probably to figure out whether I'd known already or not. I guess from the look of shock on my face, she figured out I hadn't.

"So, this means we'll have to either let this entire thing drop or make him an offer."

"Do you think he'll take it? I mean, he's thinking about creating a museum and has redone his grandmother's cottage. He looks pretty settled in here," Uncle Harris commented.

"Yes, but he needs money for that museum," my aunt countered.

"Not really," Josiah added. "He could sell a few of his art pieces and have more than enough to renovate that property and turn it into an amazing museum. He doesn't have to sell the resort to get the money he'd need."

Aunt Monica glanced at her son, and I could tell his insight annoyed her. My aunt loved to have leverage when she was making a deal, and it appeared she had none here.

"He doesn't want to run the resort—" I said, "—and Peggy made it clear from the beginning she doesn't either, not long-term. You could appeal to that concern. Besides, he's about to become a famous singer."

That revelation killed the entire conversation, and I knew my family was about to barrage me with a dozen questions if I didn't explain myself quickly. I took out my phone and played them the video, holding it up, so even those on video call could see and hear it well enough. "Wow, that boy has some pipes," I heard Mom say through the monitor.

"He's amazing. I saw that performance too. That's the night I met him."

"Wait..." I heard Sierra say, and looked to see typing furiously on her phone. She must've been looking the video up for herself. A second later, I received a text from her.

Sierra: *The video was uploaded by someone called The Deputy. That's you, isn't it?*

I sighed. My sister didn't follow me on YouTube, but leave it to her to figure out my username in less than a minute.

Me: *Damn, Sierra, don't tell anyone. Cam doesn't know it was me who recorded him.*

Sierra: *Wow, he's got a ton of views.*

Me: *I don't know how this happened. I only put it up because I didn't want to lose it. You know my phone was corrupted last year.*

Sierra: *Brother, you have to tell him. It'll bite you in the ass otherwise, and you know it.*

I felt my face flaming.

Me: *I will, but right now we're still meeting about the purchase of the resort. We should stop texting before anyone notices.*

I looked up to find the entire family staring at me, even Amelia and Aunt Monica, who were usually all business. "What? Purchasing a multimillion-dollar resort here," I said a little too defensively, getting chuckles from my siblings and cousins.

I shoved my phone back into my pocket and refocused on the family matter at hand.

"Hunter's right. We need to discuss the possible purchase of this property," Uncle Harris said.

"Or decide not to purchase," Amelia replied. "It's nice, but it's in the middle of nowhere, not to mention it's dated." She looked around the room, her lips pursed. "*Really* dated. Wouldn't we be better off trying to purchase one of the other resorts OMS owned?"

"Yes and no," Aunt Monica said. "This one is unique, and it's open year-round. Not only does it have a resort with very desirable slopes, but it's also special in that it has a reservoir as well as the natural hot springs. With a few strategic moves, this resort could compete with some of the more affluent ones in the state. The other OMS properties are rundown and not well-regarded. We'd be fighting to bring those properties back from the brink. Avid skiers already have a bad taste in their mouths regarding those resorts."

I nodded before adding my two cents. "I've spent a lot of time skiing in Colorado. More than most since I used all my comp time to come here to ski over the years. Peachleaf is special. It has something for everyone, and that's not just a cliché marketing scheme. The resort is beautiful and old. It has historical relevance, and if Cam does build his museum, that will make it even more so. The hot springs offer a spa option for people who come to the resort, and in the summer, our revenues can compete with skiing in the winter. I don't think anything like Peachleaf exists anywhere else in the state, if not most of the country. At least, not as something we could afford to invest in."

The entire group fell silent. "We need to make our move soon," Aunt Monica said. "If Cam has just learned that the property is his, he may look to unload it sooner rather than later. If he's on the fence, making an offer might help persuade him to lean our way."

"Monica," I heard my mom's voice say. When Aunt Monica turned toward her on the monitor, she continued. "I'm more than happy to invest my part. I was always thankful that your dad included me in the trust. But Hunter, Sierra, and Deke either depend on that money now or plan to in the future. And I know the same goes for your children. Are you sure this is worth the risk we'd all be taking?"

Aunt Monica looked at those of us in the room, then back at the monitor, and sighed. "As we said before, I can't promise. No one can. It's a risk, just like any other risks people take in business. Harris and I agree that after the initial investment, we could probably find funding to pay you all back, but that could take a few years. At the very least, it'd take twenty-four months." She paused for a few moments before she continued, giving us a chance to process that information. "But I'm good at what I do. I wholeheartedly believe this resort has potential that outweighs the risks of anything we've done before, and that includes the Cabot resorts Harris inherited from his family."

Aunt Monica was looking at Harris, who was nodding in agreement.

"I'm in," Josiah said, and I forced myself not to look at him for fear of laughing at how quickly he'd agreed with his mother. Truth be told, it could be either the museum or his potential newfound love that prompted the fast response from my normally reserved and contemplative cousin.

"I'm in too," Sierra said.

"Yeah, me too," Deke said. "But if this goes belly up, you're all giving me cash for birthdays and Christmas, 'cause medical school hasn't been cheap!"

We all chuckled. It ended up coming down to Amelia, who sighed dramatically, then smiled. "Yeah, me too, but I'm not moving here," she said. Her sentiment was understandable. My overly stylish, influencer cousin wouldn't survive in this little town for long, even if it was an amazing place to be.

"Okay, with the trust and the money our company can invest, we can offer Cam a reasonable amount for the property and still have some left over for the renovations," Aunt Monica said, sounding more upbeat than she'd been the entire meeting. "But I warn you, we probably won't get full ownership. It's unlikely we have enough to convince him to part with all his shares."

"Will he retain the management rights?" I asked.

"No, and that's where we have to draw the line. If we do this, we need to control management and oversee the improvements so we can strategically ensure what we do maximizes our return."

I smiled. Aunt Monica was back on her footing now, spitting out terms like we were true business partners.

When the meeting ended and everyone went their separate ways, I hung back to talk to Aunt Monica alone. When she saw that I hadn't left, she sighed. "I wondered if you wanted to talk."

"I like him, Auntie. I like him a lot, and I'd rather this didn't come between us."

She looked sympathetic and shook her head. "Son, I can't promise it won't. Business has a way of screwing with personal relationships and vice versa. But if he likes you too…"

She hesitated for a moment, as if coming to some sort of conclusion, then added, "We're going to offer him a fair price for the property. More than fair, considering we're trying to convince him to give us a chance. So, you don't have to worry about that, okay?"

I smiled at my aunt. "You're always fair. Tough, and you grab a good deal with both hands, but you treat people right. I've always admired that in you."

Aunt Monica's smile lit up her face. "I have tried," she said.

I left her and quickly headed back up the slopes. I didn't want to come face to face with Peggy and accidentally let the cat out of the bag.

# 41

# CAM

"Wow, already?" I asked between takes. Mom had texted, saying she needed to hear from me sooner rather than later, so I gave her a call.

"Yeah, apparently they wanted to let you know they're interested in purchasing right away."

"What are they afraid of, Mom? That someone will beat them to the punch?"

"Honestly, I couldn't tell you, just that when Monica dropped the offer off, she seemed nervous, which was an emotion I never expected to see from her."

"Well, I mean, that's cool, I guess." Someone called my name, probably Madonya. I swear the diva was about to do me in.

"Listen, I've got to go, but Mom, can you have the attorney look it over? I want to know all my options before making a decision. Oh, and you and I need to talk about what this means for you too."

"You don't worry about me, honey. Your grandmother took care of me. But yeah, you need to have Mr. Pauley look it over. You don't want to end up in the legal mess your grandmother was in. You probably need to get an appraisal done as well."

"Cam, we need you!" Madonya came around the corner and stood with her hands on her hips. "Did you hear me call?"

I put my finger up to stall. "Mom, if you can arrange it, I'll reimburse you for your time, but the dragon bitch is breathing down my neck. I gotta go."

Mom just laughed. "Don't worry about it. I'll send the contract to the attorney and get the appraisal set up."

"Thanks, Mom, love you!"

When she hung up, I turned to Madonya. "Listen, I get it, you need me, but damn, I'm trying to deal with a multimillion-dollar property too, so I can't just jump every time you snap your fingers."

Madonya looked at me funny with her Corey face, and sighed. "You're right. I'm sorry. I've just gotten so caught up in all of this. Will you forgive me?"

Corey still had his Madonya eyelashes on. Most of the queens around the show kept something on to indicate their personality, even when out of drag. The eyelashes were so very much Madonya. Currently, she was batting those big things at me.

I laughed. "God, you're a pain. Yes, I forgive you, but try to give me a little leeway, especially with all this stuff I'm dealing with back home."

She came over and kissed my cheek. "Baby, you can have all you want after we get this damned performance over. The Bitter Bitch From Hell over there wants you onstage, so they can decide where to place you during the show."

Just then, the six-foot-seven, if she was an inch, diva walked toward us, and said, "I *heard* you, Jezebel," but she was laughing. Madonya just huffed and walked me toward the stage, playing up every ounce of the manufactured drama. God, she was so in her element.

I should've been more nervous than I was about my performance. This was national television, and when I thought about it, I did freak out a bit, but truth be told, the performers were so fucking hilarious. Just like Madonya, they were all in full drama mode. Bickering, throwing shade. Oh, and they were all flirting with me like there was no tomorrow, each of them trying to outdo the others.

Of course, flirting with me made absolutely no sense. They were assigned total hunks to escort them on stage. But despite the overabundance of exposed muscles, it was me they targeted, which I actually sort of enjoyed.

Not that I was going to flirt back. Even now, I wanted my sexy ski patroller more than ever. God, I wished Hunter were here. I would give so much money to watch my muscleman fend off all my drag queen admirers. Maybe it was a bit naughty wanting to watch that, but it'd be worth every penny.

Even as filming began, I was weirdly chill. It just felt like another night at Madonya's place back when I'd been a regular performer. I watched from the sidelines as the queens strutted their stuff, and the judges threw a whole shitload of shade at them. Then, it was my turn.

The new song was everything I wanted it to be, maybe that's why I felt so relaxed standing on my mark while waiting for my cue. As I'd done during rehearsal, I conjured up an image of Hunter making love to me. As the bass began to move along with the dance beat, I almost felt Hunter's deep sexual chuckle roll deliciously down my spine.

The music came naturally, as did my performance. Seeing the queens sashay down the runway to my music just felt right. Like it was a culmination of my life and work with music. The melody, the bass, the rhythm. It was me.

As soon as the song ended, I was escorted offstage by the sexy hunks, not unlike the divas. I watched in the backstage monitor as the cameras panned toward the judges.

"Well, shit," the head judge said. She was another giant of a man dressed in remarkable drag that would give the ultimate diva RuPaul a run for her money. "Girl, bring that bitch back out here," she said to one of the hunks.

I didn't realize at first that she meant me until the same hunky escorts came over and led me back on stage. "What the fuck?" I said under my breath, then forced myself to smile before I was thrust back into the limelight.

"Bitch, where did you find that song?" the diva asked.

I chuckled. "I wrote it."

One of the other judges, some famous DJ I didn't know, leaned into his mic, and said, "That was one of the sexiest songs I've heard in a long damn time."

I smirked and nodded, because damned if I didn't agree. My inspiration for it was damn sexy too.

"Well, girl, I'm so worked up, I'm having a hard time concentrating. You, over there," the head judge said to one of the escorts. "Get all the judges some ice water. We got work to do here. Shame on you." She directed that last to me with a lot of sass, but all the judges were smiling.

"My pleasure," I said, and earned applause from the queens around me.

"Well, you go away before one of us comes up there and attacks you. Now, back to the actual fucking show."

I chuckled as I was led offstage again. When one of the escorts pulled a slightly sweaty notepad and pen out of his tiny G-string, I almost lost it. "Can you sign this for me?"

"Um, if you tell me how you hid that in there with… all that," I said, pointing at the rather large package he was sporting.

He grinned. "I could show you," he said, and winked.

If there had been no Hunter, I would definitely have taken him up on that offer. Instead, I winked back, opened his little notepad, and signed it, *Thanks, but maybe next time, The Gay Nightingale.*

It was unlikely, but shit, I loved to flirt and no harm, no foul, so long as I wasn't gonna touch.

After the show, I was attacked by the judges and contestants alike. "That was amazing," the head judge said. Madonya was standing next to me, basking in the praise but also keeping a wary eye.

"He's beyond amazing, and if you want to sign him again, you can give me a call." She handed out her business cards and quickly whisked me off the stage and into the dressing room I'd been assigned.

"Wow, possessive much?"

"I am, and that bitch was just about to try to crowd my position. She's a talent scout in real life, after all. I'm gonna say this again. I'm not sharing you. If she wants to bring you into her little world, bitch is gonna have to go through me." Madonya snapped her fingers in the air, and I grinned. Madonya could be a giant pain in the ass, but she was also a fiercely devoted friend, and, apparently, manager.

"Yes, Mother," I said, and kissed her made-up face. "But don't play too hard to get. I liked doing this tonight. I'd like to do it a lot more."

"And you will, baby. In fact, I'm guessing we'll start getting more calls than you'll have time to perform. Now, we just need to expand your repertoire. That one song can be recorded as a single, but I'm not here for a one-hit-wonder. We're gonna take this bitch all the way! For now, I'm going to go back out there and sell you to these hoes, then my sugar and I are going to take you out to celebrate, before you get too famous to be seen in public."

I laughed, I couldn't imagine that would happen too soon, if ever, but hell, it was a lot of fun to dream.

# 42

# HUNTER

My family were all fit to be tied. It'd been three weeks since Aunt Monica delivered the proposal to Cam. So far, there'd been no word from him about it.

He called me at least every other day, but usually, he was so exhausted all we did was chat about our days, his being filled with performances, interviews, and recording studios, mine filled with shutting down some of the resort's summer activities as we transitioned into the shorter fall season and prepared for winter.

I'd be the first to admit, I was jealous of his new career. Not of the fame and fortune aspect, but because it felt like I was competing against it for his attention. Hell, we'd only just agreed to being boyfriends before Cam had left, and nearly a month had already passed since I'd last seen him. Now, he was some superstar. What would he want with the likes of me, a glorified ski bum? I answered his phone calls, excited to hear from him, but my gut told me our relationship was teetering on the edge of nonexistence.

I tried not to think about that, tried not to think about Cam in general, but the harder I tried not to, the more the man filled my thoughts. I knew that when the final blow came, I was going to be crushed. More than losing my job as a deputy. I just hoped he'd have the decency to break up with me in person rather than by phone, or worse, text message, otherwise I'd likely end up chucking my cell into the reservoir.

"Have you heard from Cam?" Aunt Monica asked, startling me from my thoughts. She'd been gone for over two weeks herself, off visiting some other Cabot Management-run properties, and had just returned today. Also, she never came into the patrol hut.

I shook my head. "Not about the deal, no. I'm sorry, Aunt Monica, but as I told you before, I'm not comfortable bringing it up unless he does."

"I know, Hunter, and I understand, but we do need to know something soon. If Cam is receptive, I'll need to set up the financing that the trust won't cover."

"I thought that was approved already."

"It has been, tentatively. The money we all have in the trust is a good down payment, which the bank required, and we have perfect credit ratings, but one doesn't just get a loan overnight. It takes time."

"I'm sure he knows that, Auntie. Why don't you ask Peggy? You'll get more information from her than me, and she can ask him without it being uncomfortable."

Aunt Monica sat down in a chair next to me. "I did, and she said I needed to let him come to us when he's ready." She shook her head. "Apparently, pushing Cam equals him digging in and going nowhere."

"I can totally see that in him," I chuckled, but without much humor. I understood my aunt's dilemma, but didn't feel I was in much of a position to help. "Listen, I don't expect him to tell us anything for a while. If he were going to jump on our offer, he'd have already done so. Meanwhile, Josiah has been talking to him about the art. Why don't you focus on helping with that? The more we help him reach his dream, the more likely he'll decide to work with us, maybe on several levels."

"Or he'll decide to keep it and do it on his own," she said.

"I doubt it. He'd still need us, or another company like yours, to help make it all work. Besides, how would he run this place while running around the country being famous?"

She looked at me then, her all-business demeanor fading slightly. "Oh, honey, I've been so wrapped up in the offer, I didn't realize his being away has been hard on you. Are you okay?"

I had no idea how my aunt had sniffed that out, but she was a bloodhound in so many ways. I sighed. "Yeah," I said, feeling emotional all of a sudden, "it's hard. I miss him. We had just begun getting a lot closer when his music career took off."

She hugged me. "He'll eventually have to come back home. When he does, we'll be ready, and you're right, I should go help Josiah with his project. Then I'm going to fly back to Denver and try to do some work on the other Cabot properties. Getting my mind off the waiting should help."

She stood up and walked toward the door before turning to face me, looking thoughtful. "I suggest you keep your mind busy too. It won't do either of us any good to focus on what we can't control."

Well, there it was. My aunt always made her point, and, apparently, I needed to do what I'd done my entire adult life. Throw myself into work until I could resolve the issues with Cam. Pouting and feeling sorry for myself wouldn't change things or make them move any faster.

# 43

# CAM

"Josiah, that's perfect," I said into the phone, glancing out of my hotel room window at the busy city street a few floors below.

"You don't mind selling the three older pieces then? I mean, they're something you inherited from your grandmother. I would feel bad if they held sentimental value."

"No, I don't mind selling them. Like you said, they don't fit the collection. And I really would like to renovate the mansion and prepare it to house the rest of my art collection."

"Then I'll arrange the deal. Oh, and the museum in Denver agreed to the consignment. I'll feel so much better once all that artwork is in the hands of professionals and not in your upstairs bedrooms."

"Thanks, Josiah. Why don't you have our attorney set up an official agreement between you and me? You should be getting paid for all the work you are doing."

Josiah hesitated for a moment. "About that, my mother is chomping at the bit to hear what your thoughts are on the offer."

I couldn't help but laugh. "I can't believe you were the first person in your family brave enough to ask." Josiah sighed, and I could tell he was nervous about asking. "Listen, I haven't made up my mind, and tell your mom I probably won't for at least a few more months. In fact, don't tell her, I will. I'll give her a call this afternoon. But I do need to manage all that art, and you're right, it needs to be somewhere people will enjoy it. It also needs to be somewhere safe. I'll call my mom and see if she can help get bids for the mansion renovation."

"Well, actually," Josiah interrupted, "I know a contractor from Denver who did the most recent work on the museum where I interned. I could get you his number. To be honest, even though you aren't renovating the mansion for the full art exhibits yet, you need to have someone who understands the type of heating and cooling and electrical needs you'll have. Not to mention..."

"Josiah, I get it," I said, cutting him off. Once Josiah got hold of an issue, he could go on for hours. "Yes, you're the expert, and that's why I'd love to hire you. Have a contract written up, then you and Mom can work up the plans for the first phase. At this point, I just want to get the place secured."

Luckily, with the money I was getting for the older art pieces, I could afford to do the initial work on the mansion, but even more importantly, I had enough money to hire Josiah to advise me. I didn't have enough to pay him full-time, but I'd already decided if I could find the funds, he was my first choice as curator for the museum. I was ashamed to admit that he was much more dedicated to the art I'd inherited than I was.

Regardless, I was happy that things were working out as I'd envisioned. The museum in Denver that Josiah had spoken with agreed to house my art collection while my museum was being created. He had convinced them to display various pieces for now, and when we were ready to make an official announcement about the mansion house museum opening, they would feature the collection that would be displayed there as a way of promoting it.

It was an ingenious marketing solution as well as a way to conserve and protect the artwork. I had yet to hear what it would cost to have the paintings cleaned by an art conservator, which was scary, but I was sure Josiah would figure it out. That, of course, was just one reason why I needed to pay him. I didn't like the feeling of taking advantage of his generosity.

When we hung up, I immediately called Mom.

"Hey, son, how's the world of fame and fortune?"

"Ha ha, funny. I just got off the phone with Josiah, and I guess Monica and the Cabot family are chomping at the bit to hear my thoughts about the purchase."

Mom chuckled. "Yes, that's an understatement. But, honey, you don't want to rush into a decision."

"No, I don't, and I'm not going to, but I will give Monica a call and let her know that. Did you get the appraisal results back?"

"Yes, and they are significantly more than the Cabot offer, but of course, that doesn't take into consideration all the work that needs to be done on the place."

"Yeah, I agree. Okay, so what about you? You haven't told me what you want to happen."

Mom was silent for a long time, then said, "I love working here. I fought my way up the chain just like anyone else here. Your grandmother never gave me any special treatment, even though a lot of people thought she did. But, honey, I'm into my fifties now. I'd like to travel, maybe date someone who isn't twenty years older than me. I'm not saying no to managing this for you, but..."

"Mom, I'm not asking you to manage it. I'm asking if you want to. It sounds like you're ready to move on."

She hesitated again. "I... well, that's hard to commit to, but yes, I think I'm ready for what's next."

"I wish I was there to hug you. I know this is a big step."

"I wish you were here too. Any news on when you will be?"

There was the segue. Mom was like me in that when she wasn't quite ready to face heavy, potentially emotional topics, she moved the conversation away until she was. That was why I needed to let Monica know directly that I wasn't going to be making this decision anytime soon.

When I hung up with Mom, I dialed Monica's cell, and she answered immediately. "Hello, Cam, what a nice surprise."

I chuckled. "Not as nice as you wish, I'm sure. I just talked to Josiah, and he asked about my decision on your proposal."

I waited until she asked, "Yes?"

"The answer is I'm not ready to answer that just yet. I would like you and Cabot Management to continue to manage the resort under the same contract you had with the bankruptcy court, and I promise I will make a decision on your proposal within the next few months."

There was a pregnant pause, and I could almost hear everything she wanted to say. Finally, she said, "Cam, I appreciate your situation, but I also need to consider all the options for Cabot as well as my family, who've agreed to invest their trust. Can you guarantee a decision for us by the end of the year?"

I thought about it for a few moments and knew that I'd have made my decision by then. "Yes, of course, I can let you know by the end of December. Thank you, Monica, for understanding."

"Thank you for letting me know."

I could hear her disappointment, but at least I hadn't said no, not that I wanted to reject her offer. I still didn't want to run the resort, and I knew Mom no longer wanted to, but like the art collection, I wasn't ready to just toss it away either. It meant something to me that my family had invested their lives into Peachleaf. It mattered that all of it was part of my heritage.

But it mattered more to me that I was on the verge of having my dreams come true, and that was where Hunter came in. The longer I was away from him, the more I wanted him in my life. Our relationship was new, but that didn't mean I didn't already know he was the one.

"Hey," I said when he answered his phone.

"Hey, yourself."

"So, I just got off the phone with your aunt. I know you've been curious about the offer, and I wanted to thank you for not putting pressure on me. Also, I told her I needed time. I'll let you all know my decision by the end of the year."

I waited then to hear his feedback. He remained silent on the other end, which I took as agreement.

"Now, the real reason I called..."

"Okay," Hunter said, and I could sense his hesitation. That was clearly going to be the theme of my afternoon calls today.

"So, I'm stuck in New York. I will be for a while, recording my song for the record company that wants to release it as a single. I'm also meeting with songwriters. I know, that's a lot more information than you need. What I'm asking is, can you come to New York? I miss you."

"Yes!"

I laughed at how quickly he responded. "Okay, when?"

"Well, now's a good time. We're just easing into the fall season, so things are quieter, but I'll need to be back before ski season starts."

"In that case, want me to book your flight?"

"No, I can figure out those details, but do I need a car and hotel?"

"That's a total no. I want you with me, Hunter. It's been torture not seeing you. I know I'm too much…"

"No, no, I'm the same. I miss you like stupid. I'll book my flight right away."

I chuckled, relieved I wasn't alone in my feelings. "Okay, I'll send you my schedule and you send me your flight details as soon as you book a ticket, but don't wait too long, I have a lot of plans for you. *Lots* of plans, Hunter!"

He choked, and I couldn't help but smile. "Yeah, I'll book that flight now."

# 44

# HUNTER

C AM MET ME AT the airport, and the moment he crashed into my arms, the world seemed to right itself. "God, I missed you," he said as he pulled back from our kiss.

"Same," I said, and pulled him into me again. He grabbed one of my bags and led the way outside the crowded terminal. I'd actually traveled through here once before on a vacation Aunt Monica treated me to after my father died.

I didn't remember it being quite so crowded. I did remember New York, though, and the intense traffic. That much certainly hadn't changed.

"So, I took today off, although Madonya is still going to call me and try to get me into the recording studio. But if she can't find us, she can't harass me. I've put my phone on silent."

I grinned as Cam was talking a mile a minute and just swiped my lips across his. "Mmm," he moaned, and took the kiss deeper. The cabbie cleared his throat, and we pulled apart, chuckling. "Sorry, we haven't seen each other in a while."

I leaned back as Cam gave the cabbie the hotel location.

When he leaned back, he snuggled into me same as if we were on my sofa back home. "Hunter, how have I missed you this much after such a short time?"

I kissed his forehead. "I might be wrong, but that might be what the whole boyfriend thing is all about."

"Maybe," he said. His phone started vibrating, and he muttered something about vibrate and silent modes, then just turned it off without looking at who was calling.

"Do you do that to me?" I asked. "Just ignore my calls?"

"Never. I'm sure it's Madonya, she's been calling repeatedly even though I told her I wouldn't be available today. Girl was upset that I canceled the recording session tonight."

"Are you having problems with it?"

Cam shrugged. "Sorta, but let's not talk about it. I need a break, and if you weren't here, I'd be hiding somewhere anyway. At least I can hide with you."

I couldn't help but laugh. Cam was pumped, and I wondered if he realized how happy he seemed. It was like someone lit him up. I forced down the sadness that threatened to creep up on me back down. Would his coming back to his small town in the mountains dim that beautiful light that his music had brought to his life? God, what kind of terrible boyfriend would I be if I let that happen?

"So, I thought we could go to see *Hamilton*. I've always wanted to see it, but besides the TV version, I was never able to get away, but, of course, if you'd rather stay in, that'd be wonderful too."

"Baby, I'm here 'cause I want to be with you. We can do whatever you want. Besides, I've heard *Hamilton* is good, so I'm game."

He smiled so brightly it lit up his whole face. "Oh, let's get dinner too. Did you bring fancy clothes? If not, we can go shopping, my treat."

I mostly just enjoyed the ride as he asked me questions and proposed ideas of touristy things to do. We ended up shopping at some exclusive place. I got some new clothes that cost way too much for what they were, in my opinion, but had to admit they looked good on me.

We went to eat at a small restaurant Cam said someone from the recording studio recommended, and the food was like nothing I'd ever eaten. It was delicious, although there wasn't enough of it. So, of course, we ended up eating hamburgers at a little hole in the wall while wearing our fancy clothes on our way to see *Hamilton*.

That night was like we'd never been apart. After returning to our hotel room, we cuddled, kissed, and slowly explored each other's bodies.

As our kisses deepened and tender touches grew heated, giving way to the intense need and passion I'd only ever experienced with Cam, it was somehow different than before. *This must be what making love feels like*, I thought. The sweetness of the realization made me more emotional than I would've expected.

I was definitely falling in love with Cam. It was probably stupid on my part, but I couldn't deny my feelings any longer. My heart belonged to him, even if he ended up crushing it.

# 45

# CAM

SEEING HUNTER IN NEW York was like having all the planets align. Not that I understood much about aligned planets or the solar system, but I knew it felt right and perfect having him here with me. We toured New York, mostly him letting me drag him around the city, and of course, he let me snuggle into him throughout the day.

By the time we got back from watching *Hamilton*, I thought the evening would be over, but oh my god, he proved me wrong in the most delightful ways. On the hotel sofa, on the bed twice, and once in the shower. No matter how tense I'd been before Hunter arrived, he literally pounded the tension out of me one glorious thrust at a time, and I was mush afterward.

I'd been running nonstop since the filming of *Drag Dance*. One opportunity led to another, which led to another, and before I knew it, Madonya had me meeting industry people and giving interviews all over the city. I was immediately offered a record deal for the song I sang on *Drag Dance*, and was already recording the single. Except it hadn't gone as well as we'd hoped.

Unlike when I performed onstage, the music was falling flat in the studio sessions. The beat and bass were right. That music was fine, actually. I was the problem. Something was missing inside me, some unspoken magic that happened when the music flowed through me. I hadn't felt that since my *Drag Dance* performance.

As Hunter and I made love, gentle and sweet this time, I could feel myself becoming centered again. My heartbeat began slowing down. I could feel all the excitement and anxiety bubbling inside me mellow and ebb away, leaving me in the safe cocoon of my boyfriend's arms.

"You're exactly what I needed," I said as I lay sprawled out over Hunter's body.

"Mmm," he grunted happily.

"I'm going to have to get up early tomorrow and try to re-record my song. I think the studio is getting a bit annoyed with me," I said, and started to roll off him.

"Shh, worry about that tomorrow. For now, just lie here with me, okay?"

I nodded and snuggled back in. "Tell me about home. What's been happening?"

"Hmm, well, you know it's our downtime. Switching from summer to winter, most of the crowds are slowing down with school starting back. Your mom kicked the chef out. That was entertaining."

"Really? That's been a long time coming. I need details," I said, leaning up to look at his handsome face.

Hunter chuckled, low and deep in the way that always sent shivers through me. "Well, the idiot knowingly bought a bunch of out-of-date hamburger and tried to sell it to customers."

"Wow, how did she catch it?"

"Someone from the meat delivery company tipped her off."

"Damn, that could've created all kinds of problems. Can you imagine the liability? Never mind people actually getting seriously sick."

"Yep, so your mom and Aunt Monica are now working on replacing all of the cooks."

"That's good news, at least."

"Oh, we got a new chest compression machine for the patrol. We'll be training all the patrollers on how to use it before ski season begins."

"Cool," I said, yawning and resting my head on his chest. "Hunter?"

"Mmm?" he asked.

"You love it there, don't you?"

Hunter paused for a moment before I heard him sigh. "Yeah, it's one of the most spectacular resorts I've ever been to. It's beautiful and cozy, and the staff are friendly. I like my patrols, plus the owner is fucking hot."

I grinned and kissed his chest. "He likes you."

"Yeah, and I like him."

"I'm glad," I said, and closed my eyes before falling into a blessed and peaceful sleep.

# 46

# HUNTER

"**D**AMN, I'M LATE," CAM said, jumping out of bed and waking me up.

"Late? For what?" I asked, still stunned from being woken up from a deep sleep.

"I was supposed to be at the studio by now. I've got to call Madonya and tell her I'm on my way. Hey, can you come with me?" he asked.

"Um, sure, if you want me to."

"I do," he yelled as he rushed into the shower. I didn't need another shower since we'd woken up earlier and gotten one, along with mutual blow jobs. Unlike Cam, my hair wasn't standing up after having slept on it. When I'd become a deputy,

I'd had my long hair cut into a fade and stayed with the look, so it didn't require washing to keep it looking decent.

I got up, brushed my teeth, and threw on some clothes from my bag. I hadn't had time to unpack yesterday since Cam kept me running until we got back to the hotel last night.

By the time he came out of the bathroom, I'd been downstairs to get us each a cup of much-needed caffeine.

"Okay, so we can catch the subway there. It's faster," he said as he grabbed my hand and the coffee and pulled me out the door.

I wasn't a city person. I'd grown accustomed to wide-open spaces, and there were way too many people here for me. We crowded onto the subway, and my face was almost planted on some older woman's knitted hat while some guy seemed to have his nose stuck in my armpit. I moved away from him, because I'd swear the freak sniffed me.

By the time we got to the studio, Cam was talking ninety to nothing again. I just smiled and let him pull me along, much like I had yesterday. Honestly, even the smelly, crowded subway didn't bother me as long as I was with Cam. I didn't think my heart had ever been this happy.

We were met by the same drag queen who pulled Cam up on stage last year when we had our first fateful rendezvous. "You're so busted. I had to tell them you were ill yesterday and that's why you're late today, so by God, you better act like you're not feeling well," the drag queen said, causing me to cock an eyebrow.

She looked up then, really noticing me, and wasn't even shy about giving me a thorough once-over. "Well, well, what do we have here?" she asked and faked flinging the wig she wasn't wearing over her shoulder.

"Mine," Cam said, pulling me down the hall and away from the smirking queen.

"Who was that?" I asked.

"Madonya, my manager and general pain in the ass. You can sit in the control room while I record," he said, and all but shoved me into the small room with an irritated-looking dude with headphones on.

I didn't bother to say hi. I heard Cam apologize in the microphone before the guy immediately started the music before Cam even had time to get himself together.

"Dude, give him a minute," I heard myself say before I had enough time to think.

"Fuck you," he said.

"Oh no, this shit stops now. I suggest you stop the damn music and give him a fucking minute." The scrawny jackass of a man looked me up and down, then stopped the music. "If this is how you've been treating him, then no wonder he's struggling."

"Who the fuck are you?" the guy asked.

"Someone more important than you," I said and squared the lowlife with a stare. My protective instincts were blowing up now. I would not tolerate someone ambushing Cam, even if I was overstepping.

It took him a moment to realize I wasn't backing down, then he cleared his throat and leaned into the microphone, saying, "When you're ready, let me know."

"Better," I said, sitting back in the uncomfortable chair and keeping an eye on him as we waited for my boyfriend to give the signal.

Cam, clearly unaware of what happened in the control room, scrunched his shoulders, then lifting his hands above his head, he stretched. It only took a few minutes before Cam appeared fully relaxed as he smiled our way and nodded. "I'm ready."

The jackass started the music again, but this time, I could see Cam getting into the groove. He leaned into the mic, and damn, magic poured out of his mouth. It was pure sex. Pure... us. It didn't take a genius to know he was singing about him and me.

When the song ended, he looked at me through the glass. His face immediately blushed, and that was enough to confirm my suspicion. Damn, I'd love to pull him out of that studio and do all the things to him that he'd just sung about.

"Still not quite right," the jackass said, and I turned toward him like he'd lost his ever-fucking mind.

"Play it back."

"What?" he asked.

"Play the damn music back, tell him what it is he needs to fix."

I knew he wanted to challenge me, but I was more than happy to kick his ass after how he treated Cam when we first got here.

My imagination was good enough to tell me he'd been treating him the same or worse before now.

He flipped several different switches on his mixing board, and the sultry sound of Cam's voice filled the room. "There, see how he rushed the note?"

"Yeah, tell him, though, not me."

He did, and Cam nodded. We went through the rest of the song, Jackass, as I now was calling him, telling him each time where the problems were. Each time, Cam thought about it and nodded.

"Okay, try it again," Jackass said.

Cam did, and although I was far from an expert, I thought he did better. Jackass agreed, and instead of being a vague son of a bitch, he explained what needed to be fixed again and did another take.

It took all morning before Cam nailed it enough for Jackass to crack a smile. "Yeah, I think that's it," he said, and when he played it back, it did sound perfect. Sexy and perfect. Just like Cam.

Before Cam came in, I asked Jackass, "So, why were you such a jerk to him? Is this some blowoff thing?"

The guy looked shocked and shrugged. "I mean, no and yes. The studio usually sends their knock-offs to me when they think it's just a one-off thing. They don't usually expect me to produce anything perfect."

"Well, you let them know if they ever want to do anything with him again, none of this shit will be tolerated. Got it?"

The guy swallowed hard, probably because I'd also moved threateningly closer to him. "Yeah, I'll tell them."

I nodded and turned just as Cam swept into the room. "It was awesome. Did you hear it?" he asked.

"I did, and you were, not to mention that song. Damn." I didn't bother to look back at Jackass as I led Cam out of the control room and the studio. I also wanted to distract him enough that the man didn't say anything to him. I had no idea what kind of recording deal Cam had signed, but fuck if that jackass needed to be thanked. Maybe I needed to learn a little more about this whole thing because if the drag queen was his manager, she needed to be in there handing that jerk his ass, not me.

"Okay, lunch, then we'll go meet with Madonya. I want you to get to know her."

I smiled and nodded because that was exactly what I was hoping for. A moment with Madonya. Was I being protective? Hell yes. Did I understand the industry? No, not even a little. But I knew enough about assholes to know when one was using their influence to make things difficult for Cam. And that was something I wouldn't tolerate, at least not if I could stop it.

The diva sat across from us out of drag, but even without all the hair and makeup, he was full-out nuts and funny. I watched as he interacted with Cam and figured out pretty quickly the drag queen was out of her depth. "So, Corey, or do you prefer Madonya?"

"Madonya when I've got my face on, but you can call me Corey when I'm out of drag."

I smiled. "So, tell me about your business in Colorado. It was there I met Cam. It seems really popular."

"Oh honey, it's a hoot." I listened as he talked about all the things they were doing and the guest stars, many of them legitimately famous, he'd featured.

"Wow, that's amazing, so do you manage any of them?" I asked, trying to sound innocent.

The diva eyed me and, with a cocked eyebrow, let me know he'd figured my game out quick enough. "I've managed a hell of a lot of acts and made my bar successful when all other gay bars are disappearing daily, but no, Cam is my first in this role."

I nodded. "Seems like you're doing fine."

He eyed me again, and a few minutes later, when Cam went to the restroom, he turned to me. "Okay, spit it out. What's crawled up that gorgeous tush of yours?"

I chuckled. "Today at the recording studio, the guy doing the recording gave Cam a lot of grief. Doing what he could to keep Cam off-center. I almost punched the guy before he changed his tune."

Corey tapped his tooth with his painted fingernail. "I should've caught that."

I nodded. "Yeah, Corey, I'm not an expert at anything to do with music, but I know when someone is deliberately fucking with someone, and since you all spent so much time there, I'm sure most of the problems were from that jackass."

"Oh well, shit. Yes, now that I think about it, he was a bit of an ass."

"I'm guessing that has to do with the recording company who hired him. How tied down are you to that recording company?"

"Oh, not past this single. In fact, they said they'd let me know if they wanted to pursue anything else."

I sighed. "Corey, listen. Can I be blunt?"

He eyed me, but nodded slowly. "I just started a new job. After leaving the sheriff's department where I worked for years, I took on running a ski patrol in Peachleaf. I know what it looks like when someone is out of their element because I was out of mine."

The guy stared at me without moving, so I continued, "I was lucky 'cause I ended up with a mentor who walked me through all the basics. He used to be the patrol director, so I had to push down my pride to take his advice and leadership, but because I did, I'm now respected by my crew and know what I'm doing. If you take my advice before you sign Cam up for another record deal or for anything else for that matter, I recommend you talk to someone who can help you avoid the pitfalls like you and Cam were in this morning. Cam deserves more than that."

The guy deflated in front of me and shook his head. "I'm sorry, damn. I'm just a flat-chested diva with big-breasted dreams."

"Well, lucky for you, and thanks to drag queens worldwide, you can get a good set of knockers online for cheap. You just have to be brave enough to buy them."

Corey laughed before getting serious, clearly thinking about the situation. "I worked so hard to bring Cam out. We're here because I pulled every string."

"You're here because you're great at what you do. I was great at what I did too, but that didn't mean I was prepared to do it all, not without help. Had I not gotten that help, Corey, I could've put people's lives in jeopardy. Trust me, there's nothing wrong with being a team player, in letting yourself have a partner."

He sighed. "Okay, you're right. Shit, I needed someone to kick me in the ass." He winked at me then. "If I weren't happily married and my one and only client wasn't so infatuated with you he practically salivates when he sees you, I'd let you do more than kick it."

"Aah, shucks," I said, making him laugh out loud.

"I like you, Hunter. More now than I did. Now, where is that bitch, and why is she taking so long in the restroom?"

I chuckled because Cam came out just then, smiling at the two of us.

I figured the talk with Cam's manager might help keep him out of another idiot's recording studio but, more importantly, calm his manager down enough that he'd let Cam have a life outside the business. I suspected Corey, or Madonya's, insecurities were driving this insane, unending need to push him so hard.

Oh well, at least he didn't toss his drink in my face when I butted in. That was something.

We were just about to leave when Corey looked at his phone and started waving his hands. "Oh, oh, oh, I think we have a lead on who posted your video. The Deputy."

I froze. "Um, Cam, I meant to talk to you about that." Both Corey and Cam turned to look at me, confused. "Well, I mean, I did it, but I swear to God, I had no idea it would go viral. I mean, I didn't even know anyone was really even following me on YouTube."

"*You*?" Cam asked. "You are The Deputy?"

I shrugged. "Um, yeah. Surprise?"

"Oh, shit," Corey said. "Well, that mystery is solved. I'll leave you two lovebirds alone to sort all this out."

Quick as lightning, he was gone out the front door.

# 47

# CAM

“WHAT DO YOU MEAN, you’re The Deputy?” I asked.

“Well... I mean, Cam, I didn’t even know the video had taken off until your mom showed me the number of views. I-I hadn’t paid any attention. As I said, I didn’t...”

“Wait, my *mom* knows you’re The Deputy?”

“Ugh, no, listen, she didn’t know until recently. I was going to tell you on this trip. Which I just did, horribly, but yeah, I did.”

I’d never heard Hunter babble nervously before, and it was a cross between disconcerting and pretty damn cute. My big man was genuinely nervous about how I’d react to his revelation, and rightly so because holy shit. The video mystery man had been right in front of me this whole time, not to mention behind, on top, and inside.

I looked at Hunter with all of the fake anger I could muster, then started laughing. "I can't fucking believe it. You're The Deputy."

He shrugged again, and looked around self-consciously as people in the restaurant started to look at us, then he quickly began to guide me out though I was still laughing. "Seriously, you posted that video the night we met?" I asked when we got outside.

Hunter smiled sheepishly. "Yeah, to be honest, I had my phone corrupted recently, and I didn't want to lose the video of you singing. So, I uploaded it to my YouTube account. I swear I had almost zero followers. But then, somehow, it got out, and I didn't even notice the numbers. For real, how many people upload YouTube videos that go nowhere? How could I have known?"

He was nervously babbling again, so I put him out of his misery by kissing him. "I love this story more than I can even tell you. Now that I know, it makes total sense. A Gay Nightingale though?" I asked, and he shrugged.

"I didn't get your name, and that's how they introduced you that night. So, you're seriously not upset with me for not coming clean sooner?"

"I mean, you should have, and it's a wonder Madonya doesn't claw you with her painted nails on for recording in her club without permission, but God, this is epic. One day we'll be telling our kids about it." I stopped then, realizing what I'd said. "Not that we'll, um, you know I don't expect…"

Hunter laughed then, any lingering tension brought on by the surprise revelation draining away. "Cam, I want all that too, and it's too soon, but still, you can say it. I like to imagine what that would be like with you."

I blushed, and went in for another kiss. "Get a fucking room," some douchebag said as he hurried past us on the sidewalk.

"New York," Hunter said under his breath, and I nodded.

"I think he had a good suggestion, though. Why don't we go get a room?"

We spent the day hanging out together, and the fact that Madonya didn't text or call should've been suspicious, but damn, it was so nice to be off the hook. We lounged in the room all afternoon, ordered room service for lunch, and just enjoyed making love.

The next morning, I got a call at eight and cringed when I glanced at the phone and saw it was Madonya. "Ugh, all good things come to an end," I whispered before answering.

"Hello."

"Baby, I need you to bring that handsome boyfriend of yours down to the lounge. There's someone I want you to meet. Someone who's going to help me make you the famous bitch you deserve to be."

"Okay? Madonya, are you okay?"

"Oh, more than, but you can tell that man of yours, he was right. Not that I'll admit that to his face. See you in fifteen?" she asked, then hung up without waiting for my response.

I leaned back in bed, kissed Hunter's sexy mouth good morning, and said, "My divine manager says we have to be down at the lounge in fifteen minutes. Can you come with me? She asked for you."

"Ugh," he groaned, and rolled away from me.

"Come on. I'll make it worth your while."

I slipped my hand around his waist and began to snake my way toward his cock. "Don't even start if you've got somewhere to be in fifteen minutes. I work fast, but not that fast."

I laughed. "Come on, I'll go comb my hair, and we'll see what her ladyship is up to now."

Giving up on my hair, I ended up slipping a hat on to hide my wild bedhead and looked resentfully toward my boyfriend, who looked like a million bucks without having to do a damn thing other than roll out of bed. Of course, when he did so, his gorgeous six-pack tensed, making me want to attack him all over again. How could a man be so fucking hot?

We managed to get downstairs and found Madonya, or rather, Corey, out of drag and sitting across from a vaguely familiar guy.

"Hello," he said as Hunter and I approached.

Corey smiled and said, "Cam, you remember Likalya Thunder from *Drag Dance*?"

"Well, no, I don't think we ever officially met, and certainly never when you weren't in drag."

"Well, let me make your acquaintance now. I'm Efrem Stewart. It's a genuine pleasure to meet you."

"The same, and I apologize. Someone didn't have the social graces to warn me that I'd be meeting such a celebrity as yourself. I would've at least showered if I'd known." I gave Corey my most irritated look, but he just rolled his eyes at me.

"Oh, never mind that, this was a rush thing, and *Miss Thang* here and I just came to an agreement, so if you agree…"

I looked at both of them and immediately dreaded where this might be heading. "Agree to what?"

"Well," Corey looked at Efrem with an uncertainty that I'd never seen from him, in or out of drag. "Oh honey, I'm in over my head. I've done everything I know to make it all work out, but your honey over there helped me see I needed help. So, I called Miss Thunder."

I looked at Hunter with my eyebrow arched, and he shrugged. "Okay, tell me more."

I listened as Corey and Efrem explained a joint management agreement, with Corey eventually taking over. They would split the royalties earned between the two of them.

"So, what does this mean for me?"

"It means you'll have two fierce bitches watching your backside, but mainly it means I'll be training this amazing woman here to be everything she is meant to be."

I smiled. "Okay, it works for me. But for real, I can't have you both calling me all hours of the day or night, pulling me here and there. I swear, it's more than I can do with just one of you."

Efrem looked at Corey and sighed. "Well, we'll be working on helping you find your work/life balance. That's important if you're going to succeed and not burn out. For now, your single is recorded, and Corey told me you're working on some more songs. Is that correct?"

I nodded and tried not to cringe. Unfortunately, the other songs weren't anywhere near what I wanted them to be.

"Good, I recommend you focus on those, because if the single takes off, you'll want to be ready to put an album together as soon as possible. Take it from people like RuPaul, who've released a hit. You want a complete album to follow up."

"Got it, so what about performances?"

"Needed, but not as many as you have lined up. I suggest you cancel about half and move them out on the calendar, so you're scheduled for a year or even further. But this schedule is too much. I'm tired just looking at it."

I glared at Corey, who looked sheepish. "Well, I can do the ones scheduled for New York while I'm here. There's no need to cancel those, and as my illustrious manager says, 'out of sight out of mind.' Let's not get too far out of sight."

Efrem smiled. "I agree. This is such a great introduction. And we'll get some recording done while you're performing, so there's more than your sexy boyfriend's video on YouTube when *Drag Dance* gets released over the next few weeks."

I felt so much better after the meeting, and when we stood to go, I hugged Corey and thanked him for being so brave. "Like I said…" he whispered, "…thank that man of yours for helping me see the light."

I smiled and hugged her again. "Talk to you later. When it's just you and me, you can fill me in on all the juicy bits you can't tell me now."

"Will do, now go have fun with that hunky man of yours. Mmm," he said, looking at Hunter's ass as he bent over to pick up something from the floor. "Bitch, if that were mine, I wouldn't have let him out of bed long enough to come talk to some washed-up old queens."

"Hmph. First, you aren't washed-up, far from it, and second, you didn't give me a choice, now did you?"

"Well, go on then. I'll leave you alone, especially now I've got *Miss Bossy Britches* over there bossing me around. Hell, who knows, I might end up enjoying playing the submissive."

"As if," I said and laughed as Corey all but shoved me into Hunter's arms.

"I have no idea what you did…" I said as Hunter and I stepped into the elevator to return to our room. "…but thank you."

He shrugged. "Just being The Deputy." I groaned, and he sighed. "What? Too soon?"

"God, it'll always be too soon, but come here anyway," I said, pulling him into a kiss.

# 48

# HUNTER

I SPENT A WHOLE week with Cam before Aunt Monica called asking when I'd be back. "I'm going to miss you," he told me as we stood outside the airport terminal.

"Yeah, same here. But, Cam, as soon as you can, you come home, okay? Like Efrem said, you're going to need to take breaks in between the spotlights. Otherwise, you'll burn out. Promise me."

He laughed. "You're definitely fussing over me like a boyfriend. Okay, I promise to take breaks, but this is a new career, don't expect me to fly home often. Even taking breaks, I still have a lot to do. Songs to write and learn. And I need a band, people I can rely on. So yeah."

I kissed him, knowing that as the ski season was coming closer, I'd be just as swamped with work as him. Not wanting to make either of us feel any worse, I kissed him again and couldn't resist a little teasing. "Oh well, I guess there's always phone sex. Hey, better yet, is Zoom sex a thing? Would we be Zexing?"

I snickered, as did the couple standing next to us who must've heard Cam. They called my flight then, and I still had to get through security. So, I let him go with one more deep kiss and rushed toward my terminal, not daring to look back for fear of bawling like the giant sap I'd become when it came to my boyfriend.

I got to the terminal in time, went in, and found a seat at the gate. Luckily, it wasn't a crowded flight, so I had room to stretch out and think about Cam. No surprise, he occupied most of my thoughts these days.

I was still surprised my video of Cam performing in a bar had prompted all this. I still didn't get how it went viral. Had I known then what I knew now, would I have put it on YouTube?

I remembered how Cam looked when he picked me up from the airport. Bubbly, excited, happy, even though the jackass at the recording studio was treating him like shit at the time. Cam was living his dream, like his mom had said, and it showed in his enthusiasm. So, yeah, although I was going to miss him and hated giving him up to the world, especially as we were just getting a grip on our newfound relationship, I'd do it all over again. Anything to see that look of happiness on his face.

But damned if I wasn't also going to work with Madonya and Efrem to do everything in my power to get his ass back to Peachleaf every chance I got.

# 49

# CAM

I LISTENED TO AT least a hundred songs, and only two sounded anything like what I wanted to sing. I loved the upbeat pop sound, but it was hard to incorporate without sounding too much like the nineteen eighties. Classic in many ways, but nothing that'd get me played on the radio nowadays.

I went back to working with the lyricist and composer, Megan and Pete, I'd collaborated with before on my soon-to-be hit song, as Madonya kept calling it.

"So, what's your inspiration for this one?" Pete asked, and I could tell he was either expecting or hoping for another deeply sexual song.

"Roll your tongue back in. That one needs to be special, so think more relationship, less sex."

"Aah," both Pete and Megan said at the same time. I couldn't help but laugh out loud at their looks of disappointment.

"So, my family owns a resort in Colorado. I spent most of my childhood there, skiing the slopes, so I thought, let's come up with some songs that reflect that. Here's my first idea."

I told them about the exhilaration and freedom I felt when skiing, the wind whipping in my hair, and being so in tune with nature while racing down the mountainside. Even on the computer screen, I could tell when inspiration struck Megan. She began spitting out lyrics, almost rapping them. She even correlated the adrenaline rush coming down the mountain to the feelings you had when meeting the perfect guy for the first time.

"Exactly, that's perfect. Pete, I want something upbeat, maybe even the same beat as my last song, something that gets the heart pumping." As usual, he missed it completely the first time. God, if I didn't know he would eventually get it, I'd probably throw one of my princess fits. "No, the melody might be right, but the feel isn't. Try again, think more modern, more dance in a cool club."

This time Pete got closer. "Yes, better, but not quite there. This time keep it tighter. Megan, can you try putting some of the lyrics you wrote with it?"

The last time through, Megan smiled. "It's so good. So sweet."

We all laughed because our first collaboration had been anything but sweet. This one was different, but the beat was nice and complimented the song well.

It wasn't perfect yet, but we put it on the back burner to try another. I needed about fifteen songs for an album, according to Efrem, so we couldn't get too stuck on any one number keep on schedule. If I could write at least a few with Megan and Pete's help, I might be able to put my spin on some oldies to round out an album.

I loved Queen, but I was almost afraid to ask for licensing rights to any of their music. Although, since my debut video, thanks to my sexy mystery man turned boyfriend, fans had inextricably linked me to "Somebody to Love." Ugh, I was going to have to nerve up and ask about the possibility of putting that song on my album. Or I could make Madonya or Efrem do it. That's what managers were for, right?

Pete, Megan, and I worked up three songs that were definite maybes. I would probably need to sit with them one-on-one in Denver to figure out all the nuances. In the meantime, maybe they'd be able to work some of the rough edges out on their own. Regardless, when we finished our session, I could tell all three of us were absolutely fried. Writing music was hard.

After mustering the energy to power down my laptop, I collapsed on the hotel bed. I was so sick of being in a hotel, but I had two more performances here in New York. One tomorrow and one next week.

I imagined Hunter lying next to me. The week he'd been here was a dream come true. I closed my eyes and must've dozed off because I envisioned Hunter on the slopes, the song we'd worked on running through my mind.

I hadn't spent any time on the slopes with him last winter. Now, looking back, I regretted that. I bet he was a beautiful sight coming down the mountain. My imagination went with that thought, and as I saw Hunter on the side of the mountain in my mind's eye, the music changed. Slowed down. No longer a dance beat, but heat... so much heat, the snow melted on the slopes.

Hunter's hands were on me then, his deliciously rough hands running along my sensitive skin. His lips trailing along my neck, his tongue brushing against mine.

I could feel the rumble of his laughter, and the warm breath of sexual desire whispered in my ears.

I woke up so hard it hurt. But my erection would have to wait. I needed to write this down while the notes were still fresh. Like I'd known with the other song, this one would be important.

*Melody of the Snow.* Those words popped in my head as I searched for a notepad, which, of course, I didn't find. I flung my laptop open, opened a document, and began typing the images in my mind. The whispers, the touch...

My cock ached by the time I was done. "Fuck!" I looked at the clock, It was ten at night, So still early evening in Peachleaf.

I quickly grabbed my phone and dialed Hunter.

"Hello, Cam?" he answered immediately.

"Where are you?" I asked.

"Um, I'm at my apartment, watching TV."

"Get naked."

"What?" He laughed.

"You said we could have phone sex, and I need it now, so get naked!"

He continued laughing, but complied. "Fuck, this is definitely what I need," I said as I stroked myself to the sight of Hunter's enormous cock on his video feed. Though my tiny phone screen could never do him justice, his sexy voice and sounds of pleasure as he stroked himself were enough to send me over the edge.

"You okay, baby?" he asked as I was still floating down from my orgasm, sprawled out on the hotel bed.

"Yeah, just missing you. Thanks for answering your phone."

He smiled then, looking straight into his phone at me. "I'll always take your call, Cam. I miss you too."

The next day, I called Megan first. "Hey, I have lyrics for you to work on. But I warn you, they are, um, erotic."

"Oh good," she said, and I could almost see her rubbing her hands together.

As I explained the dream and emailed her the words I'd written, I could tell her mind was already racing with ideas.

"This is our song, Megan. My boyfriend and me. *Melody of the Snow*. It needs to be sexy but hopeful. Like when you're just starting a new relationship and the sex is really, really good, but it's also... more."

"Oh, damn, my brain is spinning too fast. Okay, let me work on this. I'll call Pete when I'm done, okay?"

I laughed. "Okay, just let me know when you finish."

"I will," she said, and hung up.

*Damn, I loved my team.* Well, Pete drove me nuts, but I knew he'd eventually come around once he got used to my style. There were few things more satisfying than seeing a song idea through to fruition, well, except maybe being snuggled in the strong, loving arms of its inspiration.

# 50

# Hunter

I ABSOLUTELY LOVED MY job. The first snow hit our mountain in early September. By the time October rolled around, with the help of the snowblowers, we were back on the mountains skiing daily.

How had I survived for so long spending my days in that stuffy office or old patrol car back in Kansas? I just couldn't imagine that life now. I loved almost everything about my new life in Colorado. I mean, sure, some of the skiers were assholes, and yeah, more than a few of the patrollers could be jerks, especially about scheduling, but that was such an easy price to pay to feel the freedom of skiing every single fucking day if I wanted.

Add to that, I had the best boyfriend in the world. Cam had been back in Peachleaf for a weekend and got to ski with me a few times before Madonya and Efrem whisked him off again to perform in California. Since his *Drag Dance* episode aired, his music had gotten ridiculously popular.

I even heard his first single, the one he'd performed on the show, on my favorite Sirius XM station. I was dating a famous man, but it never felt that way when he was home. He was just my Cam. Then, I had to laugh at myself. *My Cam*. He really had turned me into a sap.

The renovations on the mansion house museum had started under Josiah's leadership. I was able to spend a few hours a day over there, helping the construction team, which surprisingly enough, they didn't gripe about. I think they were just happy to have help since the goal was to get all the wiring and plumbing done and the new wallboard up before it got too cold to work, or the snow too deep to bring in supplies from Denver.

There wasn't a whole lot to do on the old place, at least as far as construction went. The roof was made of slate, so there wasn't much repair on the outside, and what little painting needed to be done got finished before the cold weather settled in.

Josiah had rattled on and on about fire prevention and securing the paintings, but most of that was beyond me so I went about helping do the stuff I knew how to do. It felt good being a part of it, and I took comfort knowing that when the mansion's renovation was done, it would be done right. Cam's artwork would be well-secured.

After Cam left, because all the art had been moved to a secure location Josiah had set up, I helped Peggy clean up and paint the rest of the cottage's bedrooms. Now that the art was gone, it looked like a proper house. I wandered through it after we finished moving all the furniture back into the bedrooms and making it a modern home for Cam. I wondered if I'd ever be invited to live here with him.

I knew I was jumping the gun. It hadn't even been a year since that fateful night I saw him perform and we'd had mind-blowing sex. Even now, after officially becoming boyfriends, I'd only spent a handful of nights with him.

We did, however, talk every day. I'd never been this close to another person, not even friends or family. Cam had become my best friend as well as my lover. I valued both aspects equally, though I never wanted to give up the lover part, and I sure as hell wanted a lot more of it in the future.

I still wondered what kind of future we'd have. Would our relationship remain long-distance, with Cam traveling the country performing and me here in Peachleaf, and for how long? He still hadn't decided about the offer my family gave him for the resort, and he was becoming more famous by the day, and busier.

So, what would it all mean for us? Would he just disappear from my life one day? Would I see on the news he'd run off with another man who was better looking, richer, and living a more exciting life than some ski patroller in the Colorado mountains?

I shook my head. No, they were just stupid thoughts. I needed to let all that go. If things stopped working between us, he'd talk to me first. We'd try to work it out. That was what kind of man he was, and I owed it to him to fully trust him with my heart.

# 51

# CAM

"**R**EALLY? YOU'RE DOING WHAT?" I asked in shock as Tommy told me he'd taken over old man Pauley's law practice in Peachleaf. "Is there enough business?"

"Yeah, I think so."

"Um, dude, what about men? You do remember it's a sex desert up there?"

"Well, not really. I mean, there's at least one really tasty morsel up here."

I felt my eyebrows go up. "Tommy, are you dating Josiah? 'Cause the only other tasty morsel around Peachleaf is my man and there's no way in hell that's happening."

"Don't jinx it with Josiah and me. We've been out a few times, and you know I like him."

"Like more than a one-night stand?"

"Ugh, shut up. Anyway, this is a business call. I need to let you know I'm taking over your account for Mr. Pauley. I looked over the proposal from Cabot. What are your thoughts?"

"Good deflection. Okay, I'll drop it for now but not forever, you hear me?"

"Whatever, back to business, the offer."

I sighed. "I know what I want to do, but I need to talk to Mom, and I guess you, too, now that you're old man Tommy."

"Shut up, never call me that again. And okay, call your mom, and we can set up a time to meet."

"Yeah, about that, I'm going to be in Denver, but only a few days, and most of that time, I have to be working with my songwriters. Do you think you could come down? Hey, see if Josiah will come too. I'd like to see the art exhibit he set up at the museum."

"I can ask, but you probably need to discuss the proposal without Josiah in tow."

I thought about that, and Tommy was right. It needed to be just us this time. "Okay, just you and Mom. I'll call her now."

I picked up the phone and wondered if I could figure out a way to get Hunter down to Denver too. Maybe just for a weekend? Knowing Mom would be at work, I called her office, but she didn't pick up, so I called the front desk. Again, no one answered. *That's strange*, I thought.

I couldn't remember a time I'd called the hotel and no one answered. Feeling concerned, I called Mom's cell, and thankfully, she picked up. "Hey, sorry, Cam, I'm sort of buried at the moment. Can I call you tonight?"

"Um, sure, is everything okay?"

"Yeah, okay. Talk tonight."

She hung up, and I stared at my phone. Another first. Mom complained that I never called enough. She never hung up without a long conversation.

Okay, well, I guessed I'd find out what was going on with her when we spoke later. I called Madonya next, to confirm I was still scheduled to perform in Denver, and she quickly said I was before she had to handle something as well. Was I the only one who had time to chat?

I didn't have anything else to do, so for the first time in a long time, I lay down on my bed for a midafternoon nap.

I was woken up by my phone. I looked to see it was my mom calling. "Hey," I said. "You okay?"

"No, not really. You know that interview you did last week?"

"Yeah," I responded, confused about where this was going.

"Well, you said you'd inherited the resort from your grandmother. Since then, we've been swamped. Every room is booked up until Christmas."

"Wow, really? Have we ever been booked out that far in advance?"

"Not since I've been here," she said. "Anyway, you called. I just got a break long enough to call you back."

"Yeah, I wanted to meet with you to discuss the offer from Cabot. I have ideas but wanted to run them by you before I committed."

"Yeah? When are you back in town?"

"Well, that's the problem, I'm only going to be in Denver for a few days, so you'd have to come down there. I could probably pay to have your friend fly you down, though, and then take you back."

Mom thought about it for a moment. "I can probably ask Monica to cover for me." I heard knocking through the phone, and Mom called for whoever it was to come in.

I heard bits of their conversation, something about a problem with one of the rooms, and Mom sighed. "I'm sorry, Cam, but I've got to go. Text me the dates you'll be in Denver."

"Oh, Mom, you'll need to bring Tommy with you. Did you hear about him taking over for Mr. Pauley?"

There was humor in her voice when she answered in the affirmative. "I'll set it up. Just text me, okay?"

"Okay," I said, laughing as she hung up. Wow, the flood of hotel bookings could help me convince Monica and the Cabot family to accept my idea of shared ownership, similar to the agreement Grandma had with her partners. I'd decided I didn't want to sell, at least not the entire resort. I wanted to hold onto part of my family's legacy.

Unlike my grandmother, though, I didn't need management rights. I wanted, if not needed, Cabot to do that. I also wanted to ensure that I didn't end up with another backassward company like Optimum if Cabot decided to sell later. That's where I needed Tommy's help.

I was still shocked about his decision to hang his shingle in Peachleaf. It'd be a lot of fun harassing him about it. And, of course, I also needed to get a lot more information about Josiah.

I thought about calling Hunter, wanting to convince him to come down to Denver with Mom and Tommy, but if the hotel was that swamped, the patrollers would be too. Even with our regular crowd, sometimes the patrol didn't have enough manpower. I'd chat with him tonight about it and see, but I guessed I wouldn't get to see him, at least not this trip.

I lay back on my bed, thinking about the song, Tommy, Josiah, and Mom, and it came to me. If the resort was getting this much attention from that short interview I did last week, this could be a perfect opportunity to sell the museum idea to the public.

I grabbed my phone again, dialed Josiah, and waited for him to pick up.

"Hello?" he answered, and I could tell he was surprised to hear from me.

"Hey, Josiah, I have an idea for the museum. Do you have any rich friends?"

# 52

# HUNTER

CHAOS WAS A GOOD word for it, but it still didn't describe what it was like to have this many people on the slopes. The only thing I could say was how appreciative I was that my predecessor was a good guy, because with the onslaught of people, he was able to drum up several retired patrollers to help keep our guests from accidentally killing themselves.

I ended up working every day, not that I wasn't already doing that, but now it wasn't a choice. We had to have all hands on deck. I needed to talk to Peggy and Aunt Monica about hiring a few more patrollers full-time if we were going to have crowds like this all winter. I mean, it was crazy.

"Hunter," Peggy said as she entered the patrol hut.

"Hey, I was just thinking about you. We need to talk about hiring some full-time patrollers."

"Yes, we've already begun moving money around to make that work, but I spoke with Cam, and since all the rooms are booked, and you're pretty much on-call all the time right now, he said you could just stay at his place."

"What? Like in the cottage?"

She chuckled. "Yes, like the cottage." She studied me for a moment and, seeing my stunned expression, must've picked up on the fact that I was freaking out about that. She sighed and added, "It's not like you're moving in, we're just in a jam, and you shouldn't have to face snow-covered roads trying to respond to an emergency on the mountain in the middle of the night."

"Yeah, we usually reserve a room here at the hotel for that."

"We still have one, but that's for your auxiliary help. I know Cam wouldn't want your other patrollers to stay at his cottage, but you already stay there when he's in town."

"Yeah, I guess that's okay."

She smiled and patted my shoulder. "If you have volunteers willing to move to full-time, go ahead and hire them. Monica and I should have the finances moved to accommodate that soon enough."

I watched her leave and pressed the heel of my hand into my knotted stomach. I didn't want Cam to think I was moving in on him. I didn't like the idea of him thinking I was pushing things faster than he was prepared to go. At the same time, I needed to be here in case of an emergency, especially with the number of people on the slopes, and it seemed he understood that.

I ran through several things I could do to pay him for letting me stay. That way, it was more of a roommate thing. Just as I thought that, my phone rang. I sighed when I saw it was Cam.

"Hello?" I answered.

"Hey, sexy, whatcha wearing?"

I laughed despite my nerves. "Well, nothing worth looking at, especially since I have several layers on at the moment."

Cam chuckled. "Okay, Mom said you were freaking out over the cottage."

"What? Did you just talk to her?"

"Yeah, Hunter, listen, I want you to be safe, and the cottage is sitting empty. You'd be doing me a favor by staying there anyway. What if the pipes freeze or something?"

There's no way I was going to tell him I went by the cottage every day to check on that very thing.

"So, will you stay there so I know you're safe?"

"I-I mean, as long as you know I'm not like moving in or something, and you know I'll pay you rent, and stuff is..."

"Hunter, don't be ridiculous. You're staying there to help manage my freaking resort. Just stay and don't worry about it, okay?"

"Okay, um, Cam?" I asked.

"Yeah?"

"I'd prefer to stay if you were there."

He sighed. "I know, it's torture being away from you so much, but I'm working on something that might keep me there over the entire holiday. I... don't get too excited about that yet, I probably shouldn't have said anything, but I'm working on it with Madonya and Efrem."

"Cool, when will you know?"

"I'm guessing in a couple of weeks. I'm going to try to perform at Madonya's bar for Christmas, which should calm her ass down a bit, but maybe do some low-key stuff over the holidays too. My goal is to be there for two whole months. Think you could handle having me in your space all that time?"

I chuckled. "Well, yes, especially if you're willing to volunteer on the slopes. We're swamped here, and your mom said it's all your fault."

Cam laughed. "It is, and I'll make it up to you, I promise."

"Okay." I was considering getting sexy with him, but a group of exhausted patrollers came into the hut, and I knew I needed to get off the phone and take a shift up on the slopes myself. "Hey, Cam, I've got to run, but I'll try to call you tonight, and thanks for being cool with me staying at your cottage. It really will make things easier."

"No problem, and yeah, I'll call you after I'm done working with my new band members tonight."

# 53

## CAM

HUNTER'S CONCERN ABOUT STAYING at the cottage gave me pause. I'd fully intended to ask him to move in with me while I was home for the holidays, but maybe it was too soon. I'd have to ask Mom what she thought. I'd come to realize that she had a good read on Hunter.

More often than not, she helped us navigate around the stuff that might have created problems between us, butting in at the most opportune times to spell out any disasters before they occurred. Not, I thought, unlike the cottage thing.

I had one more night in Los Angeles, performing at the Fairyland amusement park, then I was finally going to sleep in my own fucking bed in my studio apartment in Denver. God, I was so thankful I hadn't given that up. In the past three months, I'd only gotten a weekend here and there to work with the song-writers when I'd flown back into town, but every time, falling asleep in my own bed was pure heaven.

I liked my new band, and luckily, all but two of them lived in Denver. The bass player was from Kansas City, and I'd played a couple of times with her while working the local circuits back in college.

My drummer was from Branson, but he and his boyfriend were considering moving to Denver now that most of the band was there.

They were flying into Denver tomorrow, too, and we were going to work with the songwriters on the remaining rough edges of several songs.

I needed more sleep than I was getting, and I laughed at the fact that I'd actually gotten more sleep while working ex-tra twelve-hour night shifts at the hospital. So, after talking to Hunter for five minutes, because he needed to get off the phone to handle whatever crisis had occurred at the resort, I fell into a deep sleep. If it hadn't been for Madonya calling and harassing me the next day, I'd probably have missed my flight.

I could tell she was as anxious as I was to get back home. Larry had managed the bar since she took me on, and although I knew she loved this life, she still missed her nightlife and her husband too.

I got home after sleeping the entire flight from LA to Denver and went straight back to bed, canceling my afternoon appointments with Pete and Megan. "I just need some downtime," I admitted.

Luckily, I felt much better the next day and was ready to go. Pete, Megan, and I had an awesome session, and all six of our original songs were spot on. Pete also worked with me to turn the songs written by other people that I'd chosen for the album into something that fit me.

Of course, I was able to work on them on my own, but now that Pete was beginning to get my vibe, he was invaluable in making the music work better for me. Megan even helped with some of the lyrics that hadn't felt right. As a result, I had a list of good songs that well-represented who I was as a musician. Most were high-energy, but a couple were perfect for a slow dance or two.

I was most proud of the songs I thought of as mine and Hunter's. Those were special, and, that's where my plan with Josiah came into play.

The mansion house museum's initial renovation was complete. That meant it was just a white shell. When we had the revenue, the second and third phases would include fixing the heating and cooling to better preserve the work, and all the other stuff I didn't fully understand that Josiah said had to be in place to protect the collection in case of a flood or fire.

Josiah was planning all that, and I'd already decided I didn't want to foot the entire cost of the renovation, especially since I'd agreed to rent the museum to a foundation I'd created with some of the proceeds from my grandmother and the sale of some of the older pieces of art.

To make money, we needed events, and with Josiah's help, I was planning on having a big ribbon-cutting ceremony at the mansion. The lower level would be open, with some of my choicer pieces of art on display, which I'd still kept at the cottage anyway, and I'd perform a concert in the mansion's grand ballroom.

Josiah sent me pictures, and the white-painted walls and refinished hardwood floors made the room look like an actual recital hall.

"I've got the perfect guest musicians too. My friend Jonas and his husband Orli are interested in coming out for a visit anyway, so I offered them a free room at the hotel and all the skiing they want if they'd perform," Josiah said.

I didn't know much about them, other than they had won major piano competitions, and Orli being a mechanic somehow made that an even bigger deal. Regardless, if it brought in donors, and Josiah assured me it would, I was happy to have them perform as well, especially since Josiah handled all the event planning logistics.

Of course, I had more than the museum in mind. I wanted to take my relationship with Hunter to the next level, which meant I wanted him to spend some time on the road with me. Madonya had told me a little about what Hunter had done when we were in New York, all but kicking the sound guy in the ass when he'd been messing with me in the studio. Something I hadn't even realized he'd been doing.

I needed that sort of person in my life. Someone who had my back and could notice stuff that Madonya, Efrem, and I missed. But also, and this was the most important part, I wanted more time with him. Granted, I had no idea if he was willing to give up his time at the resort. Mom said he'd taken to the ski patrol director position like a duck to water.

*Oh well,* I thought as I prepped for Mom and Tommy to arrive. *Maybe getting the ownership matter settled will help us all get the right staff in place, so Hunter won't have to be there twenty-four seven.* I'd also met a guy who owned a music studio in Denver I thought would be a great person to introduce my mom to. She'd insinuated that she was ready to start dating again, and if we could square away the resort stuff, maybe she'd have time to follow up on that thought.

# 54

# HUNTER

T HE ROOM WAS TENSE when I walked in late to the meeting. My aunt sat across from Cam's friend Tommy, while the rest of my family was seated around the room or Zooming in via computer. Unfortunately, I'd gotten stuck on top of the mountain with a skier who had a possible broken arm, which delayed my arrival.

"Okay," Tommy said when I sat down. "Now that you're all here, we can discuss Cam's counteroffer."

*Wow, okay*, I thought to myself. I'd swear, Cam was too damn good at keeping our business and personal relationships separate. I wasn't sure how I felt about that, because I sure as hell didn't know there *was* a counteroffer.

I sat and listened as Tommy discussed a partnership between Cabot and Cam. Not much different than what his grandmother had with Optimum. "You'll acquire the management rights, but with precise requirements. Unfortunately, your predecessor, Optimum, put a bad taste in the family's mouth regarding ownership and potential problems around that."

"Why didn't he agree to sell it to us outright?" Aunt Monica asked.

"Well, as you can see, the appraisal was significantly more than your initial offer, but more than that, I don't think Cam wants to surrender something that's been a part of his family for generations."

I could tell my aunt was upset, but I knew from earlier discussions this was what she'd assumed he would offer. Ultimately, we all understood that even though Cam wasn't here much, somehow, he belonged here.

"Anyway, you're welcome to think it over. You can contact me with any other questions." Tommy waited a moment, and when no one responded, he winked at Josiah and rose to leave.

After Tommy left, my aunt sighed. "It's not what we wanted, but it's not necessarily a bad deal. We'll own three-quarters of the resort. He's charging us less in upfront costs, but requiring we finance the upgrades, which include a new lodge closer to the lifts, parking to accommodate the lodge, and upgrading the spa."

"Weren't those things we were going to do anyway?" Amelia asked.

"Yes, but it's the ownership that concerns me. Until now, we've only invested in resorts we own outright. We've never had split ownership in a resort we've managed before."

"Do you not trust Cam, or are you concerned his mother will cause problems?" Sierra asked.

Aunt Monica shook her head. "No, I'd be begging Peggy to stay on, even if we bought the place. She's one of the best managers I've ever encountered, and she knows this place inside and out."

"So, the problem is only that we wouldn't own the entire thing?" Uncle Harris asked.

Aunt Monica looked at him and blushed. "I... well, yes, your father told me we should never get in bed with someone we didn't know."

Uncle Harris laughed. "Monica, before we married, Cabot Resort was on the verge of closing for good. My dad was a good guy, but he was never an astute businessman. You can let that one ride. I think Cam and Peggy would be ideal business partners, and besides, I appreciate the fact that we wouldn't be burying ourselves in debt to acquire the project."

Aunt Monica nodded, but I could tell she wasn't completely convinced. So, I decided to add something I knew would shift the tide.

"I sat down with Peggy this week to go over the need to expand the patrol hut since we'll be bringing in a lot more patrollers, and I noticed, over the past two decades, the numbers attending the resort have slowly dwindled. I know a lot of that has to do with location and bad décor, but I also think it's because we aren't a draw for tourists. How much do you think it'd cost in advertising to draw people to Peachleaf?" I asked.

Aunt Monica looked over at Amelia, who handled the marketing for the company. "At least a million," Amelia confirmed.

"This year alone, we've seen an increase of two hundred percent, because Cam did one interview with a small online magazine. I'm guessing if he did an interview with an even larger outlet, the numbers would be over the top."

I had everyone's attention now and was surprised to see curiosity on my aunt and cousin's faces. How had they missed this? "If Cam sells the resort to us, he'll no longer be an asset to the company. He'll just be a former owner. It seems to me Cam is one of the biggest assets this resort has at the moment."

Amelia smiled. "Well, look at that. The jock has marketing sense. Can he take over my job?"

"Hush," Aunt Monica said, and slapped Amelia's foot playfully. She took a deep breath like she always did when she was about to admit she'd missed something important, which in her defense, was rare.

"You're entirely correct," she said, shaking her head. "Cam is one of our best assets, and even if his music career doesn't last much beyond this year, he's already been instrumental in getting this little resort much-needed media attention.

"So, are we all decided?" Aunt Monica asked.

"No, not yet," Josiah said. Everyone turned toward him, surprised. Josiah hardly ever said anything in the group. He almost always just went with the flow.

"There's another option on the table, one I think we have to consider."

He paused, gathering his thoughts, and each of us giving him our full attention. "I just read a report by the Cross-Country Ski Areas Association, and the need for cross-country skiing areas has increased exponentially. In fact, the demand, when you include income brought in by renting snowmobiles, competes with that of downhill skiing."

"We don't have room here at the resort to offer cross-country," Aunt Monica said.

Josiah reached into a briefcase I hadn't even noticed he had and pulled out maps. "This is a large ranch about an hour's drive east of here. The ranch's buildings are historic. Each of them date back to a time when the ranch was a stop on one of Colorado's old stagecoach lines. I happen to know that ranch will be coming up for sale, especially if we would be willing to consider a partnership, not unlike the one we're considering with Cam."

Aunt Monica looked over the maps, then back up at her son. "You're thinking if we integrated the resort with a rustic cross-country experience, we could increase the tourism draw to the area?"

Josiah nodded. "This is Tommy's grandparents' ranch. Well, it's technically his since the property was signed over to him, but his grandparents still reside there and don't want to move. They're refusing to, actually, but they're intensely proud of the place's history. I'm sure if we can play on that, play on the fact that the ranch would once again become a place open to visitors, they'll be much happier to move to town so Tommy can properly care for them."

I looked down quickly, so as not to smile at my cousin's innocence. He was so taken with Tommy, and it was now obvious how their relationship had grown over time. At first, I thought Josiah was staying in Peachleaf, hoping to acquire the job running Cam's art museum. But it's clear staying local was as much about Tommy as establishing the museum.

I saw the same effort not to smile playing out on his mom's face, and Amelia wasn't even trying to hide her grin. She was beaming, even winking at him, and I knew as soon as the meeting was over, she'd give her poor brother untold amounts of grief.

"I mean," Aunt Monica finally said, "if we could get the ranch for a good price, and the buildings are in good enough shape to support the need, we could run shuttles from there to the resort. We could also probably put up some yurts like we did at Cabot Resort."

The wheels were turning now, and I was convinced Josiah was about to get his wish. Meanwhile, I steered the conversation back to the resort counteroffer, which needed to be decided first. "Josiah, I like the idea, and the money we'd save by accepting part-ownership, as Cam proposed, could be used to purchase the ranch. But let's vote on the purchase of this resort and make it final. Cam's offer seems generous to me, and I'm not just saying that because I'm dating him. I think we'd be stupid not to invest in a place with built-in marketing."

"I agree," Amelia said. "This is a great opportunity, and with Cam's help, I can sell his ownership along with ours as a guaranteed good time."

"The museum will bring in a lot of outside attention, too, giving the resort more of a high-end feel, making it so we can compete with some of the resorts in Vail and Breckenridge. I don't think we've given that as much thought as it deserves either," Josiah added.

"There's also the family component. Cam's family has owned this place for decades. That makes it a family-owned business, which is becoming increasingly popular these days," my mother added, her voice coming through the monitor.

"And we are family-owned as well. It could be tied together," Amelia said, and I could see she was digesting all the information to incorporate into her marketing campaigns.

"So..." Aunt Monica said, smiling, "...all those in favor, raise your hands."

Everyone, even Uncle Harris, raised their hands. "Well then, it's a done deal," Aunt Monica said, sounding relieved. "We're about to buy ourselves a new resort, and this one really is going to be one our entire family owns."

I was chomping at the bit, knowing I would spill the beans when I talked to Cam. So, I waited until we were done celebrating and said, "Okay, Aunt Monica, you better tell Tommy we accept, because the minute I talk to Cam, I'm going to be letting this cat out of the bag."

Aunt Monica laughed. "No problem, I'm guessing Tommy is lurking somewhere close anyway. Josiah and he have been sneaking away every chance they get," she said, winking at her son.

Josiah blushed, but smiled. "We'll discuss the ranch concept more, Josiah. For now, maybe you can set up a time for your dad and me to take a tour. If it proves to be a viable option, we'll submit it along with the resort in our financing package."

As Aunt Monica predicted, Tommy was sitting in Peggy's office waiting for us to finish our family meeting. She'd signed the proposal, and Josiah and I hung back as she handed the signed document back to Tommy.

"So, you accepted?" Tommy asked.

Aunt Monica made eye contact with Peggy and nodded. "We accept his terms."

Peggy jumped up and hugged my aunt. "Oh, I'm so excited. I was hoping this would work out."

"So, does that mean you're going to stick around?" Aunt Monica asked her.

Peggy's joyful expression quickly turned one of sadness. "Well, for a while, through the season at least, but no, not indefinitely. It's time to hand the reins over to you all. I'm ready for a life outside Peachleaf Resort."

"Well, I have plenty of time to convince you to change your mind, but for now, let's celebrate. Well, except you, Tommy, you need to get all those documents finalized to make it official so I can take them to the bank tomorrow morning. I want to close this deal as soon as possible so as soon as ski season is over, I can finally rip that god-awful eighties décor out of this hotel."

# 55

# CAM

I COULDN'T BELIEVE HOW fast time flew. One minute, it seemed like I was introducing my plan to Josiah about a performance at the old mansion house, which was officially being renamed the Kell Museum of Art.

Now, I was preparing to perform in what was once the mansion's grand ballroom. It felt so appropriate. When Mom had been scanning more old pictures, she'd found some of parties held here in the nineteen twenties. The spacious room had been packed with flappers and men in their fancy tuxedos. Performing there almost felt like we were going back in time.

I met and fell in love with Orli and Jonas immediately. The way Josiah had described them, I envisioned something very different. Jonas was a bit standoffish at first, but when he warmed up to you, he was funny and easy to be around.

Orli was a tough-looking mechanic, his big hands stained with oil. The moment the couple sat down at the piano, though, the piece of music they played... well, let's just say it was all heart. Watching the two manipulate the keys as they gently bumped up against one another, with the occasional smile shared between them, even the hard-hearted would be taken by the sweet, romantic air around them.

Hunter escorted Josiah, the piano couple, and Tommy to the slopes for some fun while my band and I set up for our part of the performance. This was about surprising Hunter as much as a fundraiser for the museum. I'd made a point not to share the song I'd written about him. Well, written for and about him. I wanted it to be a surprise because, for me, the song was my gift to him.

We'd barely finished practicing our last set when the guests began to arrive. "That's our cue to get ready," I said to the band. "You go get pretty." Usually, we performed in blue jeans and t-shirts, but tonight, it was all about impressing the well-connected friends Josiah had invited. The more long-term funding we could secure for the museum, the better, and I hoped Josiah's deep-pocketed guests would see the value in preserving this place as much as we did.

Luckily, I saw Josiah dressed to the nines and rushing through the front door before I left. "Is Mom still at the house?" I asked, and he nodded before turning a bright smile toward an older woman who'd just been escorted inside.

Of course, all I could do was chuckle since the woman was a full two hours early. I figured Josiah must've anticipated this happening since he'd arrived dressed and ready for the night.

I kissed Mom's cheek as I rushed into the cottage and upstairs to grab a quick shower and change. The event was being recorded professionally, and the film crew would arrive in about thirty minutes. I knew Madonya was setting all that up, but at least I could go over early and ensure they had everything they needed.

I got upstairs just in time to see Hunter step out of the bathroom in a towel. "Mmm, that's a nice look," I said, stealing a quick glance downstairs to make sure Mom wasn't looking before pushing him into my bedroom and onto the bed. "Now, I wonder if I have enough time to fix this?" I said, grinding my still-clothed cock into his.

"Mmm, we could just blow off the night, and I'll blow this," Hunter said as his hand snuck between us to squeeze my hardening cock.

"I want to," I said, pouting. I crawled onto my knees, so his towel-covered cock was digging into the ass of my jeans.

"You know," Hunter said as he ran his hand over my chest. "You're doing an awesome thing here tonight. I'm... I know it sounds stupid, but I'm really proud of you."

I blushed and quit grinding on him to lean back for a kiss. "You have no idea what that means to me. It probably means more coming from you than anyone else I know."

Hunter flipped me over onto my back and straddled my legs. "You never have to worry about me, Cam. I'm more than impressed and proud of all you've accomplished." He kissed me, then crawled off so he could finish getting ready.

Hunter danced around, letting the towel slide off his sexy ass as I watched and groaned, wanting to get my mouth on that ass right then and there. Unfortunately, my own planning cockblocked me. Instead of sticking my face between those sexy cheeks like I wanted to, I stripped and rushed into the bathroom to grab a quick shower, even if it had to be a cold one.

# 56

# HUNTER

I WAS HELPING TAKE guests' coats while Cam helped Madonya's film crew set up the recording equipment.

It was nerve-racking already, with all the VIPs standing around schmoozing, everyone looking immaculate in their fancy clothes. I wondered how some of the women could handle being in Colorado's mountains right before Christmas, wearing so little.

Oh well, at least the heating worked well enough to keep everyone warm inside.

Fortunately, Peggy had hired a legitimate caterer, so the food was actually quite good. Not the hotdogs that'd become a staple for the hotel since she fired the restaurant staff for trying to serve spoiled hamburger meat.

Two smartly dressed servers were taking around plates of hors d'oeuvres. Both were very handsome men and I wondered if Peggy had hired them, or they somehow knew Josiah. Regardless, they seemed to know their way around the elite crowd.

Finally, after the longest two hours of my life, the two piano players began to perform. Peggy nodded at me, and she and I encouraged the guests to move into the grand ballroom where the recital was being held.

Once the song ended, Josiah stood up and took the microphone. "Thank you, ladies and gentlemen, for coming. We are excited to see you here tonight on such an auspicious occasion. As all of you know by now, this magnificent mansion is going to become home to one of the most complete Art Nouveau collections I've been blessed to encounter. Many of you have seen pieces from the collection on display at the Denver Art Museum, but that's just the tip of the iceberg."

The crowd applauded, and I slipped into the back, next to the recording crew, to be out of the way of filming but still able to observe everything.

"You will all have noticed we have a crew filming tonight's performances. The program is also being livestreamed, so please be on your best behavior. Especially you, Mr. Granite," he said, pointing to a very elderly-looking man who raised his Champagne glass in salute.

The entire room chuckled. "Without further ado, I will turn the floor back over to our guest pianists, Orli Hancock and

Jonas Ludwig. If you've not had the privilege of hearing these two perform, you are in for quite a treat. For those of you watching online, Orli and Jonas's information will be available in the comments."

With that, Josiah turned the concert over to the couple. I slipped out of the room then and went in search of Cam and his band. They had intentionally hidden away, because the big ask for money was, according to Josiah, supposed to happen as part of their entrance and while they were setting up to play.

I found them all sitting in what was once a butler's pantry behind the tiny kitchen. The pantry was about three times bigger than the old kitchen. People were peculiar back in the day.

"Hey, how are you all doing?" I asked when I entered.

"We're fine," Cam said, and scooted over so I could sit next to him. They were teasing each other and telling stories of the shenanigans they'd already gotten up to as a group, even though, as a band, they were still pretty new.

I was more than pleased to see how well they got along, even after such a short time. That made me feel better about Cam being out on his own, knowing he'd be with people who would have his back.

About thirty minutes later, Josiah stuck his head in, and whispered, "You should probably get ready. You'll be coming out soon."

I kissed Cam and told the band to break a leg before slipping back out the door to my position next to the recording folks.

Orli finished playing what looked like him throwing his hands all over the keyboard and got a standing ovation from the crowd.

He rose to his feet, and Jonas stood next to him. They both bowed before leaving and sitting in their font row seats near the piano.

A group of men rushed out and moved the piano to one side. Then began to set things up for Cam and the band. Josiah immediately took the mic again and asked everyone to give one extra round of applause for the amazing couple.

"As we wait for the band to set up, I ask that you look around you. This former home was built in the early nineteen twenties. At the time, Colorado's economy, just like in the rest of the country, was booming." The lights dimmed, and on the wall behind him, historical pictures of the resort and mansion were projected onto the white background. "Parties were held here that are still remembered today."

Several pictures flashed across the wall of people dressed in twenties era formal wear. "Today," Josiah said as the lights went back up, "...there isn't as much need for mansions in the middle of the Rocky Mountains. When Cam Kell inherited this estate last year, he also inherited a treasure trove of original artwork. When faced with what to do with this mansion, which had sat empty for several decades, as well as the vast art collection, he got the notion that the two should somehow be bound together. 'Art should be shared with all,' he told me while allowing me to tour this magnificent property and look at his private collection. Of course, he was right, and tonight, you all have an opportunity to help Cam's dream of sharing his magnificent art collection with the world. As you can see, Mr. Kell has generously taken the mansion through the first stages of renovation. Now, it's our turn to help complete the project."

I listened as my cousin sold the project to a group of people listening with rapt attention as he spoke. Only recently had I understood my cousin's ability to capture a crowd. But just like when he'd proposed our buying his boyfriend's ranch, catching and holding our attention, he was doing the same here tonight.

"Whether you're here with us or watching online, we encourage you to donate while we listen to Mr. Cam Kell perform some of his newest songs. Please, put your hands together for Cam Kell and his band."

The crowd clapped even louder as Cam and the band came out. No one in the audience was younger than fifty, by my best estimation, so I was surprised they'd heard of him or his music, but maybe this was as much about the museum and the artwork, and maybe even just being seen at a fancy gala, as it was him.

The first song Cam sang was the Queen song from the night we met, "Somebody to Love." I knew I was grinning like an idiot, but I couldn't help it, and when Cam glanced my way, he winked at me.

I'd heard his second song on *Drag Dance*, and damn, it was pure sex then and now. I squirmed uncomfortably as the sexuality of the music hit me where I was standing. I'd have to ask him to give me a private performance of that later on when it was just the two of us.

They performed five more songs, all amazing. Each one was Cam's take on some of the classics. Then Cam came to the mic to address the audience. "Hi, everyone, thanks for coming out here tonight to celebrate the beginning of our labor of love. As Mr. Cabot said, I inherited a home and some fantastic art when my dear grandmother passed. All the artwork passed down to me was bought by her parents or grandparents, directly from the artists themselves. I just couldn't bring myself to part with any of it. The Peachleaf Resort has also belonged to my family all these years. So, it seemed there could be no better tribute to my family, the people who loved this area, the reservoir, the ski slopes, and their incredible art, than to use this, their home, to permanently display the collection for the public to enjoy."

Cam hesitated for a moment, as if he'd been overtaken by emotion, then looked up and smiled at the crowd. Then finding me, he said, "I've fallen back in love with this property, and a lot of that is because I've met someone who has shown me how magnificent Peachleaf is. I'd forgotten that, but I never will again. This final song is for him."

My mouth must've fallen open because Peggy was standing next to me, and she giggled before reaching up and pushing it shut.

The music was soft, whereas most of Cam's other songs had been dance music. He looked right at me the entire time he sang. Laying our love out, sharing all his feelings for me and about us, with the world.

I felt a tear slip down my cheek and didn't bother to wipe it away. My heart was too full to hold back all the love I had for this amazing and talented man.

As Cam sang, it was as if the entire room disappeared, and only he and I stood there, him pouring his heart out and me feeling all he had to give.

When the song ended, the room erupted in applause, bringing me back to earth. I smiled at Cam before glancing self-consciously around the room and noticing I wasn't the only person wiping away tears.

Cam thanked everyone again for attending and donating, then he and the band disappeared through the back. "Excuse me," I said to Peggy as I slipped past her. The moment I saw Cam, he jumped into my arms, and the two of us clung to each other as the tears flowed full force.

When he pulled back, he was grinning through the tears. "I-I love you, Hunter," he said, causing my breath to catch.

I nodded, wiping at my tears again. "I love you like no other man, Cam. Thank you for what you did out there. I'm sorta scared my heart is about to burst, though."

Cam chuckled. "It's okay. Mine already has."

We probably should've stuck around to meet the VIPs and shake everyone's hand at least once, but Cam told the band to apologize for him. He pulled me out of the back of the house, and we raced through the snow toward his cottage, laughing and holding hands like lovestruck teenagers.

That night, we made love many times, worshipping each other's bodies and celebrating all we were together, especially the song he'd dedicated to me—his *Melody of the Snow*.

One with a life full of loss, the other a life of plenty; will they be able to overcome their differences, or will their pasts tear them apart forever?

**A Long Way Home**
by Blake Allwood

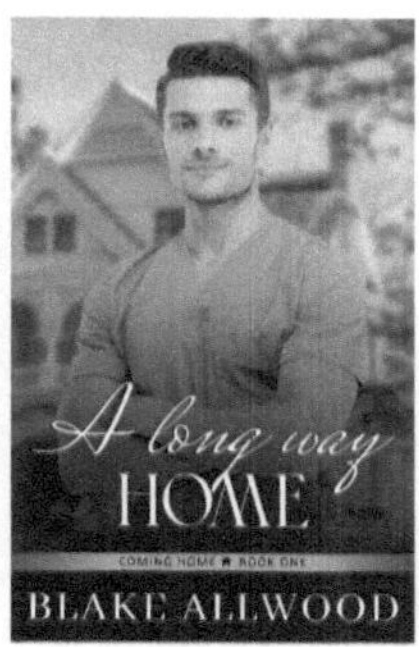

A Long Way Home is a low-heat, sweet, high drama romance.

https://blakeallwood.com/booklink/2986005

# ALSO BY

Join Blake's email list to get advance notice of new books and receive his occasional newsletter:

www.blakeallwood.com

<u>Transitions Series</u>

Aiden Inspired

Suzie Empowered (An MF Romance)

Bobby Transformed

<u>By Chance Series</u>

Love By Chance

Another Chance With Love

Taking A Chance For Love

<u>Big Bend Series</u>

Love's Legacy (1)

Love's Heirloom (2)

Love's Bequest (3)

<u>Romantic Series</u>

Romantic Renovations (1)

Romantic Rescue (2)

Romantic Recon (3)

<u>Melody Series</u>

Melody of the Heart

Melody of the Snow

<u>Road to Rocktoberfest Anthology</u>

Changing His Tune (2022)

<u>Coming Home Series</u>

A Long Way Home

<u>Novellas</u>

Tenacious

Moon's Place

Purchase at:

books2read.com/rl/blakeallwood

# BIBLIOPRIDE.COM

# BOOKS BY LGBTQ+ AUTHORS

www.ingramcontent.com/pod-product-compliance
Lightning Source LLC
Chambersburg PA
CBHW031309210726
48287CB00005B/1480